THE LITERATURE OF MY SPIRIT

A SEASON OF DESPERATION

NANCY Y. PAULIN

authorHOUSE®

AuthorHouse™ LLC
1663 Liberty Drive
Bloomington, IN 47403
www.authorhouse.com
Phone: 1-800-839-8640

Published by AuthorHouse 08/22/2014

ISBN: 978-1-4969-3597-7 (sc)
ISBN: 978-1-4969-3596-0 (e)

In memory of my mom,
my Divine Chosen Surrogate
Shirley T. Sullen

Love is the glue that holds all of our mistakes, mysteries and dreams together without destroying us. It is the plethora of celebration and reconciliation that is lost in a world that seeks for that easy thing to attain. Love is work. How much work depends on how much you want it to last.

Contents

PROLOGUE xi

One 1
Two 24
Three 41
Four 59
Five 76
Six 83
Seven 87
Eight 101
Nine 122
Ten 126
Eleven 138
Twelve 152
Thirteen 173
Fourteen 184
Fifteen 205
Sixteen 226
Seventeen 233
Eighteen 251
Nineteen 257
Twenty 268
Twenty-one 279
Twenty-two 291
Twenty-three 313
Twenty-four 320
Twenty-five 328
Twenty-six 342
Twenty-seven 346
Twenty-eight 352
Twenty-nine 365
Thirty 375
Thirty-one 386

PROLOGUE

Phyllis Hyman's, *Meet Me on the Moon* played softly as Keith took Donna into their fantasy place. It was the song that Keith had chosen for their wedding night. He said he had heard it at a party he attended while in college. The song became part of his romantic thoughts, as well as his musical taste. Every album that Phyllis Hyman made he had. But even so, it was the only song that he chose for their wedding, and it became Donna's fantasy song whenever she could not feel his touch.

As the song played softly it was in that special place of their hearts that they danced into the paradise of lovemaking. The warmth of the lyrics to the song welcomed them into the gates of consummated matrimony, while the Hawaiian sun lavishly wrapped the couple into the sands of the Kauai.

Hours earlier they paid their respect and gratitude to guests, Keith's friends and family, before promptly leaving the church's dining hall for their honeymoon. Their wedding was soft and romantic. Even the disappointing and disapproving faces of his Caucasian family members, could not stop the happy couple from seeing their forever together. Even though forever would include managing the societal differences of their skin colors, it was still beautiful.

That was eleven years ago, yet it was that moment in time that Donna played in her mind as she stood listening to the professor teaching on the struggles of African Americans in the world. She never remembered such a struggle. Her life remain memory free of struggle once she folded into the arms of Keith. His family's wealth was more than compensating for whatever she desired. And his love did the rest. So when the professor attempted to show the class the depravity of life for those of color she had nothing to reach for in her mind's eyes. Yes, she was African American, but struggle was not her memory.

Nonetheless, during the commercials of life she was reminded of the first eighteen years of her life. Eighteen years that was not celebrated with family and love, but through the windows of foster homes and orphanages. Even so, that life was behind her and never to be visited in her memories. She had managed to suppress that life somewhere so deeply in her subconscious, that even if she was to go looking for it, she would not know where to start to find it. But sitting there watching the eyes of those who attended the class, listening to the spoken words of whispers by others in the class, she was taken back. Back to the night of her wedding. Back to the moments of foster homes. Back to the revelational moment of learning she had been left behind by those who participated in giving her life. At that very moment time stood still. Clouds danced around with faces of the past. And the sun refused to shine anymore.

It could be said that she felt this happening some time ago, because it started with a morning of awakening without the usual feeling of belonging. Something in the atmosphere had been taken away, or kidnapped. She felt an assault on the life that she had come to enjoy and appreciate with a great enormity of celebration.

She thought registering for college courses would curb the nudging forebodingness, but it worsen. So she decided that not only would she register she would choose a major, focus on something that required her full attention, after her motherly and wifely duties of the day were at peace.

Still it was there, and catching up with her quite expeditiously. A reality that made its way into her life by force of a question she had yet to know how to answer. Struggle? What was that? And how was it that because she was African American, the struggle was supposed to be worse?

The night of her wedding was a symphony of love that played favorite in her mind and heart each day, and she did not want to let any other realities steal that from her. It was her wedding night, damn it. It was a place of escape after an argument with Keith. It was her place of peace when the world shouted. It was her place of love and passion when Keith was too tired to explore her body. It was her fondness memory of love's entry into her heart. She at times would consider that maybe it was so beautiful for her because of her naivety, but being a virgin bride was not the reason for her possessiveness of that night, no it was more than that. They became one. And believing it was no longer her, but they who resided in her spirit's mind and heart was her awakened reality every day. Her life before Keith was of no matter.

At least that is what she believed, and lived with for over eleven years.

"Mrs. Pennington?" The professor interrupted her thoughts. "Mrs. Pennington, do you have a question?"

"No. I do not." Donna tried to find that place again. "No, no questions."

"Let me continue." The professor's words continued to pierce her wedding reality. But Donna tried desperately to fight against them. "It is thought today that the world of racism has all but dissipated, however the influx of its disease still exist in places that we no longer choose to look."

Donna considered where to look without listening to the professor any longer. As she drew pictures of her loved ones and friends, there were no Black faces, not one. She was the only Black face she knew.

One

"Funny, whenever I looked at television as a child, and even now when I look at it, I never thought to ask where, was there a person who looked like me." Donna thought momentarily of the professor's word that imprisoned her some four years ago. "Now, I have to ask myself, when will I, ever see me more than I see you."

"What does that mean?"

"You don't know?"

"No, baby I don't know." Keith watched Donna seriously studying his face.

"Tell me Sweetie, what do you see when you look at me?"

He knew that this was a trick question. Anytime a woman, any woman asks a man, be it her husband or male friend a question of vanity, he must be careful with his response. "I see a woman of great beauty. A woman of whom I fell in love with from the very moment that I saw her, a woman who is the mother of my children and the woman who I will share the rest of my life with."

Nothing was said.

He tried again. "I see a woman who is sexy, vivacious, intelligent, passionate and irresistibly seductive." Still nothing was said. "Baby, what is it that you want me to say?" He asked cautiously.

"Do you see my black skin?"

"What?"

She sat up on the sofa. They had been lying there watching television. "Do you see the color of my skin?"

"Donna, I don't understand."

"When you look at our children, do you see the color of their skin?"

"Where is this coming from?"

"I don't know. Lately, I guess in the past year or so I have questioned my place."

"Your place where?"

"My place here at home, in the lives of our children, in our marriage and in the world." She smiled slightly. "You didn't answer my question."

"Donna, why haven't you told me about this sooner?"

"Keith, you are avoiding my question." She stood and walked over to the television and turned it off without using the remote in her hand. "Keith, you are a White American male.

2

When we met I knew that, but it did not matter. There was something in your eyes that made me feel free and uninhibited." She tried not to get emotional. "Are you going to answer my question?"

"I'm not sure what to say." He stood up. "When we met, I was fresh out of college and getting ready to begin work at my father's firm. I had also just gotten my results back from the bar association. So many things was going through my mind. Should I work with him or should I go somewhere else to establish myself without him? So much took over my thoughts. When I came into that restaurant and sat down, I only wanted a strong glass of liquor to settle my nerves. Then, there you were with those big brown eyes and those wonderful lips. All my worries went out the window."

"Are you saying you did not notice the color of my skin?"

"It wasn't the color of your skin that I was attracted too, but...."

She looked at him squarely. "Be serious, Keith."

"I am." He walked over to her and took her hand. "Darling, your skin was not what I looked at. Of course, I saw that you were not white. But it was your eyes that captivated me, and your lips that I wanted to taste." He stared deeply at her with a gentle softness that almost worked against her, but she needed to stay focused. "The way your eyes accented your thoughts stirred something inside me. So much of you is shown in your eyes. I love looking into your eyes. They make me want to make love to you. At the same time, they make me want to run and hide."

"Exactly what are you now trying to hide from?" She walked away. "Keith, you are avoiding answering my question."

"I am not avoiding your question. I answered it. You just did not like the answer I gave."

"Answer Keith, I need an answer!"

"Donna, you are Black. I never thought that you denied that part of you."

"How can you say that, Keith?" She turned to him. "Do I have any Black friends, any Black art, or any Black anything?"

"Donna, I've never stopped you from having any friends or anything that you wanted in your life."

"You never asked me either why those people or those things were never in my life." Silly she thought to herself, why blame him. "Did you not find it strange that I never brought anyone home who wasn't Black?"

"No."

"Not once did you question, even to yourself why I never had any friends that were Black?"

"Donna, why are you blaming your choices in life on me?" Keith asked.

She did not reply because she knew what she was doing, but she could not accept the blame. Not right then. "I am going to leave now." That was the best response she could give.

"And go where?" He asked.

"I don't know. I just know that I cannot be here with you." She began to walk out of the living room, but he stopped her.

"Donna, what are you doing? You come at me with things that you have never mentioned before, and then you tell me that you are going to walk out on me and on our children. Hell, what about the children? What are you going to tell them?" He felt frantic. "Donna what is going on?"

She hadn't thought that far ahead. More things had been running through her head, but she could only handle this right now. "Keith, I don't know what I am going to tell the kids. I have to get out of here."

"What in the hell is going on here?" He was angry. He grabbed her wrist to stop her from leaving. "Are you seeing someone else?"

"What kind of a question is that?"

"A legitimate one." He held her wrist tightly. "You explain to me, damn it, before you leave this house, what in the hell is going on with you."

"Keith let go of my wrist." She tried pulling away. "I just need to leave. I need time to think."

"Think about what? Are you talking about leaving our home?" Still he held onto her wrist. "If you need time to think, I will take the kids to the mall or somewhere else. But if you talking about leaving for good, you need to tell me."

"Keith, I don't know." She looked into his eyes to request that he let her wrist go. He did. "I have for months now, been thinking about my life. Sometime ago I was approached by this man, a black man. He asked me some questions relative to slavery and the struggle of the black community. When I did not have any answers for him, he looked at me as if I had committed a cardinal sin. I felt shame. Later, days later and then months later, I became even more ashamed."

"Why?"

"Why?" She replied shockingly. "Keith, I am a Black woman and nothing in my life represents that existence. Why is that?" She sat down. The room, that was built to fit a family of four, had now seem much smaller than it actually was. Much of the room was designed to Donna's dream, as was the rest of the house. But she had the design in her heart as to what a family room was to look and feel like, so Keith gave her the design pen. There was a sixty inch flat screen television, two lounge chairs, a sofa fitted for eight, and mirrors and painting from the art gallery. It took one year to build and almost as long to furnish. It had been three years now since Keith and Donna Pennington stepped over the threshold, and it each year had been just as better as the last. But then there was that day that Donna could not put out of her mind.

Much of their earlier life was spent at his parents' mansion, until Keith finally conjured up the nerve to tell his parents they were moving out on their own. This only led to Mr. and Mrs. Pennington buying them a home only ten minutes away from their home. The gift of course was turned down, in exchange for Donna's 12,500 square foot dream house, with a pool and a basketball court.

Keith was a partner in his father's law firm. She did, as all of the wives of the firm did, volunteered at the hospital or country club. She went on long trips to anywhere a plane or a train would take her, and most of the time without Keith.

It was only a year after their wedding that she became a mother. Keith and his mother of course, wanted them to begin a family right after their wedding. Even her fighting with Keith's mother finally ended and she became the star of his family, including his sisters. She was a mother now, someone that they could talk to because they too were mothers. Keith had three sisters, Lori Stephens, who married Harry just two years ago, and they already had twins. There was Daphne Jacobs, who married Daniel ten years ago, and bore him five wonderful boys. Then there was Jenny. Jenny never married, but she did manage to bring twins into the world with the help of a wonderful sperm donor. Jenny was the youngest and never wanted to marry. She would say, *'Why do I need to marry, I can have children without a man in my life'*. The family soon began to think that she was gay, but that was not the case, she just did not want a father for her children. She felt it would be better for the children if only she raised them.

Keith's father, Kevin, hated this idea but what could he do about it. He loved his daughter and did not want to lose her. Keith was the only son. They did, however, have a set of twin boys, but they died at birth. Their names were Dominic and Stanley. No one really ever talked about them because the pain cut too deep for their mother to handle, even after 27 years. Lori was the oldest of the children at the tender age of 36. Then there is Daphne who is 33, and Jenny who is 25. Keith was the middle child, who at the age of 35, was a father of two great boys who greatly adored him.

"Keith, maybe I am over exaggerating, but I feel lost, abandoned, and somewhat shallow. There is nothing in my life that dictates my heritage. I never paid much attention to this before, but when that man asked me those questions, something inside of me burst. What burst inside was not good and I have been bursting inside ever since. I look at my children and see that I failed them as their mother."

"Donna, you are a wonderful caring mother. Our boys suffer for nothing."

"They suffer for nothing because they do not know what they have not been taught."

"What?"

"How can they know what they are missing, Keith, if they have not been given anything?"

"So what are you saying, that their lives are without any substance because they don't know about their heritage? What about my heritage?"

"Keith, they know your heritage. Everything in their lives is about your heritage. Their friends, their clothes, their entire life is about you." She stood up and walked over to the mantle. Looking at the pictures of the boys and Keith's family, she pointed out to him what she meant. "Look! Look, there isn't anything about me, nor anything about my family."

"Donna, we don't know where your family is." She gave the look of death to him. "I am not trying to be mean. I am only saying that when we met you told me you were abandoned as a child by your parents and placed in a home."

"I know that, Keith." She stated sharply.

"If you want to try and find your parents, we can do that."

"It is not just finding my parents, Keith, I need to find myself." She sat again. "When I met you, I was only 20 years of age. It was two years since I had left the home. Although I had been in and out of different homes, the families always seemed to come to a decision of returning me for some reason or another. I was really actually very happy living at the home. All of my friends were there, and I could do almost whatever I wanted to do." She smiled to herself. "Memories. They are so funny. I sit here now and can remember the black friends I had at the home. Whatever happened to them? After I left the home, I lost touch with everyone there. I decided I was going to make a life on my own. I didn't know anyone outside of the home. Living in such a large city as Birmingham, I figured I could find a job almost anywhere. I had been trained as a secretary, but I wanted something different. I wanted something exciting that paid real money therefore, I decided to take the job as a waitress so that I could go to college during the daytime and work at night. For two years, I worked hard and studied hard and then came you." She looked up at him. "Keith, when I saw you I could not see anything or anyone else. You offered so much to my life that I knew nothing of. There was adventure, spontaneity and passion. I was happy to marry you, even when your family made such an argument over the color of my skin and how difficult it would be for us to survive in such a cruel world, and in a state such as Alabama. But we did it, didn't we? Eleven years now we have been married and seemingly happy."

"Seemingly?"

"Do you know when that man asked me that question almost four years ago?" She thought to herself. "It has been four years of hell and confusion that I have suffered. You haven't noticed it because if you had, you would have asked me. I wasn't quite sure how to tell you, either, since I didn't know myself. At least that is what I would tell myself. I told myself if I act as if it never happened, then it never happened. But it did, and I have been a wreck since then." Pausing to look up at him again, she continued. "I feel as if my life before that question was nonexistent, and without truth."

"Donna, what are you saying?" He was scared. Pain began to trace the outer limits of his heart. "What are you saying to me?"

"I don't know exactly. I want to tell you that it is over, but I can't because I love you so damn much. I know that to be true and I can't live without our boys." She stood and walked to the window. "So where does that leave me?"

"Donna, before you say anything more just let me say this. I don't know what is going on. I am right now, at this moment trying to grab my heart and hide from the pain it is feeling, but I can't move. You are saying things to me that I had no idea existed. I feel defenseless and angry."

"Angry? Why?"

"Are you telling me that I shouldn't be angry?"

"I guess you should."

"You guess?"

"Keith, I don't want to argue, I just figured tonight was the time to bring this out."

"Why tonight?"

"Because the kids aren't here and I need to leave before they return."

"Just where are you going?"

"I have a place on the other side of the city." He looked at her shockingly. "Before you start thinking the wrong thing, please let me finish. I rented a apartment three months ago, and I have been working now for a year with Duncan, Duncan and Jameson Law Firm."

"How? When?" Keith stammered around the room.

"Doing what?"

"Are you angrier at me for having a place that you did not know about or the job?"

"I don't know, Donna. Maybe I am just very angry at the realization that my wife, the mother of my children has been living a life that I knew nothing about!"

"You never asked."

"Why should I have to ask you about getting a place or job? Aren't those issues that we should discuss as a couple? Isn't that what we are supposed to do?"

"Keith, I did not do any of this to upset you. Besides, you knew that I was studying for the BAR, and when I passed it. What did you think I was going to do with my certification, sit on it?"

"Well, did you think that it would make me happy? Damn it Donna!" He rubbed his head like he always does when he is faced with an issue that he can't deal with. "What have you done?"

"What do you mean?"

"How are we to get over this?"

She only starred at him. "Keith, there is nothing to get over." His stare was cold and full of malice. "What I mean is I don't know what will happen to us. I just know this is something that I have to do."

"What exactly is it that you have to do?"

"Continue with my life as I have."

"How, and with whom?"

"Keith, this is not about some other man. I haven't been seeing anyone else. I don't want anyone else. I love you and you only." She felt she had to pamper his heart since she had done enough to break it. "Keith, I don't want to hurt you. Hurting you is not what I wanted to happen in this, but I could not avoid it. You and the boys mean the world to me, even more."

"The boys, yes how exactly do the boys fit into your new life?"

"I want the boys to come and live with me."

"What?"

"Keith, I am their mother and I want to expose them to a heritage that I have avoided."

"And that can't be done here, in their home?"

"No, at least I don't feel that it can."

He rubbed his head again. "Damn it Donna, I can't let you do this!" He said exactly.

"Keith, there is nothing that you can do to stop me. I am their mother."

"You sound as if you've done some investigating."

"Yes, I have. But I also know that you will not do anything to hurt them."

"You've thought all of this out, haven't you?" He rubbed his head once more. "How can you do this? Do you hate me that much? Is it because I am not Black? Is that what it is, Donna? Do you want me to go and darken my damn skin? Will that change your mind?"

"Keith, I don't appreciate that."

"What, I should appreciate what you are doing to me and my family, our family?"

16

"Listen, no matter what, this is something that I have to do. I cannot stress to you the importance of this. I need to do this for me, for us, and for the boys."

"And if you don't?"

"I haven't thought that far ahead."

"But you have."

"Keith, don't do this." She tried to walk away from his reach but he stopped her.

"Tell me Donna, what have you decided? You can't tell me that you have been living this other life for over a year now, and have not thought about what you were to do if things did not go as you had planned. Tell me damn it!" He demanded. "Tell me what my life is to be if I say no to this?"

"Keith, just please tell me that you are not going to fight me on this. I am doing this not just for myself. I am doing this for us, too."

"Oh, hey why didn't I think of this? My Black wife needs to find her Blackness, so she has to leave our home in order to do this because I am too White for her."

"You can go to hell." She pulled away from him. "If you want to be indignant about this, then we can go all the way."

17

"Where is all the way? Does that mean divorce?" He sneered at her. "Does it, Donna? Tell me what does all the way mean?"

"Keith, I am leaving now, but I will be back tomorrow to get the rest of my things, and my boys."

"Your boys?"

"Yes, Keith, my boys."

"What is going on?" Mr. Pennington asked.

"What are you talking about?" Keith replied. He went directly to his parents after Donna made her exit out of their home.

"Donna came by and got the boys a few minutes ago. She didn't look too happy, but when I asked her if there was something wrong, she just smiled and walked out. Her exit was as cold as her entrance."

"So, she has already come for the boys?"

"Keith, what is going on?" His father insisted.

"Nothing, Dad. Listen I have to go?"

"Keith, did Donna take the boys and leave you?"

"Dad, I have to go?" Keith walked out of the house and called Donna from his cell phone. "Donna, where are you?"

"Keith, I am on my way home."

"Home. Our home or your home?"

"Our home. I need to pick up some things for the boys."

"Donna, we need to talk about this."

"Keith, I tried talking to you, but you don't want to listen. You want to stop me, and this is something that I must do. Something that I have to do."

He did not respond. He had to think. He could not lose his family. "Donna, could you please wait there for me? I want to see the boys before you take them away. I want to see you, too." He felt his heart pounding, aching and running. "Donna, did you hear me? Please, I want to see my boys before you go."

"We will be there. I don't want to take the boys away from you Keith. I don't want to leave you either, but I just have to do this. My life seems like it is missing something. Something that you don't have to give."

Upon entering the house, Keith searched in the living room and then the kitchen for Donna. The house was quiet. Did she leave? He ran up the stairs and went into the boy's room. "I thought you had left."

19

"I told you that I would wait and I meant it. Besides, my car is still in the driveway." Donna said. "The boys are in the bathroom washing up. I haven't told them anything yet. I figured it was best we told them together."

"What exactly are we telling them?"

"What do you want to tell them?"

"I want to tell them nothing, but you aren't giving me that choice."

"Keith, please don't. This is just as hard on me as it is for you."

"Really?"

"Yes, really." Donna replied sharply. "Keith, I really love you and I don't want to lose you...."

"So, why are you leaving me?" He asked interrupting her.

"This is just something that I feel I have to do. My life has been so empty and without substance. But when that man began asking me those questions I felt the light come on."

"Donna how is it you've never spoken to me about this?"

"I actually did try to speak with you about what I was feeling, but whenever I did you would excuse it off to be boredom, so I went to school. I graduated and then I took the bar.

When I received word that I had passed, for a brief moment I felt like, hey this feels good, maybe just maybe, this is just what I needed. But then you informed me on how important it was for me to raise our boys and not some daycare, so I stayed home and raised our boys. But motherhood only filled a part of me that had nothing to do with what I was feeling." She sat down on one of the beds. "I've tried everything to fill the void, but nothing seemed to fill me. Then one day, while at the library I was looking for some books to read to our sons and this man approached me with questions of my heritage. When he saw that I was as lost as the Jewish guy standing next to me, he pulled me over and began to educate me just a little. But it was that little something that made the light come on inside of me. And it has not gone out since. When I realized what had happened to me, I began making plans. I knew that you would never conceive of me working, so I printed my resume and began sending them out to the different law firms. When I got the interview request from Duncan and Duncan I rushed right over and scheduled an appointment. I was scared, but at the same time I was ready to defeat whatever barrier stood in my way. I got the job. I couldn't tell you so I celebrated alone. Then it came, the time that I found my own place."

"Why do you need your own place?"

"Keith, don't you see?" She stood up. "My life is going places where you are not included, at least not now." She looked at him. She knew that she had hurt him with those last words, but they had to be said. "It doesn't mean that I don't love you because I do, probably even more than you know. But right now my life, and my dreams are leading to a place of solace, a place where I can call my own. I must do this, not just for me, but for us."

He was silent. He knew that no matter what he said to convince her to stay, she was going to leave. "Donna, I love you so much. I really don't want to lose you. I am so afraid when you leave this house, we will not be we anymore."

"Baby, I will never leave you, at least not emotionally. I am your wife whether I am in this house or in my apartment. I have a key for you. You can come whenever you want too."

"You really have thought this out?"

"Yes, I have." She walked over to him and took his hand. "Kiss me."

"Is that an order?"

"No, I just want to feel you next to me." He kissed her gently. "Keith, I am not leaving you. I am hoping that this will actually bring me closer to you."

He held her tightly. "I am so afraid."

"So am I, but not of losing you because of my leaving. But of losing you because I can't find myself." They held each other for what seem like an eternity. "We need to talk with the boys. What should we say?"

"Let's just tell them that their mother bought an apartment hoping to sale it. However, you cannot find any buyers, so you have to live there, and that you need them to stay with you for protection"

"Keith, Patrick will never go for that."

"I know, but let's give it a try anyway."

Two

It seemed as if life has begun again for Donna. She sat quietly in her bedroom and thought how much time had passed since she moved out the home she had shared with Keith and the boys. Days, months and years had brought her to this one single moment in her life. "Keith." She said. "You must get up now or you will be late for work."

"I am up." Keith turned over and took her hand. "Are you okay?"

"Yes, why do you ask?" She responded, as she stood to walk to the bathroom.

"Well, because you have been sitting on the edge of the bed for some time now. I was wondering when you were going to wake me."

"I was just thinking."

"About what?"

"My life." She came out of the bathroom after viewing her nakedness in the mirror, before returning to the room to put on her robe.

"And?"

"And what?"

"Come on baby, tell me what is on your mind." Keith sweetly requested, getting out of bed.

"I want to know what kept you from making love to me."

"You have been here in this bed with me ever since I moved out of the house we shared."

"Is that a problem?"

"Not exactly." She turned away from him. "You asked what was I thinking about, and that was it."

"But is it a problem?"

"Baby, I hadn't thought that far ahead. I was simply thinking about it." She began to walk out of the room.

"Wait, Donna. I need to know is this a problem."

"Baby." She said turning to him. "I did not think that far ahead. I was thinking about my life and your stay here. It was not a bad thought, nor was it a good thought. It was as I said, a thought."

"Maybe I should give you some time to enjoy your single life," he said sarcastically.

"Keith, do as you wish. I love you anyway."

"You know Donna, you are not making this easy."

"How is that?"

"If you don't want me to come here so often, then we need to work out a schedule for my visitation. I will at least like to see the boys."

"Keith, you are my husband, and the father of our children. You can come here whenever you like. But if you feel that you need a schedule to come over, draw up one. Now I am going to wake the boys for school, so that I can get to work myself."

Upon entering the building, she stopped and looked around. Donna always enjoyed the smell of her independence. The way everyone greeted and smiled at her made her relish in it even more.

"Good morning Mrs. Pennington." Matthew greeted. Matthew was her paralegal. When she passed the bar and was hired by Sydney Duncan she told the partners that she wanted a male assistant. When they asked why, she simply told them just to see how it felt.

"Good morning, Matthew." She liked him. He wasn't from Alabama, he was a northerner. He had moved to Birmingham to follow his then fiancé. Sadly enough though, his fiancé had fallen in love with another man, and had put him out. Instead of going back north, he decided he wanted to make a life in Birmingham. "Has Mr. Darren Duncan called yet?"

"No, he hasn't. Would you like for me to contact his office?"

"Yes, if you don't mind." She walked into her office and smiled once again to herself. This was a ritual she completed every morning. It felt good to her. It felt great! 'Damn, I did it!' She screamed in the silence of her heart. This, going back to school and passing the BAR, was the beginning. She felt it as strong as she felt the blood running through her veins. Matthew interrupted her ritualistic travel. "Mrs. Pennington, Mr. Duncan is on line three."

"Thank you Matthew." She picked up the receiver. But before she spoke she cleared her voice. Darren made her nervous. She wasn't sure why, but she did know that every time she spoke to him or was in his presence, her mind failed to perform as it should. "Darren, I need to meet with you regarding the Sanders account."

"Fine. I am available for lunch. Is one o'clock okay with you?"

"Yes, one is fine." She answered without looking at her schedule.

"Shall we say Smokey's then?"

"Smokey's is great. I'll see you there."

"Donna, before you go, have you been able to go over the Warner account?"

"Actually, I have. I finished it last night. It looks like an open and shut case."

"Good. Bring that file along with you."

After hanging up the phone she questioned what it was about this man that made her smile inside. He was without a doubt very intelligent. His father started this firm when Darren was a child of five. His life was planned for him and he did not seem to have any objections to this reality. Handsome was not a justified description of his stature. He was as beautiful and masculine as many men put together. He was a black man, a strong Black man, and he excited her. She knew that much, but what else was the attraction to him she felt she did not know.

Having only met with two clients before lunch, Donna managed to research more information on the accounts that she and Darren were to discuss during their lunch. She wanted to impress him. She also needed to impress him. That too, had become one of her rituals. She needed to always be on her toes with him.

"Excuse me Miss, can I get you a drink while you wait for your party?" The server asked.

"Yes, I will have a glass of water, with lemon. Thank you." She had arrived earlier than Darren so that she could prepare herself. Why? There were other men in the firm, but Darren seemed more than just a man. He seemed like an icon. She told herself she had to get over this. It was a must. He could never know how she felt.

"Hello Donna, I am sorry that I am late." Darren said while taking his seat.

"Only a minute. I would not consider that late." She smiled.

"Yes I know. But I always try to arrive earlier than the other party. It is one of those pet peeves of mine." He smiled back. "So, has the server--- he was interrupted by the server. I will have a glass of the house red wine. Thank you."

"Wine, for lunch?"

"Yes, I have had quite a morning." He seemed anxious. "As a matter of fact I am going to have to leave here in an hour. I have had quite a time with the Hunter's file."

"Is there anything that I can do to assist you?"

"How are you in corporate downsizing?"

"Is that what the case is about?"

"Yes, it seems that my client has been denied a separation package because his tenure with the employer was only for five years." He took his wine from the waiter. Tasting it to confirm his liking for the wine, he excused the server. "Thank you."

"What is the client wanting in return?"

"He was only asking for what is entitled to him for five years of employment. But now he is wanting more."

"Why?"

"Because the company decided that he wasn't fit for employment after he had one too many drinks while on the job."

"Was he provided counseling?"

"Yes, but that did not stop him from drinking." He motioned for the server. "I am famished. This case makes me either hungry or thirsty. So, how are you?"

"How am I?" She replied, forgetting his previous question.

"How are you at corporate law?"

"I have never tried such a case. But that doesn't mean that I don't want to try. Who is your second chair?"

"Actually no one." His smile was different. The server approached the table, and requested the orders. "I will have steak, well done, baked potatoes and green salad with Italian dressing. Donna?"

"I will have the same."

"Such an appetite for such a small woman."

"I am not that small."

"I did not mean that as an offense. You are quite a woman to gaze upon." He knew then that he had embarrassed her. "I am sorry."

"Don't be. I am fine with admiration." Now maybe he was embarrassed, she thought. "If you have more to say please don't let me stop you."

"Actually, I think that we should get to the matter at hand."

"Perhaps we should. I am not sure where to begin either case, so why don't you ask what you need from me and we can go from there."

"My, you are ready for business aren't you? I was actually hoping to speak with you about something other than work."

"Oh, really?"

"Yes, really!" He sipped a taste of his glass of wine. "I never had the chance to sit and talk with you about your decision to apply with Duncan and Duncan."

"I did not know that you were interested in knowing."

"I am actually interested in everyone that my father employs." He paused once again and then continued. "You see, I was not around when you were selected to join our firm. However, I have noticed that you do great work and I am quite interested in getting to know you better."

"Why?"

"Because I know that is what I do. I look for great attorneys to partner with and from the looks of things you seem to foot the bill."

She wasn't sure of what to say. "Darren, I don't know if that would be a good idea." Did she just say that? She asked herself.

"Oh you don't? May I ask why?"

"I don't have a good answer to give to you, I just think that right now is not the time."

"Because of your separation from your husband?"

She was shocked. "Excuse me? My what, from my husband?" The server returned to the table with their salads, giving peace to the tension at the table.

"It is my understanding that you and your husband are separated. If I am wrong please forgive me."

"Forgive you for what? Intruding into my private life or for having the wrong information?"

"Donna, I never meant to intrude. This information was given to me by my secretary, and I thought this was in your file." He sounded very apologetic.

"Why would that be in my file?"

"Listen, a week ago I asked my secretary to obtain your file and brief me on your career, and life outside of the office. I never meant for her to pry. Although, sometimes that is exactly what she does."

"Why do you need this information?"

"It is as I said, I am looking for someone to serve as second chair with me. When you started with the firm my father found it quite difficult to stop speaking of you. He said you had a fresh mind that was opened to new ideas and analyses. So, I decided to give you a shot." He paused to investigate her anger. "Donna, believe me it was not my intent to anger you. I simply found that what my father has said of you was true and I wanted to bring you on my team. That is all. I never meant to pry into your private life." She waited while the server placed their orders on the table.

"I am not separated from my husband. We are still together. We just live in separate homes." She waited for his questions but there weren't any. "Do you really mean this about me working on your team as second chair?"

"Yes, every word. Are you interested?"

"Very much," she thought to herself. "But if I am going to accept such a position, I guess that I should advise you of my home life."

"You don't have to do that."

"No, I don't, but I feel that it will help cut the errors in your investigation. You really don't think there should be any questions or doubts between us." She took a sip of wine and readied herself for the truth. "I am not sure if your secretary made you aware that my husband is Caucasian." He shook his head, yes. "We met years ago when I worked as a waitress. It was only a year before we were married. We have two wonderful boys with eleven years of marriage to cherish. As with anything in life, there comes a time where everyone begins to look for who they are in this world. Well, my time came about three years ago. Since then I have completed law school and moved out of the home that I shared with my husband."

"I don't quite understand. I thought that you said that you were not separated from your husband."

"I am not, at least not in the marital sense of the word." She corrected. "I was a child abandoned by my parents, and placed in an orphanage and many foster homes. While in the orphanage my friends were mainly Black, but once I left I led a life free of any people. Well, that was until I met my husband. It has been my husband's family and friends who have been family and friends to me. I have no friends of my own. I have no family of my own. This has left me empty and without a place in this world." Her honesty shocked even her. But he made it so easy to talk to him. No judgment was found in his eyes and neither was there any male criticism.

"So what you are saying is that you are in search of your own Blackness? Your own identity."

"Exactly!" She shouted. She was happy, embarrassingly so.

"I understand how that feels," he concurred. "For many years I wanted to believe that my older brother, Derrick, was my father's favorite. So I did everything that I could think of that would keep me within my father's favor. Derrick, however, chose a life outside of law and now works as an artist. We rarely hear from him and for some time my parents actually thought he was never going to come home again."

"Are you saying you never wanted to be a lawyer?"

"Of course not. I love the law. I love what I'm doing. But it took me years to realize this." He sipped some more wine. "You see, when I was younger I studied law only because I felt it would bring me closer to my father. But after some time off, I realize that I truly loved it. It no longer mattered to me whether or not I was my father's favorite. All that mattered was doing what I enjoyed, promoting justice."

"Well, I don't know if my search will be as easy as doing what I enjoy. As far as promoting justice, that is playing field of its own."

"Nothing is easy when it truly matters." He smiled. "I must say, it tells me a lot about you to have the courage to leave your husband and boys to find out who you are."

"My boys live with me. What kind of mother would I be if I left them?"

"It would not be as if you left them with strangers, he is their father."

"Yes, well I talked with my husband and he agreed."

"I am guessing that decision could not be as easy for your husband, as it was for you."

"No, it wasn't and we are still fighting about it. But it is as I said, something I have to do."

"May I give you some suggestions as to how to handle this freedom?" He asked softly. "Don't rush into anything. If it is yourself you are trying to find, you are never really far from the answer. Check out some books from the library related to Black History and Black women. Try to find your friends who were with you at the orphanage and try to find your parents. If you need my help with any of this, let me know."

"I don't know what to say. My husband is pretty upset with me, and here you are trying to advise me."

"Well, I am not your husband."

"Yes, I know." She said. "I really wish that I could do this with him, but it isn't possible."

"What about your boys? How are they handling not living with their father?"

"Well, we told them that I am trying to sell the apartment but could not find any buyers so I have to live there until I do. It seemed to do the trick, but I don't know for how long." She took a sip of the water. "Now that you know all there is to know about me, tell me about yourself."

"There is nothing else really to tell. I am single with no children. I love jazz, rhythm and blues, and even some country. My favorite thing to do is lay around listening to music whenever I have the time. I also pride myself in doing quite a bit of leisurely reading."

"So, are you truly serious about me taking second chair?"

"Yes, why are you asking again?"

"I don't know, maybe because there are more experienced attorneys in the firm and you've decided to choose me. Sounds very, hum, what should I say, questionable."

"No, actually it is quite the norm, at least for me. I like people whose minds are free from too much experience at law. This gives me the opportunity to learn new ideas and to grow at the same time. Usually, someone who has been with the firm for an extended amount of time can prove to be very difficult to deal with. They usually won't accept changes or new ideas and I can't have that. I like a thinking mind, not a programmed one and you fit the criteria." He was very sure of himself. "If you do not want to take second chair, you don't have to. This is an offer, and you don't have to say yes. Although I must tell you if you don't, it will be a very bad decision on your part."

"I have no desire to say no. I welcome the opportunity." She smiled. "When I decided to go to college, I wasn't quite sure what to do after graduation. Then I decided to go to law school."

"Why?"

"A better question to ask is, why not?"

"I don't understand." He took a bite of his semi warm steak.

"Should you ask the server to warm that for you?" She smiled slightly. "I mean, I really don't think that it is healthy to eat cold beef."

"Maybe, but I am sure that is not the answer to my question." He motioned for the server, who immediately came to the table and retrieved the cold steak. "Now, that that is taken care of, can we continue with you?"

"Why yes! Anyway, I realized while in college that law had become a passion of mine. I mean, I truly love it, probably more than I should. But that is neither here nor there. So, when you ask why, I can only tell you because I love it, but if you ask me why not I can give a million reasons." She smiled to herself this time. He was so easy to talk to. So wonderfully easy, she thought to herself.

"I guess then that I made the right decision."

"I would say that you have." When the server brought a fresh steak back to the table, Donna decided within herself that she was not to take this guy seriously. He was just as he is, a co-worker.

Three

As the months passed by, the closer Donna felt she was getting with Darren. They shared a friendship and a reality. He had escorted her to the library in search of history on African Americans. He had even given her the number of a private detective to assist her in the search of friends from the orphanage, and of her parents. Of course Keith knew of none of this, and neither did he ask any questions during any late nights which required that he keep the boys with him until the next morning. His visits to her apartment were short lived and soon he began calling before he used his key to come over. She felt separated from him.

Eleven years, and not one of those days did she feel without his presence, but since she began on her journey to finding herself, he seemed to become a little less than a necessary bump in the night. Which all of their lovemaking sessions seemed to become. They would put the boys to sleep and then they would have sex. She knew in her heart that they needed time together, alone. But this was impossible because of his schedule and, also her schedule.

The case that Darren enlisted her help was moving along slowly. Their client wanted more money than the company wanted to give, and they had the law firm to fight for that cause. No matter how things went, there always seemed to be a continuous granted from the judge. Besides the fact that the time spent with Darren was becoming important to her than that of the time shared with her husband, she liked what she was doing. Fighting the good fight.

When Darren came into her office, she was about to make a call to Keith to request that they get away for the weekend. She wanted to tell him of the information she had found about the history of her people.

"Donna, I was hoping that we could get together this weekend."

"Why, I thought...."

"I know what you thought, but Hartford Electronics have decided they are willing to offer our client a small amount."

"How small?"

"To the tune of $1,000,000."

"You call that small?"

"No, our client did." He came inside and sat in the chair in front of her desk. "I know what you are thinking now, but you are wrong."

"Tell me what I'm thinking."

"You're thinking that our client is being greedy and should be thankful."

"Actually, I was thinking that I really need to spend some time with my family. I feel as if we haven't seen each other in months, I miss them."

"You mean your husband?"

"Yes, my husband." She stared off into space. "I was just about to call him when you came in. Can't we work on this on Monday?"

"Yes, we could. But I would rather get it over with." He knew that she had not heard him. "Listen, it can wait until Monday. Why don't you go and enjoy your weekend with your family." Still she said nothing. The look in her eyes told him that she missed love. The touch of her husband's hands and the hugs from the children. "Donna." He reached for her hand. She still sat quietly as if she had forgotten he was there. "Donna. Is there something wrong?" He took her hand.

She awakened as he touched her. "I miss my family. I mean I really miss them."

"The look in your eyes is not the look of a woman missing her children, rather a woman who..., how long has it been since you and husband....?"

"Darren!"

"Hey, we're both adults. I consider myself a very good reader of the secrets people keep in their eyes. That is what makes me a great attorney."

"Oh really?" She smiled to hide her embarrassment. "Well, to answer your question..." She stood to turn her eyes from him. She thought that maybe he had seen enough loneliness from her. "Since I started this case, actually since I moved out of the home we shared, my husband and I haven't made love. We have shared our bodies when the other was in need." She turned back to face him. "I am not accustomed to this kind of lovemaking. What we shared as a couple was sweet, endearing and passionate at times. So passionate that I would find myself asking for time to allow my body to relax from his touch."

"Is this your way of telling me that you love this man?"

"No, it is an answer to your question." She sat, and starred into space, again. "I miss his touch. I miss his taste. I miss his love. Do you know what else? I can't believe that I am saying these things to you. I mean I have only known you for a little over three months and I have managed to tell you all of my hearts desires."

"We're adults aren't we?"

"Yes, but I know other adults, and I don't share my life with them."

"That is only because they don't listen, and maybe even they haven't asked."

"Why are you asking?"

"Because you are like no other woman I know. I am very interested in what makes you live each day."

Just like an attorney, he hit her where she was weak. "So you think that I am interesting? Now that is interesting."

"I am amazed that you don't find yourself interesting." He stood and walked over to her. "You, Donna Pennington, are a woman of many mysteries. Not only mysteries of life, but mysteries of your body, and how you like for it to be touched." He gently caressed her hand. "I knew that when I first met you and I know it now.

So if you say to me that your husband has not made love to you in a while, I know that it is important that you find the time for him to do just that, or some other man. Another man not as honorable as I am, will step in."

She quickly pulled her hand back from his touch. "You are quite observant." She tried to show that she wasn't affected by his touch. But she was, more so than she could ever imagine. "So are you telling me that I have the weekend off?"

"Yes, I guess that I am. I don't want you hanging around me with a body that is unsatisfied." He smiled and began to walk out. "You go and do your bidding with your husband. May be even throw some moves for the lonely one."

"Who may that be?"

"Well, me of course."

The only thing that mattered to her at that moment was taking her clothes off and feeling Keith inside of her. She craved for him. When he opened the door to their home, his look was not that of his missing her, but more of why was she there.

"Keith, are the boys here?" She asked walking into the living room.

"No, they are with my sister." He tried to grab her hand.

"Good, I was hoping that we could spend some time alone." She continued on into the living room. Before she could finish her thought she was halted by a visitor sitting on the sofa. The sofa she had once before shared with Keith. "I see you have company."

"Donna, I was trying to tell you but, well anyway this is Carolyn Mentz from the office. I believe the two of you have met before."

"Yes, we have." Carolyn agreed. She stood and reached to shake Donna's hand. "It is nice meeting you, again."

"Yes, well. You will have to excuse my surprise. I did not know that someone was here. I mean I didn't see your vehicle out front."

"That is because Carolyn left her car at the office." Keith added. "I didn't know that you were coming by tonight."

"Yes, well, I didn't know that I had to make an appointment." She starred at Keith, but only for a second or so. "Why don't I call you later?"

"No, I was just about to call a cab." Carolyn suggested.

"Carolyn, no. Donna, is there something wrong?" Donna was not sure of what to say. "Carolyn and I only have a couple more pages to go over and then I will be taking her home. Can it wait until I get back?"

Donna felt her heart do something, something that she did not want to feel. It hurt. "Actually, yes, it can." She turned to walk out, but remembered that it was her house that she was walking out of. She wanted to spend time with her husband. She needed to spend time with him. "I will be upstairs. If I am asleep when you return, please wake me." Keith only starred at her. His eyes were cold and unfeeling. Donna said a silent prayer and continued to walk upstairs.

Hours would past before she realized that he was not in bed with her. She had taken a long bath and tried to read a book that was part of her travel to self-realization, but she fell asleep. Her mind immediately brought to remembrance a woman, Caucasian and beautiful. She was tall, at least 5'9, and a body like a model. Her beautiful blue eyes only accented her dark black hair that extended down her back. Donna did remember meeting Carolyn at Keith's office before. She also remembered telling Keith that she found her to be quite an intelligent woman. She worked as a partner in the firm, but after six years she decided to start her own practice. The last she had heard of her was four years ago.

She wondered downstairs to find the living room empty and the lights off. When she noticed the time, her heart again began to feel that similar pain that she ran from earlier. One a.m. and he was with her. Carolyn seemed to be a woman of many talents. Talents that Donna would only allow herself to think of. The woman that Darren described the day before was Donna in her dreams. She could never let Keith see that part of her. What would he think? When she told Darren that their lovemaking was passionate, she meant in her mind and her fantasies. She would see Keith touching or reaching for her and her body would tremble. He would take her without warning and then make love to her like a man without fear. She could feel him kissing her nipples, her stomach and her body would silently scream for him. He of course would answer.

"Donna." She heard her name, but found herself still in the fantasy. "Donna."

"Keith." She tried to make eye contact but was unable to. "Keith."

"How long have you been down here?" He gently pulled her up.

"Since one o'clock. What time is it?"

"Two thirty."

"Where have you been?" She could see him now. He looked tired and frustrated.

"I told you I had to take Carolyn back to her car." He sat down next to her. "Why did you come here tonight?"

"Do I have to have a reason? I mean this is still my home isn't it?"

"Of course. That isn't what I meant." He tried to make himself comfortable on the sofa. "What I meant is that I wasn't expecting you tonight, otherwise I would have scheduled my meeting with Carolyn another night."

Her heart felt safe again. "I've missed you. Have you missed me?"

"I believe that is a question you will have to answer yourself."

"Why is that?"

"Can we talk about this tomorrow, I am exhausted?"

"It is tomorrow." She pushed him aside. "What do you mean?"

"Donna, baby please. I just want to sleep now. I am tired."

"Keith, I want to make love. I want you to make love to me."

His eyes went to her breasts. She had unbuttoned the pajama top. "Donna?"

"Please Keith. I need you. I miss you."

"Baby."

"Please, I am begging you." She began removing her top. She watched his eyes as he allowed her hand to touch and caress him gently. "I'll do whatever you ask of me."

"What is going on here?"

"Is there something wrong?" She let her hand travel to his shirt. The buttons were mostly already unbuttoned. "Do you not want me to do this?"

"No, I am just not used to you being so aggressive." He could feel her hand traveling to his thighs. She was completely naked and her nipples were showing just how excited she was.

"Should I stop?" she whispered.

"No, by all means keep going."

She placed herself on top of him and began unfastening his belt. "Is there anything special that you want of me?"

"Donna, are you okay?"

"I am just fine. I am better than fine." She kissed him roughly upon the lips and then traveled to his exposed chest. She tried to force him to lie back on the sofa to allow her more room to work her magic. "You didn't give me an answer."

"Donna, I think that we should talk." He was confused. Excited and confused. "I—I think, no, I know that we should stop."

"But baby, I need this. I miss you so much. I miss us so much. I need to feel you inside of me."

"Donna, wait!" He pushed her back with such force that she fell to the floor. "What is going on here?" He just as forcibly stood and tried to button his shirt and pull up his pants.

"What do you mean?" She tried to gather herself. "Don't you want me?"

"Yes, but first tell me what is going on. Where did this new you come from?"

"This isn't a new me, this is the old me." She finally stood, but still with some adjustment.

"This is not the, you that I know." He said while still trying to pull his pants back up. She had managed to pull them below his thighs. He was shocked at this woman whom he had known as his wife for eleven years. "I mean what in the hell is going on?"

"Keith, I thought we were going to make love."

"Who is the, we in this? Because I don't know who the hell you are. When or should I ask, whom did you learn this from?"

Her body was still very warm from her seduction. She needed his touch, not his anger. "Keith, what are you asking me?"

"I want to know if you have been with someone else."

"How could you ask me that?" She looked for her pajama top to put it back on.

"I have never seen this side of you. Is this part of your new Blackness? I mean, I have always heard that Black women were commonly more aggressive sexually than their counterparts. Is this what this is?"

She glared at him for only a moment before she could express her disappointment at his racist comment. "What in the hell did you say? How can you be so racist?"

"How can I be so racist? How in the hell can you be someone I don't know? What are you doing here tonight?" He took her by the arm. Donna, please what is going on here?"

"Nothing now." She pulled away and began walking out of the room.

"Where are you going?"

"I am going home."

"This is your home, damn it!" He yelled, walking quickly behind her. "This is your home!"

"Are you sure that you want a Black aggressive woman living here?"

"Don't be ridiculous, Donna? I apologize for my comment. It is just that all of this is hard for me. I am not perfect. I don't know what is going on anymore." He turned and walked back into the living room. "I just want my wife back."

"You never lost me, Keith." She followed behind him.

"I don't know that."

"I'm here aren't I?" She walked up to him. "I'm here wanting to touch and make love with you, and only you."

He looked into her eyes. "Who are you becoming?"

54

"Keith, I love you. Whoever I become will not change that. You are my husband, my friend, and my lover. You are the only man that I will ever love." She kissed him gently. "I guess in some ways I am becoming more aware of who I am as a woman." She caressed his hand. "But I don't see that as a bad thing. I mean whatever I am becoming, or whoever I am becoming I am sharing her with you and you only."

"So, this new aggressive sexual woman is just part of your growth process?"

"No, actually I have always been sexually aggressive. I guess that I was afraid that you would think differently of me if you saw that side of me." She sat on the sofa.

"Well if you never showed that side to me, to whom did you show it too?"

"No one, I just found a way to live only in a fantasy world with that side of me." She looked up at him. He was quite a handsome man, she thought. His dark features were as impressive at that moment, as they were the first time that they met. "Does it bother you? I mean did you not like it?"

"I—really don't know." He took a seat next to her. "Should I like her?"

"I guess it is up to you." She felt his hand sliding under her thigh.

"I mean if she is going to become a part of our relationship I need to know. But if she is just here for the time being, I...."

"Would you like for her to stay around? I mean, I like her, and I want you to like her."

"I like you." He continued with his hand up her thigh. When she could feel his hand between her legs, she looked at him. "Can I continue?"

"Can I stop you?" She laid back on the sofa and allowed him to caress her more intimately.

"Are you sure you're okay with this?"

She could only moan yes because the spasms in her stomach made her weak from his touch. "Please." She softly said.

"How do you want me to make love to you?"

"Do you have to ask?" Her body once again began to silently scream for his touch and his taste. When he saw that she could no longer withstand not feeling him inside of her. When he saw her eyes continually go to the back of her head. When he saw her ache even more intensely for his touch, he took her.

The doorbell was a sound that seemed far away. Donna thought it was the neighbor's home, so she fell back to sleep. Besides, Keith had not moved.

"Keith." The voice called.

Donna quickly awakened to see who it was. When she saw his sister, Daphne, standing in the foyer with a look of shock, she realized that they were still on the sofa and presumably naked. However, she then remembered Keith going into the hall closet and retrieving a blanket for them when the heat from their bodies no longer comforted them. So she knew then the shock that Daphne showed on her face was only because she was there with Keith. "Keith." Donna called to him softly.

"I am sorry, but no one answered when I rang the bell." Daphne said.

"I thought that I was hearing the neighbor's door." She tried again to wake Keith, who appeared to be in a coma. "Keith, baby, please wake up, the boys are here."

"What?" He was exhausted.

"The boys, baby, are here, and so is Daphne."

Keith quickly sat up. "Oh Daphne, when did you get here?"

"Just a second or so ago." She smiled at his embarrassment. "Hey listen why don't I hold the boys off a minute or so? They are still in the car."

"Yes, maybe you should." Keith suggested. Donna removed the blanket from over her slowly, so that Keith would not be exposed. Keith and Daphne were both shocked when she stood there in view, naked. "Donna."

"What is wrong?" She asked, noticing the look in their eyes. "Come on, your sister looks at a naked woman's body every time she undresses herself. The only difference is the color of our skin." She walked right by Daphne. "Keith, maybe you should follow me upstairs. The boys will be coming in soon."

Daphne once again smiled. "I will get the boys. It is good to see the two of you getting along so well. I take it she is back home now?" She said when Donna was out of view.

"Actually, she isn't." He answered standing to wrap the blanket around his waist.

"So, what do the two of you do, get together to pleasure each other whenever needed."

"You could say that."

"I did."

Four

Nothing seemed more impossible to deal with than a hot Monday. The weekend went by so quickly Donna actually felt she had missed it. When Daphne left, Keith decided to take the family to the movies and dinner. The boys enjoyed their family time, and Donna relished in the moments. She even invited Keith to the apartment for the rest of the weekend. It felt special to wake up with him as she had done so many years before.

She wasn't sure what to say to Keith when he asked when she thought she would be moving back home. Her journey, she felt had not begun. It had been months since she had moved and she only felt that she wasn't there. She still felt empty inside, lost and empty. The fact that she still could not talk with Keith about what was going on inside of her was even more devastating. She tried desperately to explain to him all that she felt, but he did not understand what she expressed. She concluded that because he was Caucasian he could not understand her feelings of not belonging, unworthiness, and misappropriation. She felt no matter what she said he would never understand her. This understanding brought on doubts of their marriage, which was not a good feeling.

She was so deep in thought that she didn't notice Darren walking into her office. The smile on her face told him that her weekend went much better than he thought. But that wasn't the reason why she was smiling. "I take it your husband proved to be a man of great staying power?"

"Actually, I am just happy to see you." She answered, finally focusing to see him. "How was your weekend? I hope that you did not spend the entire time working on this case."

"Someone had too."

"Darren, please tell me that you did not do that." She stood to take the seat next to him. "I mean, I don't want to feel guilty."

"Would you really?"

"Would I really feel guilty? Yes. Well, maybe not." She gave him a sincere smile.

"What is going on inside of that head of yours?"

"I don't know if I can explain it to you."

"Try me." She sat back and readied herself. Her stare off into open space showed Darren that maybe her weekend did not go as well as he thought. "How is Keith?"

"Keith is Keith. He is trying to hold onto a woman who he fell in love with 12 years ago. The only problem with that is this woman is different. We are both different, just in totally opposite ways." Darren did not interrupt her. "Keith is settling down, while I am growing out. It is as if I'm looking for another spirit to possess. Does that sound strange?"

"I guess it really doesn't matter if I think so or not."

"It matters. It matters because I respect you therefore, what you think of me is important." When she looked deeply into his eyes she tried to see judgment, but there wasn't any. "I mean we are working closely each day, aren't we?"

"Yes, we are."

"Yes, you are right. I guess in some ways I feel as if when we talk you understand. I wished that Keith did. I really need him right now."

"But, you moved out of the house. How do you expect for him to understand? I believe your expectations of your husband are quite unfair. You are living your life without him." She was surprised, and he knew that she was. "Donna, you forget, I am a man."

"I haven't forgotten that. I just thought that maybe you understood where I was coming from."

"Why? Because we're both Black?" He asked most certainly. "You will have to do better than that."

"Did I do something to upset you, or did something happen over the weekend that you aren't telling me about?"

"Nothing happened, Donna. I am simply trying to play the devil's advocate. It seems as though it is necessary."

"Meaning?"

"Meaning that you obviously have failed to find anyone to speak against what you are doing to your family, but your husband, and of course his family. I am guessing that their opinions do not mean much to you." She said nothing to rebuttal Darren's analysis of her decision. "So, it is as I thought." He stood and then decided to sit back down. "You know Donna, I don't disagree with what you decided to do because I am of the understanding that we do what we think is best at the time. But, I really think that it is necessary for you to not ignore your husband's feelings. You have to realize that what you have done is both dangerous and some would even venture to say, childish."

"I think childish is somewhat harsh. Besides, who are you to talk?"

"I am the same person who you felt you could talk to. If I don't say what you need me to say, what kind of a friend would I be?"

"I don't remember telling you that you were a friend." She was irritated.

"Oh, but you did when you invited me into your personal affairs." He took her hand. "Donna, you cannot tell me that you did not think that your decision to move out was a good one. You left your husband alone. Alone, each night and each morning that he wakes without you or your boys. I don't think that any husband wishes to wake up like that. I have observed you and I must admit you are quite an enemy to have in the courtroom. When it comes to affairs of the heart you seemed more argumentative and selfish."

"You are wrong." She said cautiously, pulling her hand from his grip. "I love my husband and my decision to move out of the house was a difficult one. Hell, I thought you were impressed with me. At least that is what you first told me." She stood and walked to the end of the long marble desk. "Maybe I made a mistake of talking to you about this, I mean, I barely know you."

"I am under the belief that a person opens their heart to whoever will listen. In your case you decided that that person was to be me."

"I see now that I was wrong."

"Why? Is it because I acknowledge some of the dangers of your decision? Donna, I am only saying what you know yourself. The problem is you just did not want to admit to it." He stood and walked over to her. The office seemed cold and distant. He realized that he had made her feel inadequate, but he felt he had to say something. "Tell me something, have you decided how long it will take you to move back in with Keith?"

"No, I mean yes."

"May I ask when?"

"I don't have a specific time or day."

"Just as I thought." He walked back to the door of her office and then turned to say one last thing. "Donna, you can't think that this game could go on for as long as you want. I know that you feel lost, but sooner or later you will have to decide on whether or not the decision you made eleven years ago is all that you need for the rest of your life. Even if it is not the life that you feel you should have. Maybe, just maybe, all that you are feeling is a lack of accomplishment as an individual, not as an individual with a heritage." He felt he had said enough, but he was a lawyer. "I mean what does being a Black woman mean to you, anyway?"

His words cut through her like a knife with jagged ridges. Who was he to talk to her in that manner? She knew why she moved and she knew that her decision to move was not based on selfishness. Maybe a little, but it was not the basis. Her life was empty, even with her two wonderful boys and Keith. Darren was right with one thing, she did feel that as an individual she felt a lack of accomplishment. She thought that this feeling would leave her after she graduated from law school, but it remained still and immovable in her chest. It wasn't as if she made the decision to leave her home with ease. She loved that home. She loved her family, dearly. But that thing inside of her was more deadly in its resolve to awaken her. Awaken her to life. Awaken her to a fantasy, maybe even to death. No matter what she did to shut it up, it remained a constant.

Darren's words did cut through her like cold vengeance. She did not feel that he felt so passionately opposite of her thoughts. What did it matter anyway, he was not who mattered.

When she tried to begin working on the case she second chaired with him, she found herself unable to be objective. This of course was not a good thing, she thought to herself. She needed to get away from the office, so she decided to go home.

"Hello, Mrs. Pennington, how are you today?" The doorman said, greeting her as she walked through the door.

"I am doing well, William. How are you?" She felt it necessary to always speak to the doorman. He was a small man who always had a smile on his face and a flower in his lapel. "But it is great to be home. My day has not been a great one."

"So early? I am sorry to hear that. Let me know if there is anything that I can do for you."

"Thanks William, but I think that I will be okay now that I am home." She looked at her watch. It was only 12:15. "I think I will eat some lunch and then try working on this case." She smiled and walked into the elevator. William has been working in the building since its erection seven years ago. He was a retired Marine Officer who only worked part time since age 50. He had four adult children who all lived throughout the US and six grandchildren. His wife of 53 years died last year after a painful bout with stomach cancer. Now at 73 years of age, he wanted only to wait on the day to be with her again. Until that great moment he would spend his time making the world smile each day. This was all told to Donna when she first moved into the apartment.

On the day she set out to look at the apartment, she found herself waiting for the realtor. William was happy to grace her with his life's tell. He told her stories of working with *colored* soldiers while in the service. He thought of himself as a liberal. Besides one of his daughters was married to a Black man and his son was dating a Black South African woman he met while on a pilgrimage in South Africa.

So, these relationships William felt bought him passage into the Black community. He prided himself with this heritage.

At first Donna thought it was cute. But the more she fought the voices inside her, the less attractive his quaint ideas of being part of her heritage became. She decided the best way to deal with his stories was to avoid all conversations related to race. There were moments when it seemed she would not be able to change the direction of the conversation, but something or someone would appear and he would be called upon.

She checked her answering machine when she saw the red light flashing. She knew before she pressed the button that it was a message from Darren, so she only half-way listened until she realized that it wasn't Darren, but her father-in-law. He wanted to meet her for dinner at seven. Damn! There went her day. Why did you leave? When are you coming back home? Are you coming back home? What about the boys? The questions would be endless and she was not about to answer any questions coming from him. It was her life. Yes, his son was her husband, but that does not give him the right to question her.

She argued this argument with herself for the next 20 minutes or so. But she knew to ignore his invite would only avoid the inevitable. She picked up the receiver and returned his call at his office, but he was at lunch. His cell phone ranged at least five times before he answered.

"Hi, Donna. I was hoping that you got my message. Your secretary told me you had left for the day. Is everything okay?"

"Everything is fine, Kevin. How can I help you?" Too formal, she thought to herself. "Kevin, is eight okay with you? I mean, I need to make sure the boys are settled."

"Of course. I understand you have to be a mother first." He cleared his throat as he usually does before he goes into a lecture. "I need to let you know that Keith will also be joining us." He waited for her to reject his invite, but she did not. "I feel that it will prove to be beneficial for both of us that he is there. I will meet, excuse me, we will meet you at 8."

Now she had to find a sitter for the boys. If it was going to be a long night, she needed someone who could stay the night. If she called any of the Pennington sisters, it would be Jenny, but she would probably have to work at the hospital. She usually worked late. Donna decided she would give it a try anyway, maybe she could also tell her what this meeting was about.

Dr. Jenny Pennington was the only sister of Keith who treated Donna with more than just humanly respect. She treated her like a sister. She truly did seem to love her. Donna hated the way the other family members disagreed with Jenny's decision to be artificially inseminated. It wasn't at all that she agreed with Jenny's decision, but who was she to judge her.

"Donna, how are you?" Jenny answered knowingly, having looked at her caller ID.

"I am well and you?" Their conversations were always cordial. Jenny was not really a free spirit child the family only treated her like she was. She was actually very conservative. Her decision to become a mother by means other than coitus, was only made because she was ready to become a mother, but did not have a man in her life that she loved enough to be the father of her child. She had a constant line of dates, as well she should she was beautiful in every definition of the word. To look at her meant only to look at beauty personified. Most of the men in her life were there only because she was too nice to tell them no, so, they remain friends and friends only. A romantic at heart, her heart was set on finding the man made for her. So when it seemed that her quest to be with this dream man had come short with her desire to be a mother, she made up her mind to conceive anyway. "How is Laura?"

"She is driving me to drink, but I am loving every minute of it."

"Spoken just like a young mother." Her beauty was wide as her intelligence. Jenny proved to be a genius. She graduated from med school at the tender age of 24, and later became a leading doctor in the field of brain surgery. She loved the brain and wanted to know what made it work and stop working. "I am sure you know that your father wants to meet with me tonight, and I am in need of a sitter for the boys."

"Actually, I wasn't aware of the meeting. I have been out of town for a couple of days. Remember, I told you the other day that I would be leaving to attend a conference. I came back this morning."

"Oh, I forgot."

"You see this is what happens when you move out of your family's home." She laughed softly. "Just kidding."

"I do hope that you are, because I really need to feel that someone likes me."

"Actually, I love you like a sister." She said sweetly. "I wonder what dad wants to meet with you about."

"You have no idea whatsoever."

"No, I am at a total loss. Why don't you bring the boys over on your way to the country club?"

"How did you know where I had to meet with him?"

"Come on Donna, you know my dad never eats anywhere else but that country club."

"Yes, you are right. We will be there around 7:30. I don't want to get to the club too early."

"Fine, I will be here. If I don't answer, just use your key. I will probably be giving Laura her bath then, and she really hates to be disturbed during her bath."

"Oh really?" After saying good-bye to Laura, Donna busied herself with things around the house and making telephone calls to potential witnesses for the case she was to chair with Keith.

When the sound of the doorbell ranged in her ears, she realized then that she had fallen asleep and failed to make any dinner. Karen, the sitter quickly walked away after leaving the boys with Donna. Karen was 16 and made extra cash from Donna bringing the boys home after school. If Donna wasn't home she would use the key given to her by Donna and Keith, and sit with the boys until Donna arrived from work, usually around six every weekday. The private schools that the boys attended was only a block away from Karen's high school, so she could meet the boys after her last class. Karen's dream of becoming a heart surgeon usually kept her focused on her studies and less on the boys. She had a very serious mind for a young lady, and she took the responsibility of sitting the boys as seriously as an operation she was conducting on any of her future patients. The extra cash she made from Donna was placed in her savings each week and never touched. It was the money she would use to add to her parent's college savings for her. She was the only child and seemed to enjoy the relationship she shared with the boys, even though they were of a significantly different age bracket and race than her. She treated them like the little brothers she never had. The boys returned her love.

When Donna began to feel the call of her heritage pulling at her, she naturally began to look at who was in her life, and her children's lives. The parent-teacher conferences she would attend would always be shared with parents who were of a different race than her own. The friends that the boys spoke of were all Caucasian, never one of African descent. Pulling the boys out the environment would be too devastating to them, but she knew she had to do something. So, each and every week, the boys would be accompanied by her to a community center where the children were predominantly African American. The first few weeks the boys only played with each other. But when Jeremy Price decided to ask them to play basketball with him, they never looked back to regretful moments of coming to the center. In fact, Jeremy became one of their sleepover buddies. Jeremy's father was the center's manager and would sometimes bring the boys home if they wanted to stay longer than Donna allowed. This change of heart became almost a weekly request of the boys.

After paying Karen, she quickly got the boys ready for the trip to their aunt's home. Not knowing exactly how long dinner would take she dressed them in their pajamas. This meeting with Keith's father was long overdue, but needed. What she would say, she did not know. But whatever it was going to be, it had to be good. She could not let him win.

Five

When she entered the restaurant at the country club, she carefully scanned the room to see who was there. This was not a ritual before her bout with self-awareness struck. But since then, anytime she would go into any public place her eyes would carefully scan the area, just to make sure no one noticed her.

Keith immediately stood as she walked toward the table he and his father shared. Keith was quite a looker she thought to herself. He made her think of his masculine beauty each time she planted eyes on him. He was a health nut, and worked out daily. On the days that he would have to miss a work out session, his attitude was uncomfortable to deal with. His sometimes, extreme passion to fitness was stress upon the boys as well, but only Sean gave it his all.

Patrick being the oldest did not join in this tradition of sweat and muscles. He was the bookworm who loved stories of technical conquer and risks. He was also a lover of poetry and romance. Strange combination, but it worked for him. Sean on the other hand, was his father's double. He loved the law, he loved working, and he loved his mother passionately. Patrick the protector and Sean the lover, they complimented each other.

"I was wondering if you were going to still make it." Keith said, while gently planting a kiss on her cheek.

"Yes, I was wondering the same thing myself." Kevin Pennington added.

Donna wasn't quite sure how to respond to their method of conquering her, so she only smiled. Before she could take her seat next to Keith, the server made his way to the table to get her drink request. After ordering only a glass of coke, she prepared herself for their next move.

Kevin, of course being the elder began first. "Donna, I know that you suspect that my dinner request has some underlined string attached to it, and you are correct."

"Thank you." She said to the server. "I did suspect something, but knowing you the way that I do, I figured it was not worth my stressing over it."

"Meaning?"

"Meaning, your options are numerous, and since I did not want to spend the rest of my evening trying to figure them out, I decided to let it go." She was hoping that she did not sound rude. That was not how she wanted to play the game. Keith was quiet, unusually so. "Keith, is everything okay?"

"Yes, everything is just fine."

"Are you sure?" She was not comfortable with his distance.

"Yes, Baby, I am sure." Keith quickly turned to his father. "Dad, why don't we get on with this?"

"Yes, that is a good idea." Kevin Pennington was quite a shrewd attorney. His expertise in the courtroom and boardroom were known throughout the city and even farther. His family's fortune was made from his tyrannical antics of overthrowing even the most prestigious law firms. "Donna, I asked to meet with you tonight because I have an offer to make with you."

"Yes, I know."

"First, have you had dinner yet?"

"No, I have not and neither am I hungry." She answered poignantly. "Please, Kevin, continue."

"Yes, well when Keith told me that you have been practicing at Duncan, Duncan & Jameson

Law Firm I was of course shocked, and then disappointed."

"Disappointed?"

"I was not aware that your pursuit of the law had led to your employment. When I was informed of this move, I was disappointed that you did not come to me first."

"Donna, listen you do not have to leave D, D & J. My father is only thinking of the family." Keith knew when to step in. "I have explained to my father that you are happy where you are and I don't expect you to leave."

"You did?"

"Yes I did. Even if I don't agree with your decision, I won't argue against it anymore."

"Well, I am not the one in love with you as my son here is." Kevin interjected. "I would very much like for you to consider leaving D, D & J."

"Kevin...."

"Before you say anything else let me say this." Kevin interrupted her. He positioned himself, as any attorney would do when they decide to go in for the kill. "I feel that it shows great disrespect for your husband and his family for you to practice law with the competition."

"Kevin, I mean no disrespect to Keith or his family in choosing to practice law anywhere."

"So, then it will be of no problem for you to leave D, D & J and join the family."

"Kevin, I am already a part of the family." She corrected him. "As far as my leaving D, D & J, that is out of the question. I am quite happy with where I am."

"How is that?" Kevin asked. "Keith is not happy, and neither are my grandchildren."

"Wait a minute Dad." Keith quickly jumped in. "My happiness is not for you to question, and neither is the happiness of my children." He stared only at his father. "Now, Dad when you told me that you were going to ask Donna about practicing law with the family's firm I was okay with that. But now that I see it has nothing to do with the firm, and only to do with our marriage, I see no reason why this should go on."

"Keith."

"No, Donna, let me finish." He turned to face her. "I am not happy with how things are with us right now. But I am not going to let my family make any decisions for my life." He stood and waited for her to stand along with him, but she could not move. She was so impressed with how he took over the night that she felt unable to do anything. "Donna, we should leave now." After hearing his appeal for her to stand, she stood sort of unconsciously. "I will need a ride. I drove in with Dad."

"Of course." She remembered answering. "Kevin, I guess I will talk with you later."

"Donna." Kevin stood and took her hand. "I hope that you know that I meant no disrespect in asking you here tonight. I think, however, that I underestimated my son's love for you, and in doing so, this night has ended on a sore note." He smiled half-heartedly. "I do hope that we can at least remain civil to each other."

"Kevin, as far as I am concerned this night never happened." She took his hand and shook it firmly.

As they walked out of the restaurant, she noticed the stares. Stares that never mattered before, but now seemed to have consumed her. She thought to herself that maybe it was her who was staring and not them. When Keith opened the car door for her, she took one look at those blue eyes of his and thanked him for defending her honor.

"It was not your honor that I was defending it was my love for you."

Six

"Are you ready to go?" Darren asked. Since their last conversation, he had shown no difference in his demeanor. Although Donna had decided not to let his brass advice upset her, she could not resist ignoring him at times when he would call upon her response to anything related to the case they shared together.

"Mrs. Pennington, your husband is here."

"Thank you Matthew. Please let him in." It was always nice to feel so important, but sometimes the limits that Matthew would go to, just to make her feel as she was the queen seemed to have no end. "Sweetheart, it is good to see you."

"Yes, well, I was hoping we could go to lunch." Keith said, as he gently kissed her lips. "Are you available?"

"For you, of course. But could you give me just a few more minutes? I have one more phone call to make, and then I am all yours." As she made her way back to her chair, Darren came through the door without knocking.

"Donna, listen we really need to get together ...Oh, excuse me,...Keith Pennington, correct? I am Darren Duncan." Darren extended his hand to shake. He remembered Keith from his 8 X 10 picture that Donna had placed so visibly on her desk. Darren often questioned why the picture was so large. He questioned himself, not Donna. His reasons usually ranged from her fear of tipping out, to maybe just maybe she really did love this white man. Everything in the middle was just spats of jealousy. "I have heard quite a lot about you. I feel as if I already know you."

"Strangely enough, I haven't heard much about you." Keith felt uncomfortable. Darren was tall, handsome, intelligent and wealthy. And he was Black. "My wife doesn't talk much about her job or the people she works with."

"Well, now I am sorry to hear that. That makes me feel somewhat unimportant." Darren jokingly stated. "Listen, I see you two are going to lunch. Donna, give me a call upon your return."

"Is your father Nathaniel Duncan?"

"Yes, he is."

"Quite an entrepreneur and an outstanding attorney. I have studied some of his cases and also used some of his strategies."

"Oh really?"

"Yes, really, I am truly a fan of his, even though you are the competition."

"Yes, it would seem so." Donna felt as if she stood alone in some room watching this masculine means of communication take place. "About the case?" Darren's word brought her back. "Donna, when you return please contact my office."

"I will", she answered. "Darren, is there anything wrong?"

"Wrong?"

"With the case?"

"Everything is fine. I just think that we may have limited our client's ability to find other employment."

"Meaning?"

"When you return." He left her office without speaking another word.

"That guy is very intense."

"I believe that is an understatement." Donna said. "He is a very different person. I don't think that I have met anyone quite like him before in my life."

"How is that?" Keith asked.

"Just like I said, he is very different from any man, or woman that I have ever met." She took one last look at herself in her compact.

After deciding all was okay, she stood to leave. "I guess in many ways, it is because of him that I decided to stay on."

"What does that mean?" Keith asked quickly.

Donna noticed the urgency of an answer, decided not to let his jealousy take over. "Baby, understand one thing, I love you and only you. Darren is a man of great intellect and intensity that I enjoy working with. He is a great attorney and I am learning a lot from him. Not just about law, but also about life as a Black person." Keith had nothing to say. He wasn't even sure of what to say. Donna's description of Darren was bold. "I know that....

"Never mind. Listen, why don't we leave now?" His interruption of her thoughts told her one thing and one thing only. This was going to be a long, exasperating lunch.

Seven

No matter the day, Alabama's weather was at most, the same, warm and with a lot of color. But during the winter months the beautiful scenery did not prove to be in this case. November especially was not one of the months. The cold air seemed to follow you even when the heat from a fireplace tried to comfort your body. November was always a cold month, and so was the family's reaction to Donna attending the yearly Thanksgiving Day dinner. Not that she really wanted to go, but it was for Keith, and she could not say no to him.

It was only right she thought that she should attend the annual family dinner, but her mind was not really ready for the usual conversation of children, law and what the neighbors did not have anymore. Neither was her mind ready to deal with Keith's sisters.

Darren had remained the same distant partner as he had been three months ago when they argued. Donna wasn't quite sure what happened in their unscheduled friendship, but whatever it was, she did not try to find out. In the interim they worked on the case together, won it together and celebrated it apart. Apart from each other, apart from the firm and apart from the clients they shared. Even though they won him more than what he had asked, neither mentioned the win to the other.

Many nights were spent working on the case, many long and stressful nights. Even when Donna tried to converse about topics that did not have any relevance to the case, Darren would answer quickly and immediately go back to the case. She could not figure out where his anger stem from. All she did know was that he wasn't the one to be angry.

"Donna, before you leave for the weekend, I would very much like to speak with you." When he spoke, she turned quickly to make sure that it was indeed Darren. Her motion was so abrupt that she almost dropped the punch served during the Thanksgivings Day celebration. He avoided her most of the day, and now he was speaking with her as if they had had conversation the entire day.

"About?"

"Just let me know before you leave."

"Actually, I am leaving now." She stepped back into her office, after putting down the half empty punch glass. "Why don't we speak now?"

As he followed behind her, she tried thinking of what he was going to argue with her about. She knew it wasn't a case because after their last case, he did not request her assistance on any other case. She sat in the chair behind her large mahogany desk and prepared herself for what would be there last argument. At least she saw it that way.

"I have been doing some research on the detective that you should consider using for your search of your parents and friends."

What she felt was shock. What she thought was shocking. What in the hell was he doing? "Darren, what is going on here?" She sat closer to the desk.

"What do you mean?" He did not sit when he came into her office. But he decided to take a seat after her question.

"What is going on here?" She tried to control her anger. Besides why was she angry? "I don't understand something. You...never mind. What is the name of the agency?"

"Actually, it is just a one manned business, but he is good. I always use him on cases that require a personal touch."

"Darren, forgive me if I am out of line here, but you haven't spoken a word to me about anything other than business for over three months. I mean, what kind of game are you playing?"

"I don't play games, Donna. Children play games." He said with certainty. "I simply wanted to give you this information because I knew that you needed it. You are still trying to search for your beginning, aren't you?"

"Yes, but I...."

"Well, I am here, as I said before to assist you." He stood and reached into his vest pocket and sat down again. He was of course, a very well dressed executive man. Suits and more suits, was all that he wore. Maybe on the weekend, or after work, he would put on a pair of designer slacks and comfortable designer shirt to match. He, too, always smelled like a man. Only the most masculine, yet soft smelling cologne would complement his masculine, yet soft personality. "Do you still want my assistance?"

"Yes, of course. I just need to.... You know what never mind." She decided to give up. There was a game being played, but she was not going to be a pawn. "So, you say this guy is good? I haven't actually given much thought to using a detective. I haven't thought much in finding any of the people who were with me in the home. And I especially haven't given thought to finding my parents."

"But I thought you were serious about finding yourself."

"I am."

"Well, maybe then I am misinformed."

"By whom?"

"By you." He sat back in chair and placed one leg over the other. "When we first met you spoke of this time of your life with such passion and conviction. I thought that you were serious. But it would seem that you are becoming complacent, or maybe fearful of doing what comes next in this journey of yours."

"I would say that I haven't become either."

"Well then, why don't you call this guy up and get him started?"

"What is his name?"

"His name is Michael Walker. He has been in the business for over 10 years, and I am sure he can find anyone you ask him to look for."

She sat back and thought to herself for a minute or so. Finding her parents had never been a thought for her. She gave up on finding them or them finding her years ago while still in the home. She remembered thinking to herself what kind of people would leave a helpless baby alone with people they did not know. Did it mean anything to her now, after all this time? NO! But was it important to her existence? Yes. "So you say this guy is really good."

"I am saying that if you want to find someone, anyone, he is the man for you." He stood, and turned to walk out of her office. "Oh yes, are you spending Thanksgiving with your husband?"

"Yes, I am." She tried not to look shaken by his question, and his new interest in her life.

"Okay." He smiled softly. "Well, have a nice weekend."

The long drive home allowed for many moments of thought. Thoughts of her marriage, her children, her childhood, the parents she never knew, and the friends she met at the home. She knew after talking to Darren that she did want to find those friends, but the jury was still out on finding her parents.

What kind of parents would leave an infant? If this Michael Walker person does find her parents, what will she say to them? What will they say to her? Do they want to find her? So many doubts, but she knew she had to try. Most of her time spent not talking to Darren made her lose focus on her journey, but she was back, and in full force, and she needed answers.

"Darling." Keith greeted her as she walked through the door of the apartment. "The boys and I were thinking of ordering pizza. What would you like on your side?"

After giving him a kiss on the cheek and then the boys, she put her purse down and walked into the bedroom, not answering his question. "I have had quite a day." Keith followed her noticing her separation from him and the boys.

"Are you alright?" He asked.

"Yes, I'm fine. Why do you ask?" She slid out of her high heel shoes.

"Because I asked what you would like on your pizza, and you totally ignore my question. Now what is wrong?"

"Nothing, really. I just have some things on my mind."

"Do we have to play twelve questions? Or are you going to tell me the whole story?" He sat on the end of the bed while she went into the closet to change.

"Darren told me today about using an investigator."

"What are you talking about?"

"He thought that I should try and find my parents, and may be even the friends I had at the home." Keith did not say anything as she walked back into the room, so she continued. "What do you think?" She slid on a pair of jeans and one of his t-shirts.

"Is this something you've thought about?"

"Yes."

"Well, are you ready for this?"

"I really don't know. I mean I gave up finding my parents years ago. I don't believe that I have given it too much thought since then. I just realized one day that they weren't going to rescue me from the home. When I did that my life seemed easier. I don't know if I want to believe in it again. There are so many what ifs in the reality of it. If this investigator was to find my parents, I don't know if I would want to see them."

"Why did Darren suggest this to you?"

"He feels that my parents are the beginning of my journey to finding my lost heritage."

"What do you think?"

"I don't know." She was sitting next to him on the bed when the boys came into the room. Her eyes planted softly on both of them. She thought of how nothing and no one could make her choose to leave her boys. How could her parents choose to leave her? Her thoughts made her feel childish. Maybe there was a logical reason why they had to leave her, maybe? "Maybe, I will call this guy."

"I think that you should." Keith agreed.

"May we order the pizza now?" Patrick asked.

"As soon as your mother tells us what she wants on her half."

"Mommy, what do you want on your side?" This time Sean stepped in to ask the questions. Sean was always more persistent than Patrick. He was also more passionate in getting what he wanted. Patrick was more passionate in love.

"I will have whatever you and your brother want." She said kissing them both gently on their foreheads. "Patrick, why don't you order the pizza? Your father and I will come in the living room after we finish talking."

"Thanks Mom." Both boys gladly ran out of the room before another word could be said. Patrick knew exactly who to call and how to tell them his address. He had ordered pizza in the past a few times when Donna did not feel like cooking.

"I thought that we finished talking." Keith quickly said. "I mean you have already made up your mind, as you have done before." He remained seated on the end of the bed while Donna stood to address his cynicism.

"What does that mean?"

"It means exactly what I said." Keith stood and took her hand. "Baby, listen, this whole thing has been of your doing anyway. You don't need my advice."

"Keith, you are wrong. I do need your advice." She, too, stood. "I know that it may seem that I don't need to hear what you have to say about what I am going through right now, but I do. I really do."

"If that were true, you would have come to me before you bought this apartment."

"Are we still there?"

"We never left." Keith said with certainty. "Listen, I know that it may seem that I have been alright with your actions, but I am not. I need my wife at home where she belongs. Not in a totally different house than the one we share together. I don't even want to mention how this decision of your, has affected my relationship with the boys."

"I don't want to get into this right now, Keith. I only wanted to know what you thought of my choices. I simply asked you a question regarding my life and you can't even answer that." Keith did not give a response verbal in nature. He exited out of the bedroom as if no one else remained after him. Donna saddened by his departure sat back on the bed. When Patrick entered the room, she did not notice him. He sat next to her and took her hand in his.

"Mommy, are you okay?" .

"Oh baby." She answered finally realizing his touch. "I am doing just fine."

"You're lying to me. Why?" He held onto her hand. "Is it because you think that I am too little to understand what is going on between you and Dad? Or is it because you think that I won't understand that I am Black?"

"What?"

"Jeremy told me that I am Black and that dad is White."

"Oh baby." Many words ran through her body, but none seemed to fit what was necessary to say to Patrick at that moment.

"Is that why we are living here and dad is living at home?"

"Oh baby." Words seemed to still fail her.

"Is it? Are we ever going back home to live with dad?"

"Do you want to go back home?"

"I want to go only if you want to go."

"Baby, listen, if you want to live with your father, it is okay with me. As long as you leave time for me."

He seemed sad. "You don't want me, mommy?"

Only fear found its way to her heart. Fear that her child felt like she did not want him. Fear that he did not know what he meant to her. "Patrick, I know that right now you're not old enough to understand what is happening between your father and me, but I need you to know that it doesn't have anything to do with you or your brother. The two of you mean the world to both of us." She held him close to her. "Patrick, I only told you that you could go live with your father because I don't ever want you to feel as if I have taken you from him. Your father and I did not spend much time talking about this move. Believe me when I say this, your father had nothing to do with my decision to leave. He wanted me, us to stay home with him, but there are some things that I have to find out about myself. Things that right now at your age you would not understand. But the thought of leaving you and your brother behind to find out what is going on with me was too painful for me to deal with, so I told your father that the two of you had to come with me. He agreed only because he loves me, and because he knows that I love him."

"I will stay with you. You need protection." He said looking up at her.

"I need protection, you think?"

"Yes, I do. You are a girl, and girls need boys to protect them."

She smiled softly. "Okay, then you can be my big protector. What about your brother?"

"Well, he will stay, too. But only as my backup." Keith stood by the corner of the door listening to the conversation. Patrick laughed as children do to things that they really don't understand, but had at least made an attempt to try.

Eight

Thanksgiving Dinner started as it always did with Mr. Pennington saying the family blessings. However, this year proved something all, together different for Donna. She felt the need not to bow her head and close her eyes. She instead decided to keep her head up and watch the others. As she scanned the room, all she could see was the White faces of people she did not know. People who at one time in her life was the example of what family life was to be, but as she looked at them at that moment, all she could see were strangers. Only her children were recognizable to her. Even Keith felt like a distant stranger.

The Pennington home was already decorated for Christmas. Thanksgiving was just the month to share old memories and future plans. No one really celebrated it. The food was always catered and supremely delicious. The dinner table was set only for the adults, while the children were given a table of their own. The nine room mansion was furnished in contemporary furnishing, because Mr. Pennington thought it always necessary to stay ahead of the times for the occasional possibility of entertaining possible clients.

When she felt his hand squeeze hers, she tried not to catch his stare, but his grip became tighter. She whispered softly for him to loosen his grip, but he held her hand even tighter. She knew then that he had caught her in her observation of his family. And she could also tell that he was not happy. She told herself then that she would not mention the moment to him because she did not want to argue with him. All they did was argue. At times when they were trying to be nice to each other, they would find the passion to make love, which had begun to reach a new level of happiness of its own.

Keith had decided it was okay for her to be sexually aware. He decided that he was not intimidated by her moments of torrid sensuality. He in fact enjoyed not having to make the first move. She enjoyed the liberty of touching him wherever and whenever she wanted. That is of course, if they weren't arguing.

"Donna, how long is your vacation?" Mr. Pennington asked carefully. "I mean, I understand that you are taking one."

"Two weeks." Donna tried to answer carefully. She really wasn't upset with Keith's father, but Kevin seemed to think that she was, so she played the game with him. "I decided to take time off so that I could spend it with the boys, and of course your son."

"Well, that is a good thing." Keith's mother stated.

"Why is that Marianne?" Donna asked quickly.

"It is your place as their mother to be home with them." Marianne was not one to hold her tongue. This personality trait was always visible. Donna figured it was because she taught in public school that she was so verbal.

"You decided this when Marianne? Before or after you retired from teaching?"

"Donna, I will have you to know that I did my time raising my children. Taking a job in teaching only came when my children were old enough to care for each other when I wasn't at home."

"Don't you mean the nanny?" Jenny intercepted.

"Thanks, Jenny, but I can handle this one." Keith defended. "Mother, I do believe whatever decisions my wife and I make for our lives, are our decisions to make."

"If I recall correctly, you weren't consulted on the decision until it was made." Marianne was as shrewd an attorney as her husband, but it was never to be her reality. She had decided to teach instead of entertaining the law since the money was running short for the family. When the future looked financially prosperous for the family, she had decided that her time had passed and that teaching was enough. But there were moments when it seemed she would have proved to be a great attorney. "Perhaps, had you been included in this matter things would not have turned out this way."

"What way Mother?" Keith asked demandingly.

"Your wife at home where she belong."

"My wife belongs where she wants to be, mother."

"Keith, it isn't necessary that you defend my decisions with anyone." Donna finally tried to speak. "Marianne has a right to say whatever she wishes, this is her home. But it seems that I don't have the right to be here, so I will just leave."

"Donna that is not what I meant." Marianne quickly stood and said.

"Well, it is how I feel." Donna stood from the dinner table. "Keith, when you and the boys have finished your dinner, I will be home waiting for you." She realized that she should advise which home. "Not the apartment."

"Donna, please don't leave." Kevin insisted. "My wife can sometimes be more abrupt than necessary. I am sure she did not mean any harm."

"Well, I am sure that she did, and I do take it as such." She kissed Keith on his cheek. "I will see you at home."

"Donna, please don't go." Jenny stood this time. "My mother is not the only person in this home. Besides, she did not mean to be so rude."

"Jenny, really it is okay. I don't feel welcome here anymore." Donna looked around the room at the faces of those whom she had known for years, but once again they were faces of strangers, White strangers. "What is going on inside of me now, is something that I cannot ignore. I have tried for the past two years to ignore it, but it haunts me. I don't feel that I am being a good mother to my boys, or the wife that Keith deserves. I feel lost and unwanted. This is not your fault or the fault of your "rude" mother, it is just how things are right now, and I am comfortable with that."

"Have you tried to talk with anyone about this? I mean someone who is trained?" Jenny asked.

The rest of the family, including Mr. Pennington remained quiet. This was strange enough but Donna knew that she did not have strength to do anything about it. "I don't need to talk with anyone."

"Donna, why don't you sit down? The boys are here and I am here and we are your family." Keith finally said something. Even though what he said wasn't what Donna wanted to hear. He stood and tried to take her hand. "Don't leave Donna."

"Keith, there isn't any reason why I should stay."

"I thought that I just gave you at least three."

"That isn't what I mean." She realized that she had hurt his feelings and she did not want to do that. "What I mean is that your family does not want me here, and I don't want to be where I am not welcomed."

At this Mr. Pennington felt it was necessary that he should stand and say something. He had remained quiet only because he did not want to destroy what was left of his relationship with Donna since their last dinner. But Marianne stood. "Listen Donna, don't you think that you are taking this finding your Blackness thing a little too far. I mean look at you. You are not about to walk out of the home that welcomed you, and in doing so, you will be leaving your husband and children behind. Is that what you really want to do? Is walking out on your family the only thing that is going to help you in finding yourself?"

"Mother." Jenny exclaimed.

"Jenny that is okay." Donna tried to settle her. "Your mother is right, walking out is all that I can think to do when I don't want to be where I am not welcomed. But leaving my family behind is not." She began walking away from the table. "Listen, this is not easy for me. I don't want to be many places these days, but leaving my family is not what I am trying to do. I love Keith, and I love our boys. But my life is not my life right now. I am not happy, and I...."

"What do you mean you're not happy?" Keith asked. She hadn't said that before.

Donna only looked at him. The boys sat quietly at their table with the rest of the grandchildren in the day room. The children were already eating their dinner and had not thought to look in at the adults. Donna realized that she was still standing and that the conversation she and Keith were about to get into was not one that they should discuss in front of his family.

When they lived with his parents they could never have an argument alone. She could see those moments coming around again, but she refused to let that happen because enough had been said. "Keith, I am going to leave. I will be home waiting on you and the boys to return."

"Donna, I asked you a question!" He insisted that an answer be given. It wasn't that he was in front of his family that he felt he should continue, and she knew that. Keith just could not end an argument without a resolution. She knew that in his mind she was walking out on him again. He stepped toward her direction. "I want an answer Donna."

"Keith, I am not going to have this conversation here."

"Donna, Keith, please don't do this now." Lori, who usually thought of herself to be the voice of reason, spoke loudly. "Your children are here. Why don't you two stop this, now!"

"Lori, stay out of this." Keith demanded. He was getting angrier by the second, and Lori was about to feel the brunt of it. "Donna, I need an answer."

"Keith, I am not going to answer your question." She turned from him and started walking to the foyer. Keith followed her footsteps. And so did everyone else.

"Donna, don't walk away from me! You will give me an answer! And you will give it to me now!"

When she turned to look at him, she saw only anger, anger and pain. The pain of rejection was one thing, but the pain of a loved one walking out on you was quite another. How she should handle the situation was not to her understanding. If she should handle it was not clear either. But she did know something had to be done. Touching him was of course, out of the question. Even though she really wanted too, she knew that it would only produce more of what he was already feeling. Besides, if he felt her touch, he would only feel her confusion.

"Donna, answer my question!" By now he was in her face. She could feel the rhythmic beats of his heart through his silk shirt. "I do believe that I am warranted that much."

"Keith, I am not going to do this here."

"But you are." He took her hand and held it close to him. "I refuse to let you leave here without answering me."

"Son, you must let her leave if that is what she wants to do." His father insisted.

"Father, stay out of this!" He turned his anger on his father. "Donna is my wife and I will deal with her as I see fit! Now, every one of you leave us alone!"

"Keith, are you out of your mind? Let go of my hand!" She pulled her hand from his grasp. "I am not going to discuss this with you, now!"

"Damn it Donna, you aren't going anywhere!" He took her hand again and pulled her to him. "I need you home! I need my family home!"

"Keith, I thought that you understood, but...."

"But what?" After letting her hand loose, he turned to see the boys starring at them. "Boys, go back to the dinner table."

"Daddy, is mommy okay?" Patrick walked into the foyer without being noticed by either Donna or Keith. When he saw the stress in his mother's eyes and heard the anger in his father's voice, he felt it necessary to step in.

"Your mother is fine Patrick." Keith affirmed without looking back at the frightened, yet gallant boy. "Now go back to the dinner table."

"Patrick, I am okay." Donna stepped away from Keith's grasp to reaffirm her position. "Your father and I are having a conversation right now."

"But daddy sounds angry."

Keith still refused to face Patrick. His anger had taken him to a level of embarrassment with his family and now with his son, eye contact could not be made. "Patrick, go back to the dinner table."

"I will if mommy goes with me."

"Come on sweetheart." Donna took his hand and began walking him back to the table. "I will walk back to the table with you and then your father and I will continue talking."

"Are you leaving us mommy?"

"Of course not baby. How could I leave you?"

"Well, when you finish your conversation with daddy, will you come back and sit with me?"

It was always refreshing for Donna and Keith to listen to the intelligence of their children. Listening to Patrick trying to protect her made Donna smile. That was until she looked around to see the adults of the family standing in front of her. "I am going to walk you back to the table and after your father and I talk I will see what I can do."

"Donna, I will walk Patrick back to the table." Kevin said.

"No, I will do it. Please, everyone just go back to having your dinner." No one moved at first, but as she and Patrick passed by, they decided it was safe to do so. Keith still refused to turn around. He was very angry. Donna knew that he was, but she could not defuse it this time. It would be up to him to make light of what had become a horrible moment in time.

As she walked through the dining area to the day room, she tried to avoid the eyes of Keith's mother, who had remained there instead of running to his rescue with the others. The day room was simply what Kevin Pennington called the room for the children to dine in, during the daytime. Any dinners that were not held during the day light hours allowed the children the privilege of sitting with the adults or upstairs with the nanny. It was furnished with the same furnishing as the dining room, with the exception of two or three baby chairs. Usually, the nanny would sit and feed the children, if need be. During Patrick and Sean's infant years, Donna sat in the day room to feed them. She never wanted any other woman to feed her children. She was their mother, and it was her duty.

"Now Patrick, sit and eat your dinner. When you are finished I will be waiting for you at home."

"But I thought you were going to wait for me here?"

"Aunt Donna, are you leaving now?" Lori's daughter Sara asked. Sara was always interested in Donna's coming and goings. She was also very interested in why her Uncle Keith married a woman who was colored. No one in the family wanted to answer the question. Even at 10 years of age, Sara still asked the questions why, but the questions is more politically correct, or as politically correct as a 10 year-old could be. Now, it was why did he marry a Black woman? Not that the color of Donna's skin made a difference

113

in how Sara related to her because she loved her. She trusted Donna with all of her secrets. Maybe it was because of her black skin that Sara felt she could trust her. She was different, which meant she could be told all the things that you could not tell your parents.

"Yes, I have to go to work. But Patrick I will be home waiting for you and Sean."

"But I don't want you to leave mommy. Please don't leave." Patrick begged.

"I have to Patrick. Please don't make this any harder on mommy than it already is." She gently kissed his forehead. "I promise I will be home waiting for you and your brother. She felt terrible making her children feel responsible for her problems, but it had to be done. It was selfish and unforgivable. But it was also because of her selfishness that she would someday teach them the way of her heritage. That she felt would make up for her betrayal, today. "I will see you both when you get home." As she kissed both of them on their cheeks, she felt something inside her turn. She knew that something was going to happen that she had not exactly planned on. As that thought ran through her mind, Keith had made his way into the day room.

"Donna, we need to talk."

"Keith, there is no more to talk about." She quickly said as she walked out of the room.

"Listen Donna, I am not allowing you to leave until we finish this conversation!" His anger had gone beyond the norm. It was almost violent in tone. "Donna, turn around and talk to me now!"

As she made her way back into the foyer, Keith quickly approached and grabbed her wrist. "Keith, let go." She demanded as quietly as she could. She didn't want the kids to hear.

"If you leave Donna, don't bother to come back!" She opened the door leading out of the house.

"What did you say to me?" She tried to turn face to face, but he refused to release his grip.

"I said, if you leave don't bother to come back. And I mean exactly that!" He released his grip only so he could speak freely. "I can't take this anymore. I need my wife at home. I can't take you not being with me when I go to sleep at night. I can't take my kids not being with me. I need my family with me, in the house that we share together. If you don't want to be with me, then I think we need to do something about it." He was calming down, but it was painful, heart wrenchingly painful.

"What is that something, Keith? Are you talking about divorce?" His answer would either break her heart or make her think twice about coming home sooner.

"If you aren't coming back home, yes, I guess I do mean divorce."

Her heart broke. She could feel the valves bending and the chambers doors closing down quickly. "Is this what you're using to control me? You're threatening me with a divorce."

"It is not a threat, Donna." He walked passed her and out the door. "I don't want to do this anymore." He said as she closed the huge door behind her. "I don't have the strength."

"I don't know what to say."

"What do you mean you don't know what to say?" He turned to her shocked by her statement. "Do you love me, Donna?"

"Yes, Keith, I do love you."

"Well, what is the problem?"

"Keith, this does not have anything to do with my love for you."

"That can't be possible. It has everything to do with your love for me. I mean how else, could you come to the decision to leave me."

"I did not leave you, Keith."

"What in the hell do you think your living in a different home than the one we share together is?"

"Keith, please." She had to do something because she was losing him. "I don't know how to explain to you what is going on inside me. Nor do I don't know how to share it with you. It is as if my life is lost in this abyss." She sat on the doorsteps. The front doorsteps were her favorite of the house. They were once thought to be the place where she and Keith would go share thoughts of their future. They loved that special place on the doorsteps. Now, all of a sudden it had become her nightmare. "So, you want a divorce?"

"If you're not coming home, I see no other option."

"Just like that you want a divorce." She continued to look at him hoping for a no.

"Isn't that how you moved out? Without conversation, and without considering my feelings?"

"So, to get back at me, you're divorcing me?"

"It isn't about revenge Donna. It is about me being a lonely man. It is about my needs."

"Keith, I am going to leave now." She stood quickly, hoping to avoid his next statement.

"What?"

"I think I should leave before we both do or say something else that we will regret in the morning."

"Donna, I have given this a lot of thought. This isn't something that I just thought of." He tried to continue before she took another step. "When you left I thought I would never get over it, and I didn't. But one night just before I fell asleep alone, I thought of you. I thought of us. I thought of how selfish it was for you to tear our family apart on a search for a life that you never knew. After much more thinking, I realized that you weren't worth my lonely nights."

She stopped breathing. At least she thought she did. "Are you saying that you don't love me?"

"What I am saying is that if you are as selfish as you have shown yourself to be in the last six months, then you aren't the woman I

118

love. The woman I love would never do what you are doing to our family."

"Keith."

"No, Donna, I am not going to listen to your excuses anymore. If you want to leave our home, you are going to do it the right way." He waited for her to say something, but no words were spoken. "I know that you will want the boys to live with you, and I won't give any objections to that. That is as long as we share custody." Still she was unable to speak. So he continued. "All of our properties, your alimony, and child support will be handled generously and equally. I will fulfill my duties as our boy's father and your ex-husband."

"Keith."

"If you want the house, I...."

"Keith."

"Yes." He wanted to finish what he had rehearsed earlier. "Donna, I haven't come to this conclusion easily. As a matter of fact, my heart is breaking up into pieces that I am sure I will never find again. I love you, Donna. I love you even more as I look into those brown eyes today, but I can't keep doing this anymore. This whole thing is tearing me apart."

She felt the cold air claiming her body. Funny she thought to herself, the cold air did not exist when she first walked out the door. She remembered taking her coat from the closet, and putting it down in one of the chairs when she walked onto the porch, but she did not remember being cold. But now, now the air felt as if it was going to take her away. She wished that it would claim the pain she felt in her chest, but that was not to be. "Is this really what you want?"

"No, it isn't what I want. It is what I need." He turned from her. "Donna, I can't, I won't let you destroy what is left of me for someone else."

"Is there someone else?" She dropped her head sullenly. The next word that comes out of his mouth could either permanently destroy her or give her some time to correct what had been wronged.

"Donna, how could there be someone else when there is you?" He considered his words. "I am not a man who wants to be a bachelor. I like having a woman in my life. I like having a woman to cuddle with at night. I thought you were to be that woman, but I see that is not the case."

"I am that woman, Keith."

"Don't do this, Donna."

"Don't do what?"

"That night when you walked out on me, I told myself that I would do whatever I had to do to get you back. But then I woke up one morning and realized that it was not my fault that you had left. I realized that if you wanted to come back you would have to come back without my interference." He took her right hand and gently stroked it. "My dear wife, you chose to leave me. You and you alone decided that our marriage was not enough for you. So, I decided on my own that your leaving me was enough for me. I will not let you destroy me anymore than you already have. If you want to find yourself, do so. But you will not do that at the expense of my heart. Not any longer."

"Keith." The tears started to fall before she could stop them. "I don't want a divorce."

"What does that mean?"

"I don't know." She pulled her hand away from him. "Keith, I really don't know."

Nine

When the sun's rays found their way through the rain, and then through the blinds of the bedroom window, Donna quickly turned over to face the other side of the bed, but there was no one there. It was cold outside, very cold, and with the rain sounding against the window, Donna wanted only to drown herself in the darkness of her mind. The memory of the day before had not climbed through the worries of her mind. It had not manifested because she refused to let it. She realized that she could not keep this up for long, but repression had been her partner since childhood. Repression was the one thing in this world that she could count on when life's miseries claimed her self-worth. And it would be repression that would get her through yet another catastrophe. She did remember leaving the boys with Keith. This was after he suggested that it would be better that they stayed with him so that they could spend more time with their cousins.

Usually, a great many things would be done on the day after Thanksgiving, participating in the scurry of Black Friday was one of them.

Even though there was truly no need for the Penningtons to shop for sales, it was thought to be just a day to be together with the world outside. It was their way of staying connect with those less fortunate. Besides, the shopping done would be for purchases to give to different charitable organizations. But no shopping with Keith's family would be done this year instead she would go to work and write the brief for her client that she had put aside on Monday. She would smother herself with work. That of course, would be easy since her name had become quite important to the firm because of the cases she shared with Darren.

Darren's father was very complimentary of her work on the case. Although Darren never told her of this achievement, the grapevine provided by her paralegal was communication enough. Since Keith had decided it was best that the boys stayed with him the rest of the weekend, she could focus on work. So that was what she would do, work and more work.

When she entered the office building, she tried to shake what water she could off of her umbrella. The guard, Stanley, looked up from his small screen television to greet her. Her hair was not looking its best and neither was the sweat suit she decided to wear. She was sure that Stanley was surprised to see her, but she did not give him time to question her about it. She took the elevator to her office on the 15th floor. While on the elevator she took a deep breath. She had found that taking a deep breath had become her duty in order to keep a clear head. Her desk still had the file of her client on it. She remembered telling Matthew not to file it since she had planned on coming in during the weekend. She placed her purse in its usual spot in her closet and then walked over to her desk. When she opened the blinds to let what was left of the sunlight in, her heart felled victim to the repressions that she had tried so desperately to bury.

She fell to the floor as if she was experiencing an epileptic seizure. Her body trembled unmercifully. She tried to wrap her body within her arm's span, but she shook so she could not hold on. The tears that fell from her eyes felt as heavy as the rain that fell from the stormy sky. They burned her cheeks. She tried again to cradle her body, but still was unable to do so. She tried to pull herself up to her knees to pray, but her strength felled her. She began praying fervently.

"God, please make it stop! Make the pain stop. Please, God." She could feel her lungs shutting down, she could not breathe. "God, please!" When it seemed that the pain was going to be the death of all she knew, she succumbed to the torture of her heart, and fell asleep.

Ten

Many days had passed since the volcano in her heart erupted, many, many days. But the smut and burning sensation still resided. Keith brought the boys to the apartment on Sunday and left without saying a word to her, except to say that he would pick up the boys for Christmas. No time after that did she hear from him, or any member of his family. She had expected to hear from Jenny, but she had not called. Something was different, not wrong just different. Patrick seemed somewhat distant from her since that Thanksgiving Day, and she figured it was because she did not keep her word to him. He wanted her to come back, but she could not face him or his brother after her fight with Keith. Patrick and Sean spent most of their time at the center, and she spent most of her time at the office.

When she got the divorce papers she knew then that she would soon have to tell the boys of her failure to hold on to their father. She did not think that he would go through with his threat of divorce, but he did. She tried to reach him at his office, but he had refused to speak with her until she signed the papers. He said he did not want to barter with their lives anymore. It was all so strange and fast. But it also explained why his family was so controlled during the Thanksgiving dinner, they all knew. It had all been planned. She would arrive with the boys and then he would ask her about moving back to their home. She would refuse, as Keith knew, and then he would tell her that he wanted a divorce. Keith had met with his attorney to draw up the necessary papers before the Thanksgiving holiday. This she found out during her meeting with him and the attorney handling the divorce. Everything was divided equally, with the exception of his alimony payments, which were more than what she ever expected. Alimony would be paid until she remarried. The court ordered and she agreed to joint custody of boys. Keith would pay child support payments and make specific monetary provisions for their college funds. A trust fund would also be set up for the boys, to be granted to them respectfully at the age of 21. Between their college and trust funds, the boys would be multi-millionaires. The accounts would be managed by both Keith and Donna, and they would require both of their signatures should any withdrawals be requested.

Christmas was only a couple of days away and telling the boys of the divorce would destroy their celebration. Donna decided to hold off until the holidays were over. She would let the boys spend the holidays with Keith and his family. If they had a question as to where she was going to be, she would tell them that she had to work. And just to make what she said true, she would go into the office.

She gave the house to Keith since it was a gift from his parents. It was also the only home that the boys knew, and she did not want to take them out of that environment. Keith argued against keeping the house, but his words went without her actually listening. She did not want the house. She was comfortable with the apartment. The four bedrooms, three full baths and a half 4200 square foot luxury apartment had more than enough space for the boys to play and spread their wings.

Everything happened so fast, even looking back at each moment of change, Donna could not account for when she lost her husband. She thought maybe it happened when she walked out of the door of his parents' home. Maybe it was before then. Maybe it was when she woke one morning and realized that she was a Black woman without a heritage. She could have told him then, but what could she say that he would understand. Maybe she did not want him to understand.

The air was cold outside and the rain that was there during the Thanksgiving holiday was still there. The sound of the lightning only made her loneliness increase. The boys were with Keith and the sounds of their voices were missed. When she could no longer deal with the silence and the nagging pain in her heart, she rendered her services to her client. The more work she could do, the better.

"Hello." Donna was not familiar with the voice that came from her office door. She figured she was the only person in the building since not even the guard was at his desk when she came through the lobby. The parking garage was also empty. With Monday being Christmas day, most businesses were closed for the weekend.

"Excuse me."

"Yes, listen, I am Halley Duncan."

"Yes." Donna said. Still she did not know this woman, who seemed to be quite at home in her office.

"My father, Nathaniel Duncan was supposed to meet me here. I wonder have you seen him."

Donna felt silly, a lot less silly and more ignorant. Was she that far gone that hearing the name Duncan did not awaken her senses? "Forgive me." She stood and walked from behind her desk to shake Halley's hand. "I did not know."

"That is fine." Halley assured her. "Not many people know me here. I lied, mostly everyone knows me." She said walking further into the office. "You are...?"

"Yes, I am Donna Pennington....

"Oh yes, Donna. I have heard quite a bit about you from both my father and my brother, Darren. You are said to be a powerful attorney. How much of that is true?"

"I guess it would depend on who you ask."

"I am asking you." Halley asked in her most authoritative voice. She was not at all like her name, soft and gentle. She was a woman whose presence was as alarming and commanding as her brother's. She was a lady, a beautiful lady who knew what she wanted and how to get it. Donna could see that just by looking at her. If it took using feminine wiles or intellectual combat, she was ready. She was in most surrounding of business, an intimidating person, partly because she was a woman, and partly because she was a Black woman. She was comfortable with her presence. She seemed to even relish in its glory. But as intimidating as she seemed to be, she was just as humble. These two characteristics of her personality were not at all allies to each other, and with that realization Halley disciplined her mind to control the attack on others, and maybe even herself.

"Well, I am not sure how to answer that question without sounding arrogant."

"Arrogance is fine, as long as you have the backing to defend such a description of your abilities." She smiled curtly and then gestured to take a seat on Donna's sofa. "As I said, my father speaks very highly of you, and I would love to hear what you think of yourself."

"Why?" Donna asked, consenting to the gesture to sit. Rather than taking the seat next to her, Donna ventured back to the front of her desk and sat on the edge of it with her arms folded in front of her.

"Why not? Who is best to judge one's action, but the one who is in question?"

"Still, I ask you, why is it so important for you to know?"

"Just as my brother stated, you are quite an example."

"Example?"

"Example of a woman on the move." She smiled softly this time. "Have a seat, please."

"I have been sitting for some time this weekend, I'd rather stand." Donna stated. After all it was her office she should be the one who offered the seat.

"Tell me about yourself."

"You first."

"Okay, I will." She positioned her body to a more relax soft like state and then began the tale of her life. "I am 35 years of age. I practice law with a firm that my father dislikes and I enjoy. I have been engaged to the world's greatest man for one year. I have no intentions in marrying this man, but I will forever be his wife. I love my family, and I love being a Black woman. I have always felt that there is something great in being who I am as a Black woman." For a moment Donna felt she was listening to the voice in her head, but she knew that it could not be since she did not know what it meant to be a Black woman. But listening to Halley expressing her love of being a Black woman with such conviction made her feel that a part of her was speaking. "Not many women, Black women that is, are comfortable with being a Black woman, but I make love to it every day that I wake."

"I am not sure of what to say."

"Is there something to say, or do you have questions to ask?"

"Your fiancé, is he aware that you will never marry him?" She was afraid to ask anything else.

"Of course." She placed a smile on her face that was both conning and honest. "We only became engage to lessen the questions with my family about our relationship. I could remain his lady friend for the rest of my life. I love him. I love him more than I love myself, but marriage has never been a road that I've wanted to travel." She uncrossed her legs and lean against the shoulder of the sofa. "My parents are devout Christians. My brothers and

I were raised to believe in the Old Mighty Bible, and every Word of God. There is but one interpretation of that Word, and I believe that to be true. However, I have not found the courage in my heart yet to trust someone enough to give my life to him." Donna was quiet. "If my memory serves me right, I think that my brother informed me that you are married to an attorney yourself, right?"

"I was." The pain that she had forgotten had found its way back to her reality. She tried to go back to sit in her chair, but could not move. She was paralyzed with sorrow. "I -I ---

Halley saw the anguish in her eyes. "Is there something wrong?" Go away. Donna said to her heartache, but it was relentless. "Donna, are you alright?" Halley stood and walked over to her side. "Donna?"

"Yes."

"Are you okay?"

"I just need to sit down for a minute or two." She found her way to the chair in front of her. "I just have a lot on my mind."

"It would seem like you do."

Donna looked up at her with tears in her eyes. "I am sorry." She tried to wipe away the tears with her hands.

"About what?" Halley retrieved the box of kleenex on the desk and placed it on Donna's lap.

"I guess when I think about it, you aren't the person that I should be apologizing too. I should be asking for forgiveness from Keith."

"Keith?"

"Yes, Keith, my husband." By now the tears had all but dried and her emotional balance was once again found to handle the situation at hand. "Listen, I really should get some work done here."

"Donna, are you okay?"

"I am fine." She stood and walked to finally sit in chair behind her desk. "Are you sure that your father was supposed to meet you here?"

"There are few things in life that I will allow myself to overlook, but a woman's tears are not one of them. Talk with me. I promise, I won't bite."

Donna looked at this stranger who wanted her to open her heart and smiled gently. "Halley, thanks a lot, but really I can handle this."

"Handle what?"

"You can't get the hint, can you?" She began to mettle with the paper on her desk. "I am trying to be polite, but you are refusing to concede."

"I am not refusing, I am simply not going to stop asking until you tell me what made the eyes of a woman with such character as you possess, shower me with tears."

Donna thought for a few minutes while starring into Halley's eyes. She could not bring herself to opening up, not to Halley, not to anyone. She had failed, and admitting to this failure was not easy for her to do. "Right now is not a good time."

"Well, tell me what are you doing for the Christmas holidays?"

"I haven't given much thought to that. I will probably be here working."

"No one works on Christmas."

"This year I will be." She sat back in her chair. "My boys will be spending time with their father's family, and I...."

"Then why don't you join my family?" Halley saw the pain in Donna's eyes, so she interrupted what was going to obviously be the difficult last words for her to speak.

"I can't do that."

"Why not?" Halley asked. "My father would love to have you. He loves Christmas. The more the merrier. Besides, I would love to have someone other than my brothers to talk to." She waited for Donna's answer. "Please don't say no."

"Are you sure it will be okay?"

"Of course. Why don't I give you the address because dinner will be at my parent's home?"

"Halley, are you sure this will be okay? I mean I am sure that you have other people you could invite."

"Yes, but none are as intriguing as you." She stood up. "I believe that I see now what my brother sees in you."

"And that is?"

"Invitation. You seem to offer yourself to the world quite honestly, but with strong reservations. Quite a contradiction of personality, if I would say so myself."

Eleven

When Keith ranged the doorbell, Donna thought initially that he would be alone, so she came to the door with only her robe on. However, when she opened it Carolyn stood there looking as beautiful as she did that night when she last saw her, Donna forgot what she was to say. Keith who saw the shock in her eyes nonchalantly invited Carolyn and himself into the apartment. As they walked passed Donna she felt the familiar pain that she had become one with since Thanksgiving.

"Donna you know Carolyn Mentz?" Keith was cold. "Are the boys ready?" She heard what he said, but she could not believe that it was true. Did he hate her that much that he would bring this woman to her home and show her off to her boys? "Donna, are the boys ready?"

He had won. She was defeated. "I,...Keith, may I speak with you in my room, please?" She finally closed the door. "Carolyn, if you could please excuse us."

"Carolyn, please have a seat." He walked Carolyn to the sofa, and waited for her to sit. Donna walked to her bedroom passed the boys rooms. Keith followed behind her without missing a step. "Donna, what is it that you want?"

Donna stepped behind him and closed the door. "Keith, do you hate me this much?"

"I don't hate you at all, Donna. And if you are asking that asinine question because I am with Carolyn, you are way out of line."

"I'm out of line!"

"Yes, you are out of line."

"Keith, we have only been divorced a couple of weeks and you already have someone in your life."

"How long was I supposed to wait, Donna? I mean it is not as if you have been in my life for months now. I told you before I have needs."

"So, this is what she is all about, your needs?"

"Yes, my needs. Is there a problem with that?"

She stopped for a moment and turned away from him. "Keith, do you not know how much I love you?"

"I would say that none of that really matters anymore."

"What?" She turned quickly to face him. "Are you telling me that you don't love me?"

139

"I am telling you that how I feel or don't feel about you doesn't matter, any longer. It hasn't mattered to you for months, so why should it matter now." He turned to walk out of the room. "I am going to get the boys."

"Keith, please don't do this. You are killing me." She was desperate. "I gave you the divorce because you asked for it. I never wanted a divorce."

"Let's not do this now Donna. Carolyn is waiting."

"Carolyn is waiting!" She was wounded. She did not know who he was. "What about me? What about us? What about our family?"

"Donna, all you have been thinking about is you." He turned back around to face her. "You haven't thought about us or our family since this whole thing began with you. What in the hell makes you think that I should continue to live in this warped world of Black and White?"

"Are you sleeping with her?"

"Have you talked with the boys about our divorce?"

"No."

"Well, I suggest you call them in here now so that we can do it together." He was serious.

"While you're doing that I will let Carolyn know it will be a bit longer."

When he walked out the room she felt as if he would never return. He was gone. Patrick and Sean would not want to hear what they were about to tell them, but she knew that they had to be told. She slowly walked to the boys' door and knocked gently. It was a dream, a nightmare. That's what it felt like inside of her head. All she had to do was pinch her arm and this would be over. "Patrick, your father and I need to speak with you and your brother. We need for the two of you to come into my room."

"Is this about your divorce?" Patrick asked. He put down the control unit to his video game. Sean continued to play.

"Patrick?"

"Grandmother told us."

"Why didn't you say something to me?" She walked further into the room.

"We figured that she was not telling the truth because you and daddy did not tell us." When Keith walked into the room, Sean put his unit on the bed and ran to him.

"Daddy, are you leaving us?" Sean wrapped his arms around Keith's leg.

Keith looked at her with great disappointment in his eyes. "Don't look at me like that." She defended.

"Couldn't you wait until I returned to the room?"

"Keith I did not say anything. Your mother told the boys."

"So, it's true." Patrick asked.

"Son, sit down." Keith took Sean into his arms and walked him over to his bed. "Your mother and I decided that it was best that we do this."

"Don't say that." Donna insisted. "If we are going to tell them, let's tell them the truth."

"Meaning?"

"Meaning, tell them that it was your idea, not mine."

Keith only looked at her for a moment, and then he realized that it was true. "Your mother is right I decided that we should end our marriage. Now you boys aren't old enough to understand this yet, but I, we both want you to know that this does not mean that we do not love you. Our love for the both of you is as strong, if not stronger than the day you came into our lives."

"Why did you want to leave us, Daddy?" Patrick asked. Sean was quiet. The look in his eyes was of confusion and lost.

"Patrick, I could never leave either of you." Donna turned away from the conversation. She did not want to become a part of his reasoning. When she heard Keith's voice quivering she turned back to them, but still remained quiet. What was she to say? She could say that Keith was doing what she did. He was lonely, confused and angry at life and the world for failing to fulfill him with all that he thought was true. She could tell them that she had failed as a wife, a friend, a lover and a mother in keeping their family together. She could say all of that, but then why should she? She was still very lonely, confused and angry at life and the world. "You boys mean the world to me, and even more. Your mother and I found ourselves in a place in life where we could no longer be together as man and wife, so I did what was necessary to make that legal."

"Do we have to live with you or with mommy?" Sean finally said something.

"We decided that the both of you would live with your mother. I will continue to pick you on the weekends or on special days."

"Mommy, are you coming with us today?" Patrick asked. He was sad.

"No, Patrick. But I will be here when you return."

"Are you going to spend Christmas alone?"

"I won't be with you boys, but I won't be alone." She took his hand. "Listen, this Christmas you can spend with your father and his family, and next Christmas you will be here with me."

"No." Patrick exclaimed.

"Patrick, it is okay. I will be okay."

"No, I will stay with you. Besides we haven't opened our gifts."

"Patrick, we will do that tonight when you return."

"No, I will stay with you, and Sean can go with daddy."

This was not how it was supposed to go. The presence of guilt filled the large room and conquered it. "Patrick, you can stay with your mother."

"I want to stay with Patrick." Sean insisted.

"Boys wait." Donna took both of their hands. "Your daddy wants you two to be with him this Christmas. Why don't you give him this day because he doesn't get to spend that much time with you, as I do? Besides I don't want you boys separated from each other."

"No." Patrick held her hand even tighter.

"Patrick, please don't make this difficult for us." Donna looked only at him. He was not responsible for their feelings. Hell, he wasn't even old enough to understand what those feelings were. She knew that Sean was only going alone with Patrick because he refused to be anywhere without his big brother. "I promise I will be here when you return tonight."

"Mommy, no. Daddy told me that I will have to take care of you when he is not here, and he won't be here today, so I have to stay."

Keith, who had sat on the edge of the bed, stood and sadly smiled. "He's right. I have always taught him to take care of you. Well, why don't we do this? Why don't I come back later tonight with your gifts and we can open them together."

"Keith, no I can't ask you to do that. They have to learn to accept that you are not going to be around, and so do I."

"Mommy, please, let daddy come back." Sean requested.

"Sweetheart, I mean Donna. It isn't a problem. I will have dinner and come back later tonight, about seven."

"Alone." Donna quickly said.

"Yes, alone."

"Good." Sean was very happy. Then again, he was always happy when he got his way. He was his father's son.

Halley was more than happy that the boys were coming with Donna. The more the merrier. She only hated that she did not have any gifts for them. Donna advised her that they had enough gifts anyway, and anymore they would have to find another room for just their gifts, alone.

Donna thought long and hard how she would participate in the activities of the family that holds her paycheck. She hadn't spoken with Darren on a personal level in quite some time, so she wasn't sure how she should socialize with him. The other problem was that no one knew of her divorce, and that was how she wanted to keep it.

The drive entrance to the home was almost as long as the home itself. Donna felt that her Mercedes S600 Sedan seemed but like a bug on the street. The Duncans lived in one of the wealthiest neighborhoods in Birmingham. Grant Woods was filled with rolling hills for golf and huge homes for the wealthy. Keith's family refused to live there because of its distance from the country. They chose to live in Quail Ridge, instead. They could afford any house in the neighborhood of Grant Woods, but his father refused the drive, not that Quail Ridge was not adequately equipped with all of the desires needed by the wealthy.

The population of Black families living in Grant Woods was almost five, which wasn't saying much since there were more than 30 homes in the expensive part of the world. The Duncans were one of the first Black families to move into the area, and their welcome wasn't a nice one. But as time passed, the community became more comfortable with their presence and started inviting them to parties held at their individual homes. Some even became clients of the Duncan's Law Firm.

"I hope that you found the place alright." Halley said walking to the doors of the huge home to let them in before the butler could perform his duties. "Can you believe that I spent most of my childhood in this home? Strange, every time that I come here, I am still shocked at the enormity of it."

"As well, you should be." Donna said after giving her coat to the butler. "I was afraid the guard at the gate wasn't going to let us in."

"I have the same problem." Halley jokingly responded. "Listen, the rest of the kids are in the game room. If your boys would like for me to show them to the room I will be happy to do so."

"No, we will stay with our mother." Patrick said gallantly.

"Patrick, I will be just fine. Why don't you and Sean join the other kids, and I will check in on you in a few minutes?"

"Are you sure Mother?"

"Yes, I am sure. Now go along."

"Donna, Harry will show you to the living room where the other adults are. I will join you as soon as I have the boys playing with the other kids." She smiled and walked off.

Donna felt alone, even with Halley standing by waiting to direct her way. When Darren came in view she almost ran to him. He was dressed in a silk suit, with a vest. My god, he is just beautiful she thought to herself. Dark, tall and beautiful. How could any man be much better than Darren Duncan? "Well, hello Mrs. Pennington." His voice was as deep as the color of his skin. He shook her hand with the familiar grip of confidence. "When my sister told me that you were coming to have dinner with my family, I was somewhat shocked."

"Why?"

"Well, I would have expected that you would be with your family tonight."

"Yes, well when your sister Halley invited me, I could not turn her down. I mean she is after all my boss' daughter." Donna responded sarcastically, releasing her hand from his grip.

"Yes, I guess you could look at it that way." He was going to want answers. "So, where is that husband of yours'?"

"He was unable to make it." That was the best she could come up with. Darren was the last person she wanted to tell that Keith had divorced her only three weeks ago. It would prove him right and also make her available to touch him. "Besides, we do travel separately at times."

"Yes, you have proven that fact, quite eloquently, haven't you?" He looked at her as if she was a mannequin he was undressing with his eyes. "You are a beautiful woman. Forgive me if I am out of place, but I have wanted to say this to you since the day I saw you on the elevator."

"And what day was this?" She could feel her body warming up to his words.

"The day you came in for your interview."

At first she was unsure of what to say. The thought of him watching her for so long, and admiring her for so long, made her feel more beautiful and more sensuous than she had felt in some time. "Well, I must say you look as gallant as you always do. And thank you."

"Darren, can you escort Donna in with the rest of our guests?" Halley interrupted their visual lovemaking. Donna welcomed her interlude. She did not like the fact that her mind was so ready to knock down the walls she had so carefully built, just for protection from Darren Duncan. But now that Keith is no longer her husband, her mind is weak without foundation. Her heart, however, still called for Keith desperately.

"Let me do the honors." Darren guided her by placing his hand on the small of her back and escorted her into the room.

Twelve

"Wonderful view isn't it?" Darren had not long followed her to the gazebo. After being introduced to everyone by Darren's mother, whom she had only met once, Donna made herself comfortable to stay. The gifts had already been opened, and the children quickly took control of the holiday. After dinner, Donna decided that she needed to get away from the family's surrounding. The faces all seemed familiar to her, even though she had only met most of them that very day. She was also happy that her boys were able to experience the celebration with her. She did not have a Black family to share with them, so the Duncans would have to do.

"I would have to say yes." Donna turned from her view of the paradise that was the Duncan's lawn to face what was the vision of manliness that was Darren.

He sat on the bench next to her. "May I ask you a personal question?"

"I am surprised that you asked my permission."

"Well, I dare not ask this question unless I have your permission, as it seems it may cause you some personal discomfort."

"Why don't I answer the question before you ask?" She stood and walked down the steps of the gazebo. Darren watched her intensely before deciding to follow. The air was chilly and her coat was not enough to comfort her, but it was all she wanted. "You want to know if Keith and I, are still together, no, we are not. We signed our divorce papers only three weeks ago." When she turned to face him, he did not look at her with pity, which was what she thought he would. Instead, he gave her a hug, a long, warm and strong hug. She wanted to claim this piece of property for herself but it was not to be. She quickly pushed him away.

"Hey, what was that for?" Darren said, with his arms still in position from the hug.

"Darren, I can't...."

"You can't what?" He smiled that brilliant smile. He held her shoulders and starred deeply into her eyes. "Mrs. Pennington, when you come to me it will not be as a woman who has been weakened by heartbreak." He gently placed his hand under her chin. "You will come to me strong, and as beautiful as you were when I first saw you. Until that moment, I simply want to be here for you."

"Why?" She stepped away.

"Why not? You are here at my parents' home, sharing the Christmas holiday with my family and friends. Why shouldn't I be the one you turn to for shelter?"

"How about I don't know you?"

"Well, I thought we had already settled that. But if you feel that we haven't, tell me what you need to know to make you feel more comfortable with me."

"What is it that you want from me, Darren? I have nothing to give you. Nothing at all can I give to you to satisfy your curiosity."

"Friendship. What about that?"

"The price is too steep for me." She walked back up the steps and sat down again.

"How is that when it is my friendship that you get in return?" He joined her on the bench. "Listen Donna, we work together and I would like to continue working with you. You have become somewhat of an oddity for the firm, a good one, but one just the same. I enjoy waking each morning knowing that you will challenge me. And if becoming your friend is what it will take to keep you mentally fit, then I am willing to do that. Besides, I want to watch you go through this transformation of self-awareness. Have you called the detective?"

"No, I haven't."

"What are you waiting on?"

"Darren, I really don't know if this is something that I want to do. I am not sure if finding anyone from my past is in my best interest, especially now."

"Now see that is where you are wrong. Finding anyone from your past is especially what you need now." He was focused on her life more than she was. "Right now you are in a time in your life where all that you are familiar with has left you alone. All you have now are your boys. No family. No friends. I am not saying that this is a bad thing. I am only saying that there is more of you out there, and you should do whatever you need to do to find out what those things, or who those people are. What do you have to lose?"

"I really don't know. Right now, I just want to raise my boys, and get over this ache in my heart. I have lost my husband because of this drastic change in my life. I have lost the father of my children. In many ways I feel as if I have failed my boys for losing their father. In many ways I feel that I have failed my marriage. I should have taken different steps, but at the time the steps that I took seemed to be the best ones. I never figured that he would leave me. I never figured that Keith would leave our boys."

"Donna, you cannot be serious?" He was indeed shocked. "You cannot think that any man, no matter how well verse a woman is in keeping him satisfied, would sit back and watch his wife move out of the home and life that they shared. Do you think that you would have stayed with him had the positions been reversed?"

"I would like to think that I would." She went into deep thought. "Darren, I truly love Keith. There is no other man on the face of this earth that intrigues me as much as he does. He touches me, and my body reacts like magic. He is my drug. He has been for many years the only friend that I have had. When I decided that I would have to leave to figure out the next part of my life, it was not an easy decision, but it was one that I felt I had to make. The road that I must travel to find peace within myself does not have a lane for him to follow me. I knew this, and I fought this, but I had to make the trip." The tears began to fall from her eyes. "When he decided to leave me, I was not shocked, but it was expected. But that does not mean that I did not do all the praying and hoping that a woman could do so that he would not. I mean I begged him, but I knew that he would not listen. He is angry with me. I have hurt him in a way that he never saw coming. And because of this, I don't think that I want to go through with this search. He was my life, my existence, and I have lost him."

Darren reached into his coat and took out the handkerchief to give to her, but she refused. She had her own. "How are you able to sleep at night?"

"Sleep. Who knows what that is?" She wiped her eyes and nose. "I stopped sleeping Thanksgiving night." Her tears were heavier than she could control. "Then to top it off, he brought his new "White" girlfriend with him this morning to pick up the boys. I guess I can't call her new, he has known her for a few years now. And he has always known that she wanted him. So what does he do the minute the papers are signed? He opens his arms to her? How ironic for me?" She tried to smile, but the tears were making the

157

muscles in her face too weak to make a smile. "I mean look at this picture. Here he has his Black wife who wants to know what it is to be Black, so he leaves her and goes to the arms of the White woman who has been waiting on him for years." She ran her hand through her hair. "I mean, don't you think that it is funny? I care not to find out anything else about me, all I care about is finding a way to sleep at night. All I care about is finding a way to stop this ghastly pain that is tearing my heart into pieces. Can you help me with that, Darren? Can you bring me sleep? Can you stop the pain?" This time when he held her she did not resist.

He held her as tight as he could. He gently rubbed her hair and tried to make her feel warm. "Mommy, are you okay?" There stood Patrick. He was alone. Donna could tell by the look in his eyes that he was not at all happy with what he was seeing.

"Baby, mommy is okay." She released herself from Darren's hug. "Where is your coat?" She removed her coat to put on him. But Patrick refused it.

"Mommy, a man does not take a woman's coat. A woman is supposed to take the coat from the man." She remembered when Keith told him that. He was the goodness of her soul.

"Well, excuse me Mr. Man." She put the coat on him anyway. "But until you become a man, you will have to accept mommy's coat. Do you know Mr. Duncan?" She tried to dry her face from the tears.

"No." He had not passed judgment yet, but Donna knew that he would at any moment.

"Mr. Duncan works with mommy."

"Why was he hugging you?"

She looked at Darren who stood at attention. He seemed to offer Patrick the respect that he would give to a man of his maturity. "Mommy was upset and Mr. Duncan offered to help."

"Mommy, I told you that I will take care of you when daddy is not around." He took her hand.

"I know you will, but mommy sometimes will need to talk to someone who is older than you." She lowered herself to look him directly in his eyes. "Patrick, you do know that I love you, and that you are, and always will be mommy's son?"

"Yes."

"I want you to also know that mommy is hurting a lot right now over what has happened between your father and me. Now that doesn't mean that I am trying to find you a different father. So when you saw Mr. Duncan hugging me, he was only being nice to me and that is all. Do you understand what I am saying?"

"He is your friend."

"Yes, he is my friend." Donna looked up at Darren who remained as he had before, at attention.

"Is that okay with you, fellow?" Darren asked Patrick.

"I guess so."

The ride home was welcomed. They left the Duncan's earlier than expected, but that was fine, since she did not want to rush home. The day had proven to be quite an emotional one for her, even though her boys were with her, Donna desperately missed Keith.

Still it was good for the boys to share with her the opportunity of having Christmas dinner with a Black family, howbeit not her own. Halley asked her to lunch during the week, and there were other request for her presence. Donna figured that they all knew that she was alone now, and was trying to do all that they could to provide some company for her. She was sure that

Darren had not spoken a word of her divorce, but the mere fact that she showed up without Keith on Christmas was enough to quell the thirst of the suspicious group.

As she drove through the garage to the apartment, she did not notice Keith's car. So, she figured she had time to shower and change before he arrived. But as she was trying to lift Sean, who had fallen into a deep sleep, out of the car, Keith drove up and parked next to her. He exited his Cadillac Escalade and finished the job of lifting Sean out of the car.

The elevator ride was quiet. Patrick held to his father's hand as if it would be his last time to do so. Walking into the apartment, Donna tried to wake Sean, but he was out for the night. Patrick also looked exhausted. He followed Keith into their bedroom and laid down on his bed. Before they could get Sean undressed and ready for bed, Patrick had also fallen asleep. Donna completed the task of undressing him and then exited the room.

Keith stood near the sofa, quietly. Donna wasn't sure what to say to him. He felt distant from her. "Maybe I should just get their gifts and leave them here for the boys to open in the morning."

"Well, it is still early, yet. Maybe in an hour or so we can wake them."

"I don't know they both seemed really tired. I guess they had a good time."

"Yes, I guess they did." She sat on the sofa. She too was tired. "Have a seat."

"No, I think that I will go and get the gifts, and then I will leave."

"Keith, I really don't think that that will be a good idea. I mean you did promise the boys that we would open the gifts together."

"What are you suggesting? I cannot stay here for the night."

"Listen, do what you want. I am tired myself." She stood slowly. "You do still have your key don't you?" He shook his head yes. "Well, I am going to go and take a shower. If you want to leave the gifts here, just place them under the tree, and I will make sure that they open them in the morning."

"Donna, I...."

"Keith, I am not going to argue with you about this. I will explain to the boys that they were asleep and it was late. I am sure everything will be fine. Maybe you can come back in the morning, just before we open the gifts."

"I can't do that, I have plans." Donna was walking away, but she turned back to face him. "Carolyn and I will be leaving for a trip to Jamaica in the morning, and we won't be back for a week."

"As I said, do what you want, Keith." She turned quickly because she felt her body becoming limp from the pain in her chest. She walked into her bedroom and closed the door behind her. She fell to the floor and held her chest as if someone was trying to pry it from her. She knew that she had to get up because he could not see her like she was. As she found her way to the bathroom, she turned on the shower, undressed and stepped in. All the steps she made to get to that very point in the custom shower were maneuvered as if she was a robot. But now with the shower water spraying from all directions, she could cry and not have to worry about anyone seeing her.

The hot water felt good gently beating against her body. She would spend yet another night without Keith, but this time, her dreams, she knew would take her to Jamaica. She would be forced to think of him with Carolyn, making love to her, laughing with her, doing all the things with her that they had once done together. She tried to focus on the water, but found that she could not because her heart ached too much.

After spending what she knew was too long in the shower, she dried off and got into bed. She thought of checking to see if Keith had actually gone, but was afraid to do so. She laid in the bed for a few more minutes, and realized that she could not avoid checking any longer.

When she came into the living room, Keith had made a bed for himself on the sofa. He, too, had fallen asleep, or so she thought. He woke to see her standing next to the sofa totally nude. "Donna, what are you doing?"

"What do you mean what am I doing?" She gave no thought to the fact that she was naked. "So, you're staying?"

"Yes, I can't let the boys wake without me being here. I called Carolyn and advised her that we will have to take a later flight. She is fine with it."

"Oh really?" Still she stood in front of him, still without noticing her nakedness.

"Donna, are you going to put on something?"

She looked at herself, and felt ashamed. "I am so sorry. I guess I just didn't think." She ran back into her bedroom to put on the silk robe, which was in her closet. When she came back into the living room, she found Keith sitting up.

"Are you trying to seduce me?"

"No Keith, I just didn't think. It isn't that we've been divorced that long."

"Well, things are different now, and I'm going to ask that you are more respectful toward me."

"What is this Keith?"

"What is what?"

"Does being in my company anger you that much that you plan on berating me every chance you get? If this is going to be the gist of our relationship, then I can see that there are going to be some problems." She sat down next to him. "Keith, I am very sorry for what I have done to our family. I am very sorry for hurting you as I have, but you cannot continue to punish me every time that you see me. It isn't fair."

"I will tell you when it is not fair." He shouted sternly.

She stood again. She looked down at him and felt herself beginning to cry again. "Keith, do whatever you want." With saying that, she walked hurriedly off to her bedroom, so that he would not see the tears flow. Closing the door behind her, she went into the bathroom and sat in her vanity chair. Her head ached from the constant attacks of her heart. She felt she could no longer take his berating and her guilt at the same time. It was becoming too difficult to manage. Right then she decided not to let this situation tear her down, she would survive. Who was she fooling? She wasn't at that great point yet. She had not suffered enough.

Keith stood at the door when she returned to her bedroom. He said nothing to her. He simply walked up to her, took her into his arms and began kissing her gently on the lips, and taking claim of her tongue with his. When she felt his hand cup her breast, she melted into his arms. She wasn't sure what was going on. She only knew that it felt good feeling him holding her with such tenderness, again. The tears that were flowing from her eyes were no longer tears of pain they were now accompanied with joy, ecstasy and an unquenchable thirst for the man who made her body ache with intense spasms of rapture. She slowly unbuttoned the silk shirt that covered his wonderfully slender chest. His body was that of a runner. Tall, slender, tone in all places needful. She moved slowly. She did not want to move too quickly because she was afraid that he would awaken from his dream of seeing her naked again and stop her from loving him. As the shirt hit the floor, she began to work with the slip lock that held the pants on his body. She could feel him throbbing for her, she was happy. He soon reached her breast with his kisses of love, which aroused her nipples to their full explosion. He too moved slowly with removing her robe. She knew that to be his way. He loved caressing her body. He would tell her that it was her body that made him become a gentleman. They avoided each other's eyes. Neither wanted to look for fear that what they were about to explore would end.

While removing his pants, he allowed her only for a moment, to pleasure him, as he ran his hand through her hair. She could see his head fall back slowly as the look of ecstasy cross his face. His eyes were closed, but still she could see his desires. She knew his body as well as he knew hers. She knew what to do to make him ache, and she knew what to do to make the aching succumb to the call of passions. But she did not want that to happen, so she came to her feet and allowed her robe to drop to the floor. Still they did not look into each other's eyes. He lifted her and took her to the bed. As he placed her on the bed, he slid to her thighs, kissing and gently nibbling on them. He knew that she liked what he was doing, and he knew that she wanted more. Traveling further along her body, he kissed her toes and played softly with them. Donna was so far away from the pain that had only moments ago imprisoned her that she walked assuredly through the gates of pleasure. Keith, with the hands and tongue of her experienced lover took great pleasure in caressing and tasting what lied between her legs, sending her mind to the skies of eternity. She softly called for him to give her more, and more he gave.

She did not know that he was now climbing on top of her, because he had, as he always did, taken her to the world of unbelief. But when she felt him enter her, she reached only for his wrists. The pleasure of feeling him inside of her again was more than she could handle. Keith saw the look of finality in her eyes, and softly told her to come with him. He did not want to stop making love to her. He then looked into her eyes and told her that he loved her, and that she was his wife. He dried her tears with his lips, and continued to stroke inside of her as boldly as he had begun. After seeing that she was his, he turned over so that she could take control of the love that they were sharing. How could she continue with her body constantly in a state of probable eruption? She knew that once on top of him, she would have to go slowly. Her ride would have to be as a trained woman of the night. She could not let it end so soon, she would not let it end. She looked deeply into his blue eyes and pleaded for him to help her. Help her to hold on. Help her to make it last forever. She loved the way he loved her, but she hated the way he brought her to elation so quickly.

"Come to me." She said softly. "Come to me and help me make you feel me again." Keith came up to her and began kissing her passionately. He moved with her. Every thrust that she made, he made with her. When he once again maneuvered her body to get behind her, she grab the sheets so she could welcome him enter her again. He cupped both her breasts, while he single-mindedly thrust himself back and forth, bringing her pleasure with every push. She bit down on the sheets between her teeth because the pleasurable pain that she felt as he pleased her made her want to scream aloud, and she did not want to awaken the boys. He pulled himself out of her and laid her down to begin his conquering of her breasts with his mouth. Then his lips traveled to her stomach, her thighs, and then to that which belong only to him. She tried desperately to move below him so that she could taste him in her mouth once more, but he had not completed what he seemed to have dreamt about. No part of her body was left without his the touch of his tongue or his lips. He gently turned her over and began kissing her back, her butt, and her thighs. All of her is what he desired to claim, and she did not resist.

He allowed finally, for her to lead. She began kissing his neck and then his chest. As she lowered herself, she heard him say softly to make love to him. She heard him quietly say that he had missed feeling inside of her. She heard him say in a whisper that he had missed her tasting him in that special way that only she knew how to do. She took him into her mouth and began sliding up and down his long, more than ample manliness. He tasted of her. She gently caressed the twins that accompanied his object of her desire. She looked up to see him again taking intense pleasure in the joy she brought to him. Before she could go any further, he stopped her. "Come here." He quickly took her and placed her on top of him, and began thrusting himself inside of her, harder and harder. Faster and faster he pushed himself. She tried to hold onto his chest, but he moved so quickly that she could not. She grabbed his wrists and felt herself, too, beginning to move faster. "Damn, I can't stop loving you!" He said breathlessly. Quickly he turned the script and placed her on the bed below him. With her legs spread, and tightly held, he continued his drive to exploding. She could feel him inside her. She could see that at any moment it would be over, so she danced with him. She begged for him to give her more of him. She wanted to feel all of him inside of her.

"Baby, please, all of you. Please give me all of you. I want to feel all of you inside of me.

Please baby, all of you." She said quivering from his passion.

"I love you, Donna. Do you hear me? I love you so much it hurts." He amazed her. Never had he taken her here, this place where she could only see eternity through his eyes. He had always made her feel like a lady when they made love, but this, this she had never felt before.

"Keith. Keith." She screamed. As they gave into the pleas of the moment.

Thirteen

Donna was awakened by the sound of Patrick's voice laughing at something that Keith said. She thought that maybe she had dreamed that last night they made love, but she could still feel his moisture between her legs. She could still smell his cologne on the sheets. She smiled to herself, and rejoiced at having him back in her life. She found his shirt and put it on.

When she walked into the living room, Patrick ran to her. "Mommy, look what gifts we have. We were going to wait for you, but daddy said he had to leave soon, so we had to open them now."

Donna looked at Keith, who had avoided eye contact with her. "Keith, are you leaving?"

"Yes." He said, standing to his feet. "I told you yesterday that I changed my flight time to later in the day, but I need to go home to shower and change." He fiddled with a toy that Sean anxiously wanted to play with.

She looked at the sofa, and then back toward her bedroom, she thought maybe last night was a dream. She refused to let the pain surface, something was wrong. "Keith, are you serious?"

173

"What do you mean am I serious?" He finally looked at her. "I told you last night that I would stay the night and then leave in the morning, after the gifts were opened." He showed no resistance in voicing this statement. "I am not sure if it was okay, but since I had already purchased this gift for you earlier in the year, I brought it with me."

Donna walked back to her bedroom. Once again he had won. He made love to her. He told her that he loved her and that she was his wife. Was it a game? Was this part of his pursuit in tormenting her? When he tapped on the door, she refused to say anything. She could not let him win like this. He could not see that he used her love for him at the highest level and then dropped it. She quickly opened the door. "Did you need anything?"

"No, I just wanted to make sure that you were okay."

"Why wouldn't I be? I was going to put on my robe so that I could give your shirt back to you." She removed his shirt and gave it to him. She stood in front of him completely in the nude, and then turned away. "If you could wait with the boys for a few minutes, I need to shower."

"Donna?"

"Yes?"

"Your gift." He handed the box to her, as she turned back to face him.

"Oh, thank you. I will have to get you something later. I didn't think that we were going to exchange gifts. You know with the divorce and everything else."

"Yes, well, as I said I had purchased this gift earlier this year." She walked off toward her bathroom. "Are you going to open it now?"

"No, I will open it later. Right now, I just want to shower. I feel dirty." With that she closed the door behind her, and once again fell to the floor in silent agony.

Her shower had taken longer than she said, but she needed it. Keith sat playing with the boys when she entered the room. "I hope that I wasn't too long."

"No, my flight doesn't leave for three hours. But I think I will go now." He stood and gathered his things. "Donna, about your gift?"

"Yes."

"I'd like for you to open it now."

"I would rather not."

"Mommy, don't you want to see what daddy got you?" Patrick asked.

"I will open it later, baby. Right now, I am going to make breakfast for you and your brother."

"Mommy, let me open it." Sean eagerly requested.

"No, I will open it later." She looked at Keith, who had made his way to the door. "Keith, I want to thank you for the gift and last night."

"Thank me? What kind of thing is that to say?"

"Forgive me, but it is the best that I can come up with right now." She walked into the kitchen, and heard the door close behind her. Keith had gone, but his touch still remained on her body.

The sound of ringing in her ear is what brought her back from the fantasy of last night. "Hello."

"Donna, this is Jenny. How are you?"

Donna was surprised to hear from her. She was surprised to hear from anyone in Keith's family. "I am fine. I was about to make breakfast for the boys. How are you?"

"I was hoping that I could visit you today. Do you think that it is possible?"

"Well Jenny, anything is possible. Is there something you need?"

"I need to talk to you about Keith."

"I don't believe that will be necessary."

"Donna, do you not love my brother? If you say no, then I will not bother to come over."

Donna wanted to say no, but she knew that it would be a lie. "Jenny, I really don't want to deal with this right now. Keith just left here and I am having somewhat of a difficult time accepting what has happened."

"That is precisely why I want to talk with you. I will be there in an hour or so. Is that okay?"

"I guess. But Jenny, I don't know what our talking is going to solve."

"Maybe nothing, but I just can't sit back and not do anything. You have been a sister to me for years now, and I really don't want to lose our friendship."

When the doorbell rang, Patrick got up from the breakfast table to open the door. Patrick loved Laura. She was his protégé. When he saw that Jenny had not brought Laura with her he was unhappy. "Where is Laura?" He asked, when Jenny bent to kiss his cheek.

"I left her with the sitter. Is that okay with you, sir?" She smiled graciously. "Where is your mother?"

"She is in the kitchen with Sean. We were eating breakfast. Do you want something to eat?" Patrick escorted Jenny into the kitchen and waited for her to sit after she had made her rounds of kissing Sean and Donna.

"No thanks, I ate before I came." She looked at Donna, and smiled softly. "How are you doing?"

"I am doing well. How about you?" Donna drank some of her orange juice to control her heart. "Boys, why don't the two of you finish your breakfast in your room?"

"We get to eat in our rooms?" Patrick asked happily. Both he and Sean moved quickly, just in case Donna changed her mind.

"Don't make a mess. I will be in to get your trays in a little while." Donna placed their plates on the trays and gave them back to each of them. Sean struggled with his for a little, but soon took control and walked confidently behind Patrick.

"Donna, did Keith stay the night?" Jenny asked pouring herself a glass of juice.

"Yes." Donna began to stare off into space. She was brought back to the night she shared with Keith, and how much it hurt when he left only an hour ago. "He stayed the night, and then he left this morning to go to Jamaica with Carolyn. I guess that I should have expected this, but who can prepare themselves for heartache."

"Carolyn means nothing to him."

"That really doesn't soften the spot for me, Jenny." Donna began removing the rest of the dishes from the table. "May I ask you something?" Jenny nodded, yes. "Why are you here? I mean since Thanksgiving I have yet to hear from anyone in your family, and now out of the blue you decide to call me. What do you want from me?"

"Friendship." Jenny stood up and walked toward the sink where Donna was making water for the dishes. "Donna, when my brother came to me and told me that he was going to tell you that he wanted a divorce, I laughed at him. Then he asked that I not say anything to you. I stopped laughing. He was serious, crazy, but serious. I asked him why was he thinking of doing such a stupid thing, and he refused to say. I knew that he was not handling the distance your choices put on your marriage, but I thought in time everything would be okay. Then time went on, and you never returned home. Keith loves you, and I know that he loves you."

"Jenny, I love Keith too."

"I know that Donna, and I never doubted your love for him. I mean, even after you decided to move out, I never questioned whether you loved him or not. What I did question was your decision to move out." Jenny walked back to the table. "Could you not have found your heritage in the home you shared with Keith? Why would it require such a drastic choice on your part?"

"That is the problem, I didn't see it as a drastic choice. It was a choice that I had to make. It was a choice that I felt if I did not make, I would not be of any purpose."

"How is that, Donna? I mean, just because you're Black does not mean that you are the only person on this earth who has problems with understanding who they are."

"Jenny, it is not because I am Black that I am having problems understanding who I am. It is because I forgot that I am Black." Jenny looked at her with misgivings. "Jenny, just know that this is something that I have to do."

"Even, at the expense of losing your husband?"

"I would have to say that that has already been decided for me." Donna began washing the dishes. "How is Laura?"

"Laura is great." Jenny took another sip of her juice. "Are you sure that you want this?"

"Jenny, if I don't do this, I will be without existence, and without purpose. I need to do this. I never meant to lose Keith. I guess I never expected him to leave. I mean, I did question it a time or two, but we have always been there for each other, and I figured that this would be one of those times. I was wrong, terribly wrong."

"So, what do you do from here? Are you going to try and get him back? Or are you just going to sit back and let this happen?"

"Jenny, how can I win him back when it was him who left me? Besides, if I don't move back into our home, Keith would not want me back. I cannot move back, not right now." Having made that statement, Donna realized the revelation of her divorce. "I am alone now more than I can ever remember being. After being in the home for so many years without knowing who my parents were, I sort of accepted being a child of no ties. But then your brother came into my life, and I found a reason. It was great! I had meaning. My life had meaning. When Patrick was born I knew that life was worth living, and then Sean came along and I did not think that I could want anymore. Boy, does life have a way of showing you how small you are on this earth. I can remember waking, to the sound of emptiness. I can remember looking at myself in the mirror and questioning who I was, who I belong too and who loved me before Keith, if anyone did. After that I could not go back to yesterday. I could not find the peace I needed to continue smiling each morning. I needed to find my reality."

Jenny wasn't sure if she understood what Donna was expressing, but she did know that she was not coming back to her family, at least not then. "Donna, if ever you need a sitter for the boys, or just to hang out, you do know that you can call me?"

"Of course Jenny. We are still family aren't we?" Donna smiled gently. "I hope so. And let's not make this sound like this is the last time we will hang out."

"Just to make sure of that, we will schedule lunch each week." Jenny wanted to make sure of the plans.

"Are you sure that you are going to be able to keep the lunch with your schedules?" Donna rinsed the dishes.

"Donna, I will admit I don't understand what is going on with you, and neither does my family. But as long as you understand it, I guess that is all we can ask for. I will call you tomorrow with our lunch schedule."

Fourteen

The Christmas holiday went by, and the first of the New Year came right along with it. Keith continued to pick up the boys each week, and Donna kept her lunch dates with Jenny. Their conversations were always invariably about Keith, and his relationship with Carolyn. Jenny did not think that there was anything to it, but Carolyn did make sure that she was available for dinners with the family. Even more presumptuous was Carolyn's request to move in with him. Keith told her no. He did not give her a reason, just an answer. Jenny knew all of this because Keith told her everything. They were the closest of the siblings. Maybe Jenny was a free thinker, and Keith needed such a thinker in order to clear his demons.

Donna also felt that Keith told her all his personal information because he knew that she would tell Donna. Maybe there was still a chance. Or maybe he just needed someone to talk too. Their luncheons would end with hugs and kisses and promises of getting the children together.

Jenny was the only person from Keith's family who would talk with her. Not even his father would call. The boys would visit with them when Keith had them, but only then. Donna didn't know if they were told to stay away or if they never liked her at all. She would admit to herself when no one was around, which seemed more often than she wanted that they never liked her, and she never liked them. She would only admit this to ease their rejection. If she was to admit that she liked them and that they also liked her, then she would feel a fool for leaving her family.

Halley called a month after Christmas and asked her to dinner at the park downtown. Donna thought the invite was silly, but said yes anyway. She wanted to see Halley again. Since Christmas dinner, Darren was all but gone from the office, or was doing a good job of avoiding Donna all together. The cases that they were to chair together were given to another attorney in the firm, and he took on other cases. Donna tried to speak with him about his cold separation from her, but he denied such actions.

"Well hello, Donna. How are you?" Halley greeted her with opened arms. It was only

185

six o'clock and the sky was still clear. The winter's cold was not as hateful, but her body shivered still. She was waiting for Donna near the water fountain.

"I am doing fine. And you?" Donna tightened the belt of her long black trench coat. "Why here?"

"Why not?" Halley smiled genuinely. "Actually, I need to be here. I am speaking here next month."

"Speaking. May I ask for what?"

"First, can we cut it with the formal speaking? I thought we were beyond all of that." Halley was serious.

"I am sorry."

"Don't be sorry. Let's just do this thing." She took Donna's hand and walked away from the water fountain. "I will be speaking during a heritage day celebration for Black History month." Donna only looked at her. "You are familiar with Black History month aren't you?"

"Of course."

"Have you ever attended any of the celebrations?"

"No."

"Why not?"

Donna did not want to answer, but she knew that Halley would not be satisfied until she gave her one. "I just never had an interest to do so." When she looked at Halley she wanted to avoid her eyes, but Halley would not allow that.

"Tell me about yourself Donna." Halley asked taking a seat on the bench.

"Can we talk inside a restaurant?" Donna was cold. "We could go over to Reggie's and have the dinner you said we would have." Halley agreed and they left in separate cars. The time it took for them to get to the restaurant wasn't enough time for Donna to conjure up the nerves to open up to Halley. She exited her vehicle to let valet park it, and then waited for Halley to pull up behind her.

"Donna, do you always eat here?" Halley exited her silver Jaguar XK8 Coupe.

"Yes. Would you rather go somewhere else?"

"No. Here will be fine." Entering the restaurant they were greeted by the host. He was very friendly with Donna, as he walked them to a table in the center of the room. "I take it you come here often?"

"You could say that." Donna waited for the host to leave their table and then continued her talking. "My husband, excuse me, my ex-husband and I use to dine here all the time." Reggie's had yet to deal with the dinner crowd, but there were still quite a few couples enjoying the Italian cuisines. Reggie's was more of a restaurant set for sharing that special night with the one you love, but the ambiance also allowed for a meeting of the romantic at heart. Donna was that person. All of the furnishings were handpicked by Reggie himself shipped from Rome, Italy. Reggie and Keith were college pals, and Keith was the first to invest in the restaurant. The first time that Keith brought Donna there was to propose to her. From that point on whenever there was something to celebrate, or a night of romance planned, Reggie would set aside a special seat for Keith or Donna to spend in enchantment.

"It is as I thought?"

"Yes. We have been divorced now for a little over a month." The words were flowing from her mouth. Maybe it was familiarity of Reggie's, or maybe it was the remembrance of Keith and happier times that made her feel comfortable. "Time heals all wounds, right?"

"That is what they say." Halley ordered a glass of wine, and waited for Donna to complete her drink order. "Where are the boys tonight?"

"They are with Keith. He picks them up every weekend."

"You seem to be handling this really well. I mean with the time being as short as it is."

"Actually, I am dying inside every day. The person you have before you is only a figment of a woman whose heart no longer belongs to her." Halley could now see her sorrow. "When you called, I was happy. I needed to get out. It seems that I always need to get out now. Work is not enough to keep my mind from wondering where he is or my heart from breaking."

"May I ask what happened?"

"I thought you wanted us to get rid of the formalities." Donna tried to smile.

"Yes, but I can tell by the look in your eyes, formalities are probably the only thing holding you together."

The smile went away. "Tell me about your speaking engagement." She could not tell her heart to stop from breaking, so she changed the subject, just in case her tears also refused to listen to her.

"Well, I am the chairperson of my firm's Heritage Club. So, every year we circle the world for a public figure to speak during our park celebration. This year however, the Club did not want to do that, instead they asked me to speak."

"Then this is an honor?" Donna took a sip of the white wine that had been brought to her table. "Are you going to write your own speech or, are you going to solicit the help from a professional?"

"I am a professional. I travel extensively making speeches for not just this Club, but also for other organizations that I chair." Halley requested a few more minutes from the server before ordering her dinner. "I asked you to dinner tonight so that I could persuade you into participating in the event."

"Participating how? I mean I don't know much about planning an event of this magnitude." Donna knew that that wasn't the truth, but it sounded good.

"We will do this together. I just thought it would be a good idea for you to get involved." Halley motioned for the server and made her selection. Donna also ordered, but only the salad. "Donna, listen I need to be straight with you. Darren has told me quite a bit about you. My brother, in his infinite wisdom has decided that you needed someone, a Black someone to guide you." Donna did not make a move. "I am not sure if he is in love with you or, if you have become an excuse for him to ignore his loneliness."

"What?"

"My brother has many great attributes, but opening up to a woman is not one of them." She took a sip of her wine before continuing. "When we were younger, Darren watched many of his friends become shells of the men he admired because they fell in love. He has always thought of love as being something that hinders a person. No matter whom I would bring home to introduce to him, he would push them away with his inability to feel. He is so much like our father it is scary. How my mother put up with it for so long I cannot tell you." She took another sip of wine. "My mother said he was like that when they first met, but she loved him so much she could not let him go. But after so many years together, and father's continued emotional emptiness, she became distant."

"They seem so happy together." Donna was listening intensely.

"Yes, but that came after 25 years of a cold marriage. When my mother sheltered herself away from him, he became afraid that she was getting ready to leave him. I don't think any of us were ready for his transformation, but it was well needed. Now you can't stop him from calling her in the middle of the day, or from bringing a gift home just because it is Tuesday. Darren, on the other hand has not accepted this change. He is uncomfortable with it."

"His interest in me is solely to help me figure out who I am as a Black woman."

"That I don't believe." Halley sat back. "But if that is what you want to believe, we will leave it at that. Anyway, Darren thought it was a good idea that we sort of hook up. Are you game?"

"I guess it really depends on whether you have patience enough to deal with my ignorance of the subject."

"You can't be ignorant of your heritage. You only think that you are." Halley waited as the server placed their dinners on the table. "Sometimes as Black people we think that we are to walk around a certain way, but that is not the case. Just as there are many shades of the color black, there are many different cultures within the community of those whose heritage is that of a Black person." She tasted her salmon and then continued. "There are different cultures within the Black community right here in Birmingham. The one thing that really ties us all together is that no matter where we go in this world, no matter how light, dark or both your skin maybe, the rest of the world will see us as Black. Some of us may speak with an accent of the south, north, east and west. We are still the people who were taken from their homeland and forced into slavery, sanctioned brutality, illiteracy, and self-degradation." Halley saw that the look on Donna's face was of a person who did not belong to her community. "Tell it to shut up."

"Tell what to shut up?" Donna wasn't aware of what Halley's was speaking of.

"That little voice inside your head that is saying I have heard this sad story before, get over it. Tell it that I have more to say. Tell it that I have a reason to say what I am to say, even today, because today what was done over 200 years ago is still even more prevalent today. Tell it that time has not healed the wounds, that it has only allowed for the scab to cover it. Tell it that no antibiotic has been given to it to cure the damage done, only a placebo. Tell that voice inside of your head that I must say what I am saying to you today because sometimes silence is an evil that can prolong pain." Donna could not respond. "That is what is going on inside of your head, isn't it?"

"Halley, listen, if this is your way of educating me on the history of Black America, then it is not necessary. I have studied African American history before."

"Studied it, you are living it." Halley was in a zone. "Tell me something while you were studying African American history, what did you feel?"

Donna paid no attention to Halley's sarcasm. "I felt the way any other human being would have felt. No one wants to read or hear about the murder, rape and uncivilized treatment of another human being. Or even an animal for that matter."

"You failed to realize something in your study, Donna. You are not just another human being. You are the product of those human beings that were the subject of your reading. So, just as it is for a woman to read of another woman's pain from divorce or the betrayal of a man, you should have felt a personal connection to the lives of those of whom you read about." Donna remained quiet. "Did you know these souls? Did you feel what they felt? Did you share in their convictions to rid the earth of the torment that they suffered? Did you think even for one minute that if it had not been for those souls, you would not be sitting here in this ritzy restaurant being waited on by a White server? But rather the places of the two of you would be different with you serving him, and him treating you as if your existence on this earth was only to serve him, and others like him?"

"Halley, can we change the subject?"

"Donna, we could change the subject, but that would leave us with talking about your divorce. If I remember correctly you did not want to talk about that either."

"Well, why don't we talk about you?" Donna tried to eat the cucumbers out of her salad, but her mouth felt dry. "It was nice meeting Thomas at the dinner."

Halley starred at her for only a moment. She could feel her heart racing. She needed to calm herself. Civil Rights were a passion for her, and she could see that it was not a subject that Donna could relate to with the same intensity. She took a deep breath, then released it, and then repeated the needed pause again. "Donna, please accept my apology. I am who my father says that I am a victim of my own battle."

"Please don't apologize."

"I must. You see I tend to get more engrossed in this plight to cure the disease of racism, and its side effects than the person in front of me. This sometimes pushes people away from me, and I don't want that to continue to happen. So, please accept my apology."

"Really Halley you don't have to apologize. I understand what you are saying. I know that I have separated myself from my heritage. I know that because today I am without a husband."

"What?"

"The reason Keith and I aren't together anymore is because I don't know who I am, anymore." There it is, done. The room was not spinning around. She had not become ill. No, everything was okay. "I am sure Darren told you that my husband is Caucasian. I mean if he told you everything else, he had to tell you that." Halley did not give any indications either way. "I moved out of our home and took the boys with me. I had this grand idea that we would live separately until I could come to terms with my feelings, but he decided that he did not want to play the game, so he divorced me."

"I must say that took some nerves."

"It took more than nerves." Donna replied. "It may have been the death of me."

"This is why you're so sad?" Halley tasted more of the already cold salmon, a sip of more wine, and then ate some of the vegetables from her dinner. "I can't say that I would have done the same. But who knows?"

"I wouldn't recommend it." Donna knew that the pain she felt was too agonizing for her, so why advise her actions to someone else. "You know each morning that I wake now, I think to myself, 'this is the day that he will come back.' But then it hits me 'if he does come back where would he live?' I mean I can't move back in with him."

"Why not?"

"Don't you see? I moved out because I felt trapped in this world that did not belong to me, it belonged to him. My entire life belonged to Keith and his family. Not even my boys belong only to me. My identity in them was shared with his identity in them. I needed to find my own. If I continued living with him, this thing would sooner or later tear us apart."

"So, you moved out thinking you would beat it to the jump?"

"Something liked that."

"Before I let you go on, Darren never told me about your marriage. He only told me about your search." Halley motioned for the server to remove the rest of her half eaten dinner. "Which is very interesting."

"Why interesting?" Donna also allowed the server to remove her salad, which she had only taken a bite out of it.

"Never mind. So, are you going to assist me in producing this year's celebration? Or do I have to talk to my brother to coax you into it?"

"I will be happy to assist. You just tell me what you need of me and I will be there. Besides, this will give me a chance to not focus on my divorce."

"How long were the two of you married?" The server brought coffee to the table. Donna refused, but Halley accepted.

"Eleven years." Time crossed Donna's mind slowly. "He told me that he loved me when he first looked into my eyes." A noticeable smile appeared. "I was a waitress in the diner down the street from his father's firm. He asked me out right then. His family was not happy with our being together, but as time passed and they saw that he was not going to let me go, they gave in. He loved me. I wasn't sure how much I loved him until years later. I believe that I started loving him when we had our first child. Before then he was my White horseman. I knew that he would protect me. He never made me feel less of a woman or a person. He took me out of the dismal world of being a waitress, and gave me a home, a huge home to live in. We traveled. We did all of those things that young couples do, but it wasn't until our first son, Patrick, was born that I realized that I honestly loved him."

"Your eyes light up when you talk of this past life you shared with your husband."

"Strangely enough, I can't feel that light that you see. This divorce has caused me so much sorrow that I refused to see any goodness because it makes me feel dirty."

"Thomas, my fiancé, I think is the greatest man on the face of this earth. That is after my father. But marrying him will probably never be a consideration for our relationship." The server brought the checks. "Let me get this?" Halley took the checks from the server, reviewed the cost and gave him her credit card. "Marriage is unnecessary to me. I mean I will love Thomas with or without a certificate."

"How does he feel about it?"

"Thomas is divorced. It wasn't a civil one. It was full of drama and fighting for custody of his son. I don't know if you remember meeting his six year old son during the Christmas dinner, but he is as wonderful as his father. Thomas was awarded custody, and his ex has left the country. She only wanted custody of their son because she knew it would destroy Thomas." When the server brought her card back, she asked for another cup of coffee, and continued talking. "We have dated for three years now, and have yet to consummate the relationship."

"Are you serious?" Donna almost came out of her chair after responding to Halley's revelation.

"Are you really that surprised?" Halley played with the rim of her coffee cup. "I mean, is sex that important to your existence?"

"I wouldn't say that it was that important. No, I take that back, I would say that it is important. I mean it is not that I am an experienced woman. Keith is the only man that I have ever had sex with. But having it with him has shown me that it is without a doubt a part of my life that I do not wish to give up." Donna answered cautiously.

"Well, I would not know that to be true." Halley sipped some of her coffee. "I am 35 years of age, and I have never felt the touch of a man inside of me. To me that isn't shocking. It is the life that I have chosen."

"May I ask why?"

"Why not? I mean, if you can choose to have sex, why can't I choose not too?" Donna was still somewhat stunned, so she could not come up with an appropriate answer. "Thomas has been trying since day one to get me into bed with him, but I won't do it."

"Are you afraid of something?"

"What is there to be afraid of? Thomas is a sensitive, loving man, whom I know if I were to sleep with him would be gentle and respectful with me."

"I must admit I would not have expected you to still be a virgin. I mean, I don't expect anybody in their thirties to still be a virgin." Donna sat back in her chair. "And Thomas is okay with this?"

"I didn't say that he was okay with it. He is actually going out of his mind, but I just have no desire to be with him in that way right now."

"No desire whatsoever? Thomas is a very handsome man."

"I have thought about it, but I don't know, I am just not comfortable with the idea yet." Halley's teen years ran through her mind. Memories of childhood boyfriends, high school dates, senior prom dates, dates for graduation, and dates for the weekend surfaced in her thoughts. No matter how devious the plan of her date to make love to her, not once did she give into his carnal desires. She did come close once with a chance encounter. She had only considered sleeping with this man because he had that special thing in his eyes. He was in control of everything around him, and everyone around him. Halley soaked up his energy that night, and almost gave into his lines of a night filled with unbridled passion. But she turned him down because he mentioned that he knew her father.

"Don't you miss it?"

"How can I miss what I have never had?" Halley readied herself to leave. "I guess we have had enough revelation for the night. I am tired, cold and sleepy. What say I come to your place tomorrow and we can begin working on the plans for the celebration? Most of it is already completed. All we have to do is put the program together."

"Halley, may I ask you another question?" Donna did not want to rush home. She needed to spend as much time away from home as she could. The apartment was cold and lonely without the boys. The ironic thing was that she never noticed this emptiness until Keith left that night. "Did Thomas know of your decision not to have sex when the two of you first dated?"

"Of course he did. I told him. Besides that, Thomas has known my family since high school. He knew then that I was a virgin, and I advised him that the situation had not changed." Halley answered. "I told him that I did not see this decision changing because he was in my life. Now don't get me wrong, there are moments, when we kiss my body reacts as it should when the man that you love touches it. But I have become quite accustomed to sleeping alone."

"Do you think that it is fair of you to ask this of him?"

"I did not ask this of him. He decided this for himself."

Fifteen

The good thing about spending Saturday with Halley was not just that Donna did not have to be alone, but that she now had a Black female friend. Halley Duncan was a character to socialize with. The news of her virginity was more than a stunning revelation to Donna, it was a sweet and innocent proclamation of another side to her. It made her appear softer than her intimidating exterior presented.

Sunday went by quickly and as usual so did Keith. Since Christmas night he had become all but a shadow to her. He would call so that the boys could meet him outside of her apartment. And whenever she tried to set a date to speak with him about his behavior, he would always come up with a skipped appointment or a client that he needed to see. She had given up seeing his face again.

Patrick would tell her of their day with Keith. But Sean had become like his father, distant. His hugs were no longer as tender and neither was his smile as joyful. Donna tried to talk to him about it, but how could he explain what was going on inside of him. He was a child with only that of a child's understanding. She did speak with Keith over the phone about the situation and he promised to address it with Sean. He did not mention their conversation again. Donna felt he took some satisfaction seeing Sean separate himself from her.

Darren walked into her office without notice, and demanded gentlemanly time with her. "How are you?"

"I am great." Donna tried not to act surprised. Whatever the feeling was that he made her feel and she would not refuse. It was now one that she began to welcome into her body. "I take it Matthew was not at his desk?"

"Yes, he is." He sat down in front of her desk. "I have something here for you." He placed a red folder on her desk.

"What is this?"

"Open it and find out." He smiled as if he had in the folder the cure to the world's problems, or at least hers.

Donna felt very uncertain about the contents of the folder, and hesitated a few minutes more before opening it. "Are you playing some sort of a trick?"

"Come Donna, have you ever known me to play jokes?"

"I wouldn't say that I have, but still...." That was the side of him that she was not comfortable with. He did not make her laugh. He made her smile like a schoolgirl. "Still, I don't know if I want to open this folder."

"Well, then let me do the honors." He opened the folder slowly, keeping a constant stare into her eyes. His dark brown eyes sparkled. "I can't believe that you are afraid of me."

"Afraid of you, never." But she was. "So are you going to open the thing or not?"

"I asked you months ago about hiring the detective to find your parents, remember?" She shook her head, yes. "Well, after realizing that you were uncertain of your decision, I felt it necessary to speak with him myself." She remained quiet. "I hope that you don't mind, but as I told you before I am very interested in helping you."

"What did he find?"

"Before we go on, I need to know if you are angry with me."

"Please Darren, I think that we are beyond my anger right now. Now tell me what did he find?"

"Actually, I have decided that you should open the folder and find out what is there." He closed the folder and pushed it toward Donna. "I believe I have done enough meddling."

"Darren, I don't think that I can open it." She starred at the folder as if it contained some form of a disease. "I know that I can't."

"Well, I won't be the one who does." He stood and walked out of her office.

Donna still could not open the folder. So much of her life was to be revealed once she did. She sat for minutes after starring and desiring to turn the cover, but found that she could not. When Matthew buzzed her, she quickly brought her mind to the present and answered him. "Yes, Matthew?"

"Patrick's school is on line two."

"Hello, this is Ms. Pennington."

"Mrs. Pennington, this is Nurse Johnson. Patrick is in my office right now complaining about a severe stomach pain. We have contacted the hospital and will have him transported to the emergency room in just a few minutes." Nurse Johnson was quiet, but Donna did not give a response. "Mrs. Pennington, did you hear me?"

"Yes, I am sorry this is all taking me by shock. What hospital are you taking him to?"

"Greater Hope."

"Have you contacted his father?"

"Not yet. Our policy is to contact the mother first in the case of any emergency."

"I will call him. And please tell Patrick that I love him and I am on my way now to be with him." Donna knew that she had to settle down, but her heart did not. Was Patrick in pain? Was he afraid?

"Ms. Pennington, is everything alright with Patrick?" Matthew asked as he walked into Donna's office.

"Matthew, could you please call my husband and tell him to meet me at Greater Hope." She moved quickly from behind her desk, grabbing her purse as she exited the door.

"Your husband?"

"Matthew, please don't correct me right now."

"Yes. Are you okay to drive?"

"Yes. Matthew just get him on the phone." She pressed the button for the elevator, but was unable to wait. She ran to the door that led to the stairs, but was almost knocked to the floor by Darren as he opened the door to enter the hallway.

"Donna, are you alright?" He asked trying to retain his grasp of her shoulders.

"No, I am not. Patrick's school just called. They are transporting him to the hospital."

"Why don't you let me drive? You are not in any condition to drive."

"I will be alright. I just need to get to my car." She tried pushing away from him.

"No, I insist." He looked at her squarely in the eyes to assure her that he would get her to the hospital quickly, but safely. "Now, let's take this elevator." He escorted her back to the elevator. "Now, what did the school tell you?"

"The nurse said that Patrick was complaining of stomach pains and that was it."

"Have you called Keith?"

"Matthew was doing that as I left the office", she answered. "I should call him."

"Maybe you should, but wait until we get into the car." He motioned for her to notice others in the elevator. When the doors opened to the garage, she exited first and began dialing Keith's number. But before she could complete the dial, her phone rang. "Hello."

"Ms. Pennington, this is Matthew. Listen I tried Mr. Pennington's office and his cell, and there was no answer. I did leave a message for him to contact you on your cell."

"Did you speak with his assistant?"

"No one answered."

"Matthew, please keep trying and let me know when you reach him." Donna knew that if his assistant did not answer, Keith would be at home. Before she dialed the number however, she sat for a moment to gather her thoughts. She had to deal with the matter at hand. She had to see her mind's eye that Patrick was doing fine. Once she could see that she could call Keith and talk with him calmly.

"Donna, are you alright?" Darren touched her hand gently.

"Yes, I just have to be calm. Everything is going to be fine. I have to keep telling myself that."

"Donna, Patrick will be just fine. The doctors will make sure of that." Darren took her hand and held it gently.

"Yes, I know. I just want to be there to hold him."

"I will have you there as soon as I can." Darren was steering in and out of traffic dangerously so, but cautious of every movement his vehicle made. "I think you should try to reach Keith again."

"Oh yes." Donna tried calling Keith at home, but still did not get an answer. "I don't know where he could be. I have tried his office, his cell and home and there is no answer." She knew that Samantha was at the hospital, so he could not be there. She did not want to call his parents. Neither had spoken with her since Thanksgiving. As she dialed the number, she made up her mind that they deserved to know. Patrick was their grandchild and they loved him. "Hello Marianne, this is Donna. Is Keith there?"

"No, he isn't." His mother insisted.

"Listen, I am on my way to Greater Hope Hospital. Patrick is being transported there because of severe stomach pains. I haven't been able to reach Keith, anywhere. Do you know where he is?" She got no response. "Marianne, do you hear me?"

"I'm sorry. I... is he going to be alright?" Marianne removed the condescension from her tone. "Keith is in Montgomery with Carolyn. They left yesterday." Donna could say nothing. "I will try and reach him at the hotel where they are staying."

"Yes, will you do that for me? I am pulling into the hospital now."

"Donna, is it okay that Kevin and I come to the hospital?'

"Of course, Marianne. Patrick would want you to be here." Donna tried not to think of where Keith was. Where or who he was with was not of any importance at the moment. But her heart ached.

"I am going to drop you off here and park the car. I will meet you inside." Darren stopped the car in front of the emergency entrance and waited for Donna to exit the Mercedes, but Donna did not move. "Why don't I go in with you?"

"No, I'm okay." She protested uncertainly.

"Yes, but I think that I will go in with you anyway." Darren stepped out of the car and motioned for the attendant, who then quickly opened the passenger door for Donna.

"Darren, thank you." Donna sweetly agreed. She was disturbed quite noticeably, but she knew that she had to keep things in check. Patrick needed her. Upon entering the hospital, Darren urged the whereabouts of Patrick from the desk nurse, who viewed the computer monitor and advised him that he would need to speak with the doctor. Donna asked what the condition of Patrick was, but the nurse repeated that she would need to speak with the doctor, who was on his way to prep for surgery.

After being given the directions to follow in order to find the attending doctor, Donna waited as patiently as she could before demanding that the doctor appear for an explanation. Darren follow up with trying to temper her frustration explaining to the nurse the fear Donna was feeling, not knowing the nature of her son's condition.

"Mr. and Mrs. Pennington, I'm Dr. Bavelich."

Both turned their attention from the nurse, who was happy that they did. "I'm Mrs. Pennington, Dr. Bavelich. How is my son?"

"Patrick is being prepped for an appendectomy." He saw the concern in Donna's eyes, but knew that he had more to tell her and that it would add to her stress, so he directed his words to Darren. "Mr. Pennington."

"Darren." Donna spoke quickly.

"Darren, Patrick has taken a turn for the worst since his arrival. "Dr. Bavelich continued. "He now has a temperature above 104 degrees, and he has protracted vomiting. Have you taken Patrick to his primary doctor before?"

"Yes, a couple of times?" Donna answered, interrupting Darren's thought process. She was somewhat more calm and willing to listen. "Why?"

"Did he diagnose his condition?"

"He said that Patrick needed to stay away from foods difficult to digest. He thought maybe he was suffering with some type of gastric problem."

"Appendicitis is difficult to diagnose in a child Patrick's age. But he is here and we will take care of him. You can see him now, but he is not in the best of condition. Hopefully, we will be able to get him into surgery soon. But right now filling him with fluids and antibiotics to fight any infections is all that we can do."

"Dr. Bavelich, we are ready." The nurse urged.

"Yes, thank you." Dr. Bavelich immediately turned to leave. "If you will excuse me."

"Dr. Bavelich, will he be alright?" Donna asked frightened by the answer not yet given.

"Mrs. Pennington, I must go now. But to answer your question, I think Patrick will be okay. The important thing now is to keep fluids in him and his body clear of an infection. The nurse will show you to his room."

As Dr. Bavelich walked away, Donna turned to look at Darren. He took her into his arms and held her to him. "Donna, he is going to be fine." He placed his hand under her chin and tilted her head back gently. "He is going to be fine."

"I know." She smiled and kissed his palm. Donna walked slowly, but quickly. She could feel the fear that she felt she would see in Patrick's eyes before even seeing him. She wanted to take him into her arms as she did when he was but a baby, and had a pain that he could not explain and she could not cure.

When the door from his room opened, the nurse stepped aside to let Donna walk through. Patrick looked at her and cried even more. He had an IV running from his small hand, and his neck. "Mommy, I hurt". He said through the tears and pain.

"I know baby, but mommy's here now and everything will be alright." She took him into her arms for as much as she could. "The doctor

216

said you will be just fine. The pain will be over in just a little while."

"I stopped throwing up a few minutes ago. It was gross." He swallowed hard. "Where's daddy?"

"He will be here soon. Your grandparents are coming too." He looked so tired. As he fell asleep in her arms, she held him closer. She knew that sleep was not going to be his friend, so she tried to provide him with all the comfort she could. When Darren walked into the room, she looked at him and smiled knowing that all was well.

"So, how is he doing?" He asked.

"I'm okay." Patrick answered. With his head rested on Donna's chest, he looked up at Darren. "Mr. Duncan, what are you doing here?"

"I came with your mother. She seemed too nervous to come alone." Darren took a seat next to the bed. "Is it okay that I am here?"

"Yes." Patrick was in a lot of pain. He tried to position himself in order to find the way to run away from the pain. "I am hurting a lot, Mr. Duncan."

"Yes, I can see that. But you are a strong guy and this pain can't take you. Can it?"

"No, but it still hurts." Darren took Patrick's hand into his.

"Well, your mother will take care of it. Just hold onto her." Donna saw that Patrick was succumbing to the pain, so she laid him back on the bed.

"He is such a strong little guy." She convinced herself of this. She had too. "Dr. Bavelich said that it is difficult to diagnose with kids Patrick's age. I feel like I failed him in some way."

"Don't do that to yourself." Darren insisted. Donna walked to the other side of the bed so that Patrick would not hear her conversation. "You are not a doctor."

"I know that Darren, but shouldn't I have seen that the pain he was suffering was more than just simple stomach pain. I mean, I should have known something else was wrong."

Darren could see the tears streaming down her cheeks. "Donna, you are a great mother. Don't take the blame for something that you have no control over."

"If I am not to blame, then who is? Someone should have seen this coming."

218

"Donna." She turned to see Keith standing at the door with his parents and Carolyn. Darren had been holding her hand, so he let it drop to her side. Not because it was wrong, just not respectful, he felt. "How is our son doing?"

Keith walked into the room starring deeply at what he thought was a conversation between lovers. "He is asleep now. Well, as much as he could get comfortable with."

"Where is the doctor?" Keith looked at Patrick lying in the bed unknowing that Keith was now there. "What is wrong with him?" Kevin and Marianne followed Keith to Patrick's bed. They tried to act as if they did not witness Darren presence in the room. Carolyn still remained at the door. She was uncertain as to where her place should be. "Donna?"

"Yes." Donna was somewhat taken aback with the situation of the moment. She hadn't really heard the questions posed by Keith."

"Did you hear me? Where is the doctor? And what is wrong with my son?"

"The doctor is in surgery with another patient."

"What? I want a doctor here, now!" Keith was angrily disappointed that Patrick was not getting the medical attention he felt he should.

"Keith, you are going to wake him." Donna took Patrick's hand gently.

"I want to see a doctor." Keith still angry walked to the door of the room. "Donna, where is Sean?"

"He is with the sitter. She picked him up from school." She was not pleased with him questioning her as he did. "Darren Duncan, this is Mr. and Mrs. Kevin Pennington, Keith's parents."

"No introduction needed." Kevin pointed out. "I am quite aware of the great Darren Duncan." He was smiling professionally so.

"Yes, how are you Kevin?" Darren shook Kevin's hand and then Marianne, who took his hand quickly and dropped it even faster.

"Donna, the doctor, what did he say was wrong with Patrick?" Kevin asked cautiously and sweetly.

"Patrick's appendix is inflamed and will have to be removed. When they brought him in they were unable to start the surgery because he was vomiting. But since that is under control, I am sure they will take him in shortly."

"Has Jenny been in to visit?" Marianne knew nothing else to ask.

"No, she has not."

"Mommy." Patrick had awakened. "Mommy, my stomach really hurts."

"Oh baby, I know." Donna carefully rubbed his chest. "Guess who is here? Your father and grandparents are here now."

"Where is daddy?" Patrick looked around the room.

"I will get him." Darren answered and walked out of the room to find Keith.

"How is Nana's baby doing?" Marianne took his hand.

"My stomach hurts."

"I know, but the doctor is going to make it all better for you. Your daddy is going to make sure of that."

"And so will your mother." Kevin added. He gave Marianne a look of disappointment. "You know Patrick I had this same surgery when I was about your age. It was easy."

"Really?" He spoke in a weakened tone. "Did it hurt like this, too?"

"Yes, even more." Kevin answered. He did love all of his grandchildren. Marianne on the other hand, had a series of difficult moments of proving her love to the grandchildren.

"Patrick." Keith came back into the room like a tornado. "How is daddy's boy?" Patrick eyes brightened. "I am so sorry that I wasn't here sooner." Kevin stepped out of Keith's way so that he could comfort Patrick.

"It's okay."

"No, it isn't. I should have been here." Donna knew what he meant. "Well, I spoke with the nurse and she has advised me that Dr. Bavelich will be here in a few minutes. She also advised that they are going to come in and get you prepped for surgery."

"Okay." Patrick tried to smile. "Then the pain will go away."

"Yes, then the pain will go away." Keith confirmed.

The prep nurse came in soon after and readied Patrick. The family was asked to leave the room. The waiting room atmosphere was awkward to say the least. Donna made her way over to the window with Darren. Keith stayed on the other side of the room with his parents and Carolyn.

Separation of hearts, separation of races, and separation of love is what was felt in the icy cold room. Darren removed his jacket and gave it to Donna. Keith watched as the moment of caring took shape. He motioned for Donna to join him outside of the room.

"What is going on here? And why is he here?"

"I could ask you the same, but I did not." Donna tried to speak in a low tone so that no one could hear what they were saying. "Keith, I was at work when the school called about Patrick. Darren is here because he felt it was better that he drove, so that I would not have too." She knew that her answer wasn't good enough for him, but it was her answer. "I tried reaching you everywhere that I had a number for you, but as you know I could not."

"You know if I could have been here, I would have been."

"Keith, I know that. But you must know that I will do everything necessary to find the care needed for our boys. Coming in here as you did demanding to meet the doctor after I tried to explain to you what was going on was not necessary. You made it seem as if I could not do my job as a mother."

223

"Donna, I didn't mean to do that."

"What exactly did you think you were doing when you charged into Patrick's room the way that you did? I mean did you even take the time to remember that I am his mother and am quite capable of making the right decisions about his need?"

"Donna, I am sorry. I just did not know what to think when I walked into the room and saw him, I mean Darren Duncan standing there with you."

"What?" She stepped away from the door and began walking down the hall. "Darren is my friend and that is all. He offered his help as a friend and I accepted it as one. I really don't even know why we are getting into this right now while our son is getting ready to go under the knife."

"You're right." He gathered his wits. "When he is released from the hospital, I want him to come home and stay with me."

"Keith, he has a home with me, too. I am the primary caretaker. He will remain living with me. I will take time off from work, or I will work from home. Either way he is staying with me."

"Donna."

"Keith, leave it alone. I will not let you take my son away from me."

"Donna, I... I just thought if he had a familiar place to recover, it would be better for him. I mean, our home is where he has been for some time." He tried to make right his continued wrong tongue. "Is it possible that I could stay there until he is better? I just want to be with him while he goes through this."

"Keith, it would not be a good idea for you to move in."

"Donna, I need to be with my son." He wasn't asking, he was demanding. "I will not get in the way of your life."

"Keith, why don't we wait to hear what Dr. Bavelich has to say about Patrick's condition and recovery, then we can make a decision about your staying with him.

Sixteen

Patrick's surgery was as successful as his recovery. He was back on his bicycle within a few weeks, and eating solid foods in a month or so. Keith did not move in because as Dr. Bavelich explained, Patrick would only be out of school for a short period of time, and would need to be on his feet immediately. Donna worked from home during his recovery, but soon went back afterwards. Keith of course was there each and every morning, and at night until the boys went to sleep.

Keith's sisters visited every day, without fail. They never wanted anyone to say that they did not love their nephews. That is with the exception of Jenny, who provided all of the medical needs for Patrick. Sean loved to see the scar every day. Patrick had become an action figure for his younger brother. Darren bought gifts for him, and visited or called daily. Even Halley called to see how he was doing. She was quietly disappointed because Donna was not able to participate in the Black History festivities, but hopefully next year she could.

Patrick was back in school and happier than he had been in some time. Children loved to be loved, and what better way to show that love even more than with gifts. Donna realized how the months were passing her by. It was now March and she had been taken off of the trail of finding her Blackness, as Keith would say. The thoughts of emptiness never left her, but the days of working for someone other than herself had to take precedent.

She had found some joy in working from home, but not being able to have adult conversations. Facing another adult was tolling for her, as she was on her way to a new life, and this new life required company.

"Wonderful to have you back, Ms. Pennington." Matthew greeted her as she walked into her office. "Mr. Duncan came by, but he did not leave a message or anything."

"Thanks, Matthew, it is good to be back." Donna gladly walked back toward her office as Matthew followed closely behind her. "Mr. Duncan? Darren or Nathaniel?"

"Darren, of course." Matthew sounded very coy.

"Excuse me?" Donna placed her purse in its usual place of the closet.

"Well, usually Darren is the one that comes by." Matthew was embarrassed.

Donna noticed his embarrassment and decided to leave it alone. "So, have you missed me that much?"

"I will have to say that I have." Darren stood at the door of her office as gallantly masculine as any god could be. "Now that you are back, we have a quite a bit of work to do."

"Well, good morning to you too, Darren." She was happy to see him. "And what work is that?"

Matthew excused himself as Darren walked in and closed the door behind him. "How is Patrick?"

"Patrick is doing just great. And how are you doing?" Donna sat down in one of the chairs in front of her desk. "Have a seat, why don't you."

"Thank you." Darren seemed to enjoy her role play. "The work I am talking about is the work with finding your parents."

"Darren, isn't this where our conversation left when last we spoke in my office?"

"Yes, and once again you are evading the question."

"I am not evading anything, I just need time to think if this is something that I want to do. I don't know if I am ready."

"When I first met you this was one of the most important things on your agenda. What is different now?"

"Nothing is different, I am just....

"Just what?"

"Just, waiting for the right moment." Donna sat smiling, nervously. She was nervous only because he made her want to do things that she was not always ready to do. Things that she would think of doing, but was afraid to meet the challenge. "Can we please put this aside until I am ready to deal with it?"

"If that is what you want, of course we can. But please don't become angry with me if I should hint, hint from time to time."

"I won't be, but when I am ready to deal with them, you will be the first person I call."

"Well, I don't have to be the first person, but I would like to be in the running." He smiled showing those beautiful white teeth. "I put the information the detective found in the office safe, should you need to see it."

The doorbell was loud. Maybe it was just that the apartment was empty. Donna wasn't sure, but it was welcomed. Halley stood at the door with a smile of friendship, love and sisterhood on her face. Donna gave her a big hug and then invited her in.

"I must admit, every time that I come here I am impressed with the space that you have here. It makes me somewhat jealous that I did not find it first, myself. I have lived here all of my life, and not once did anyone tell me of this place. Again, I mean what is the square footage in this place?"

"Why do we go through this each time that you come here?" Donna laughed out loud. "I tell you 4200 and you say I am stealing from the government. I say that I worked hard for this, and you comment on my ex-husband's family money. When will the abuse stop?"

"When you sell me this apartment?"

"Actually, it is not mine to sell. I told you I am only renting it."

"Are you thinking about buying it? Because if you aren't, I will take it right up from under you."

"The owner has brought it to my attention that I could buy it whenever I wanted too, but I just don't know."

"What is there to know? I mean look at this place." Halley walked up to the large window that covered the living room and looked out. The master suite was on the opposite side of the other rooms. It was large, covering more than 1750 square feet itself. The boys' bedrooms were large but not as large as the master suite. The master suite had its own private bathroom, of course. There were two other bathrooms in the boys' rooms and a guest bathroom in the hallway. The kitchen was equipped with all the essentials of a master chef. "What are they asking?"

"I refuse to tell you." Donna sat down on the sofa. "Are we going out or not? I mean I am ready to go and show me off to the world."

"How long will Keith have the boys?" Halley sat on the sofa next to Donna.

"Until Monday morning. Why?"

"I thought that maybe we could go to Atlanta."

"Atlanta?"

"Yes, Atlanta." Halley knew that Donna wanted to refuse, but she wasn't going to let her. "I know that you feel that you can only stay here in B-ham and party, but Atlanta is really the place to be. I figured we could use our company's jet and come back Monday morning."

"I am not sure if I want to be away from the boys that long, Halley."

"Excuses. The boys will be just fine. They are with their father, correct?"

"Yes, but...."

"No buts. We are going to Atlanta, and we are going to have fun." Halley took Donna's hand and escorted her to her bedroom. After packing a few items, they left the apartment.

Seventeen

Snowflakes felled softly on what was once green grass. Atlanta was beautiful this time of year. But then again, snow had that effect on most things. Although it would seem too much to ask of God to make this beautiful sight easier to wear and to walk through. Part of the glamour of snow was the clothing to warm the body and the delicacy of which one had to take to track through it without slipping to their embarrassment.

Halley seemed to be quite at home. A city girl perhaps in her spirit. "So what would you like to experience first?" Atlanta was only a few hours outside of B-ham, which left much room for conversation. Halley tried her best to make the conversation less tense as she could. Donna knew that it was a struggle for her because her personality alone was intense. So, to separate Halley from her personality, to accommodate the hopelessness of others must have been quite a task.

Donna did partake in as much of the conversing as she could. She did not want to talk about Keith, so that meant that she could not talk about the boys, too much pain. She did not want to talk about Darren either, too much of something else. What was left, were the parents she never knew, her life at the home, and that was it. "Anything that you want to do, we will do."

"I don't know. Really, I don't know what it means to be out like this." Donna felt somewhat embarrassed. "Are we going to be staying the whole weekend?"

"Yes, perhaps we should put our things up first. I believe our home is a few miles from here."

"Your family has a home here?"

"Yes, of course. My father spent quite a bit of time here in Atlanta when he first started his practice. When he was able he bought a home here so that he did not have to endure the hotel reservation game. I used to love coming here for the summer, and checking out all of the stores, and more as I got older. Atlanta is truly a wonderful prosperous city for African Americans and especially women."

"Really?"

"Yes, really." Halley spoke with much certainty. "As far back as I can remember the most successful women that I have met in my life's time have been right here in the ATL. I love it. I once thought of moving here. But I decided it was better to live where I work and visit where I play."

"Don't you play in Birmingham?"

"Not like I get to play here." Halley smiled. "Don't get me wrong, I don't get wild or anything like that, but I do let my hair down. There is not much to hold me back here. Most of the crowds that I mingle with are people who have their own."

"Their own what?"

"Their own, you know. Their own dreams, so they don't try to take mine. Their own money, so they don't hassle me with games of trying to exceed. Their own."

"Is that what you look for in people?" Donna still wasn't sure what she meant, but she did know that at one point she did not fit into that crowd, and still probably did not.

"Yes, actually it is." Halley turned the Mercedes sports with smooth adjustment to the streets. Her familiarity with the car and the street proved to be almost electric for Donna. "I don't like being hassled and I don't have much time trying to help someone accomplish their dreams."

"I don't believe that."

"Okay, maybe that was a little more dramatic than I wanted it to be." She steadied her thoughts. Being in Atlanta did make Halley feel a freedom that she did not allow of herself in Birmingham. "When I am here, I just like to be free of any responsibilities. There is time for everything in life. Isn't that what the Good Book tells us and I truly believe that. And when I am in Atlanta, I make sure that the time is for me to let my hair down, and tied up in a bow ready to conquer the world's problems. Don't tell me that you don't have some place like that."

"Actually, I don't. The apartment is the closest that I have ever been to such a place."

"You mean my apartment that I want, that you stole?"

"If you say so." Laughter sounded in the car, just as they drove up to a home that was as beautiful as the thoughts in her mind of what a home should look like. "Is this your family's home?"

"Yes, you like?"

"Do I like?" Donna felt a surge of energy colliding with the racing of her heart as she tried to control herself. She wanted to jump out of the vehicle. The landscape was white with snow, and yet she could see in her mind's eye of just how beautiful the lawn must look when it was green with flavor. Not as huge as their home in Birmingham, but it was still more glamorous.

"My father, no, actually my mother designed it and decorated it. It has a coral stone exterior, 6 bedrooms, 8 ½ baths, 3 full kitchens, 7 fireplaces, sitting room, theater, ballroom, library, smoking room, game room, and a standard pool room." Halley pulled up to the door and then exited the vehicle. Before she could do anything else, the door opened from the home, and out came the butler. "Hello Dave. This is Donna Pennington." Halley gave a huge hug to Dave. "Donna, join me."

"Hello, Ms. Pennington."

"Hello, Dave." Donna was so struck with the beauty of the home that she almost missed speaking.

"Wonderful, meeting you. May I take your luggage?"

Dave may have been no more than 40, 42. Very suave and kind. He stood at least 6'5 with a slender frame. Not skinny, just slender. His suit was of course without wrinkles. He was Black and his dark skin complimented his white teeth.

"Yes, thank you." Donna joined Halley at the door of the home. When the doors opened fully it was more than Donna could absorb at one time. She spoke to each of 3 staff members that she walked pass as she entered the home, and walked toward what had to be the sitting room. "Halley, it is absolutely beautiful, just exquisite. How?...No, why would you ever leave?"

"It is necessary to do so." Halley took a seat in what had to be the most beautiful chair that Donna had ever seen. It was of leather material, Italian leather, smooth and velvety Italian leather. "I mean, my job is in Birmingham, remember."

"Yes, you do." Donna decided that it was time for her to act as if she was comfortable in the setting of wealth. I mean by all understanding she has been living in what most would consider wealth for the past 11, no 12 years of her life. Her salary alone was seven digits yearly, and that wasn't including any of the cases she worked on alone. "So, what are we going to do now that we are here in your play town?"

"The time now is 4:34 a.m. What say we change for dinner and then we will see?" Halley quickly jumped to her feet. "Our rooms are upstairs. Let me show you where you will be sleeping tonight. I do hope that it is to your liking, Ms. Pennington."

Donna recognized the extended hiss sound that Halley used in calling her Ms. It was to remind Donna that she was now single and free to do what she wanted. "What time are we looking at leaving?"

"7:30 should be fine."

"Good, that will give me some time to get a little shut eye. Hopefully, I can do just that."

"Trouble sleeping lately?"

"More like trouble closing my eyes." Donna looked at Halley, who was watching her and searching for the answer before she could receive one. "When my eyes are closed my brain works even harder at reminding me of my heartache."

"Amazing how the pain in our hearts never takes a rest, even when our bodies decide to do just that."

"Amazing, I say more like cruel."

Donna wasn't sure of what to wear for dinner, but she supposed it needed to be soft and suitable for an expensive dinner. Halley relished in her wealth. Not with reckless abandonment, but with deserving virtuosity. The law firm that she worked with handled only pro bono cases, with a focus on civil right grievances. Her father did not enjoy her working there because it did not bring any money into her pocket, not that it was needed for her to make any other money. The Duncans were very wealthy, housing over $800 million in bank vaults and accounts around the US and elsewhere in the world. An article in the fortune 500 gave the history of their family's fortune, along with professional and personal accomplishments of each child. Halley thought she would do better for the world around her by not charging them for services that her expensive college education and family name could bring them. Mr. Duncan was proud of her, and so was her mother. It was shown during the Christmas dinner. They were proud of all of the cases she had won for those less fortunate, and they admired her drive to clean the world of hate and ignorance.

When she stepped out of the room, she heard music and people. "Well, hello sleepy head. I take it your sleep proved restful?" Halley stood at the end of the staircase dressed in a suit from the St. John Collection. It was a black scarf-collar and jacket with Marie pants. It was soft style to match the evening's winter emotion. Her Valentino pumps were a definite added touch of elegance.

"Yes, it did." Actually, it was a wonderfully peaceful sleep. The best sleep that she had had in some time. At least since that night she and Keith spent together. But perhaps that was merely from exhaustion. "Is that music that I hear?"

"Why yes it is. We have company." Halley smiled as she spoke, still waiting for Donna as she walked carefully down the stairs. "It was sort of a surprise for you."

"Did I seem to need a surprise?" Donna made it down and greeted Halley with taking her hand into hers. "Am I that bad off?"

"No, it is a surprise with a twist. It does not have anything to do with your current state of being." Halley continued her loving smile. "I just thought it was better for us to stay in and have dinner and conversation here, with some of the greatest minds in Atlanta. Come on let me introduce you."

"Halley, I....

"Donna, it is actually too late to refuse. Everyone is already here." Halley held to her hand and escorted her to the ballroom. Donna tried to consider if her attire was appropriate, or at least complimentary to the occasion. She had chosen to wear something from Eskandar, a square mélange top with flat front trousers. The natural color of the top matched perfectly with the brown trousers, and accented the heat of the fireplace crackling sound, warm and dangerously provocative. Donna decided to choose her Dolce & Gabbana pumps to accent her mood.

Before she could resist, Halley had maneuver their steps quickly into the room. There were at least 15 people that Donna could quickly scan. "Everyone, this is my dear friend and sister in skin, Ms. Donna Pennington."

From what Donna could tell no one there master an income of more than $20 dollars daily. They were poor, poor and dirty, poor and dirty and horribly smelling. "Hello everyone." She tried to ignore the judgments of shame that were aligning themselves in her head.

"Donna, we have with us some of the greatest minds in Atlanta. Every time that I visit here, these are the people I visit." The people did not speak or move. They all kind of stared weary of what Donna's presence meant for them. "Please make yourselves at home. Dinner will be served in about an hour or so." Halley then left her side and began to mingle with the people, the dirty people.

Donna, unsure of what to do with her body, did as they did, she stood still. What was she to say to them? They had nothing in common, nothing at all. "Are you from Birmingham, too?" The voice was overpowered by the malodorous odor that met her nostrils before she could turn to face the person who wore it like cheap perfume. "I am John Jacobs Stringer." He smiled with what was to be teeth, but showed themselves to be brown crowns of dirt. And the smell that came from the tunnel of what was supposed to be his mouth complimented the stench of his body.

"Hi, Mr. Stringer." Donna tried desperately not to show her disgust.

"No, call me Stringer, please. All my friends do."

"I'm sorry. Stringer."

"So are you from Birmingham? Or are you one of us?"

"One of us?"

"Yes, one of us?" Stringer looked confused. "You know one of the people that Halley takes under her wings and gives them the life that they dreamed of."

"No, I don't think that I am." Donna really wanted to remove herself from his stench, but she knew that it would be rude. Besides she could not think of a good enough reason to do so. "Halley and I are friends. I am an attorney in her father's law firm."

"So you are one of us." The thought seemed to make him happy. "I mean you work for her father, Mr. Duncan. He is a good man. And that wife of his, Mrs. Duncan, is just as, if not sweeter. I don't know much about their son. What's his name...."

"Darren."

"Yeah Darren, he is something difficult to figure out." Stringer adjusted his jacket. It was torn and tattered, with strips of spoiled food or something worse on it. Not sure as to why he still wore it since the fireplace made the room very comfortably warm. He spoke with clarity and surprising intellect. Really, who would think that an intellectual person would walk around with such a horrible stench? "He doesn't talk to us much at all when he is here."

"So do you all live here?"

"Oh no, no, we don't live here. We live in a shelter downtown. But whenever Halley comes to town, she sends their driver to pick us up, and she feeds us. She also talks with us about our lives."

Donna looked around the room to find Halley, who seemed very involved in a conversation with what looked to be a young woman. Because of the degree of damage that was imposed on her, it was difficult to tell directly what her age was. "So, how long have you known Halley?"

"Only for about a year or so," he answered. "But some of the people here have known her longer. She is quite a woman. If I wasn't the mess that I am, I would love to date her. Or at least have a chance to ask a woman like her out." He seemed convinced that if he wasn't who he was right then, he would have a chance with Halley.

"Where are you from?" Donna decided she would seem interested. Halley was still very engrossed in whatever the conversation was, so she had to do something to speed the time. Besides it did not look like 'Stringer' was going to leave her side. "I mean are you from here?"

"No, I am from New York." One of the butlers appeared with drinks. Stringer took one, but Donna could not stomach it. "I left New York about two years or so, you know, after I lost everything."

"What type of work did you do?"

"I was a college professor. I taught Biology at Cornell University."

"Really?"

"I know that is hard to believe, but it is true. See I carry my identification card everywhere that I go." He took out the card and gave it to Donna. It was probably the cleanest thing he had on his entire body. "I was actually pretty darn good."

"Why are you here, now? I mean with...."

"I understand. You don't have to be embarrassed for me. I am embarrassed enough for myself." He took another sip of the tea. Donna was surprised to see that the butler served the people in fine china. "Do you know what has always amazed me about the human body? The way that it can sometimes withstand the callous interruption of cancer, but let in the intruder of a broken heart, and all of the facilities shut down, sometimes never to reboot again." His tea proved to be not strong enough to fight off the terrors in his mind. "At least it was that way for me ten years ago." He looked at the fine crystal and the contents therein and turned his face in disgust.

"I...."

"Don't worry, it isn't for you to understand my struggles, it is only for me to tell you of them." He halfheartedly smiled. "I walked in on my wife and her boyfriend of 3 years. They were in the middle of something that she had not shared with me in months, her body." No smile. "Strange how something like that affects your system. My life has not been the same since then. I have gone from one extreme of loneliness and betrayal to another, only to fall deeper and deeper into a dark hole that has become my home."

"I am not sure what you want me to say."

"Neither am I." Still, no smile. "I guess most people would tell me to shake it off and go on, but I honestly could not. She left me after that and took what was to be her half of all we own. The rest I gave away, including my career. Every night I fight off pictures of them together in my head. I can't seem to shake them, and they don't want to let me go."

"Is that the reason why you are here tonight?"

"I would say so."

"So, just like that you let all that you have go?"

"I think that it let me go. I didn't have a choice."

"What about teaching? Do you not want to go back to it? Can you go back to it?"

"What am I to teach now? I can't keep my brain focused on anything more than her and him. I can't get it out of my head." He began to shake. Interestingly enough, the stench of him left the conversation in her head and became less important to Donna. She hurt for Stringer. He walked away from her, almost in a state of embarrassment.

"Are you alright?" Halley asked. "Who was that gentlemen?"

"He said that his name was Stringer, John Jacob Stringer." Donna tried to give Halley her attention, but her eyes continued to watch the direction in which Stringer walked. "He walked in on his wife with another man. It tore him apart."

"Donna, make sure that you only try to help, not become part of the solution."

"What does that mean?"

"It means that we can't do anything to solve their issues. We can only help them find the door to get started."

"Is that why you come out here and provide for them?"

"No, I come because it is what I am supposed to do." Halley spoke without mixed tongue. Donna felt that she was speaking directly to her. Here she was leaving a husband who loved her for such selfish reason as to find herself. She became no longer the individual when she married, and so it was there that she was lost to herself. Now she wanted that person back. How selfish, yet it showered her dreams as nightmares and her thoughts as figments of black dust. "Donna, I do not find that your own struggle with life is not within the same land of devastation as these people. The only difference is that you have a home, food, and family that you call your own. These people have lost all of that and some. When I see them, I see me. I see hope, yet failure. I even see love, yet hate. Hate of self, hate of people, hate of the living, and hate of death. They have no place of comfort here on earth, and they feel no place even in heaven above."

"Halley, please, I don't mean to be so self-involved."

"I did not say that you were. Your troubles are real to you, and that is all that needs to be known to the world outside of your pain.'

"But when I look around this room, I feel so silly and foolish, for even considering such a small matter compared to these people's problems."

Halley took her hand gently. "Whatever stirs your soul to shake with pain, confusion, and loneliness is never small. Compare it to no one. It is yours, and no one has the right to tell you how small or big it is." Words of wisdom, or pity, Donna decided she would accept both. "Dinner is served." Halley announced as the butler came through the ballroom doors.

Eighteen

The weekend getaway proved to be more exciting than Donna gave possibility for. Dinner served on Friday night was fitted for a king and his guest. Halley spared no expense to show those who had chosen to come to her family's home the feast of all times. Seafood, steak, roast beef, turkey, ham, salad, greens, stuffing, corn on the cob, creamed corn, beans of all kinds, breads of every kind, fruits from every island and state and so much more. They were even given care packages to take with them. No one left without filling their bellies to the brim and some.

The people who attended were of all colors and shades of life's skin. Halley did not choose anyone to take under her wings during this visit. She had only planned to feed and share in the good time with those who elected to visit with her.

Saturday was much of the same. Some of the same people attended, and shared their stories of sorrow and cheer. Donna had many moments of jubilation and sadness, followed by questions and doubts of her future. All in all, the weekend was to remain in her mind and heart for all days.

When the doorbell rang, it was a welcoming sight to see the faces of her Patrick standing next to Keith. Sean laid snuggly in Keith's arms, deeply asleep. It was a few minutes after 8 p.m., and they were exhausted. "Hi."

"Hi mommy, I missed you." Patrick almost jumped into her arms.

"I missed you, too." Donna gave him a long hug. "And your brother, who is sound asleep." Donna reached for Sean, but Keith held to him tightly. She did not like looking into his eyes any longer, she was no longer there. There was a time when she could look into his eyes and see herself there surrounded by his love. That existence no longer was shown in his eyes, and she dare not determine what was there.

"I will put him to bed." His words were as they had been lately, cold and precisely without hope. "Patrick, why don't you help your dad out?"

"Keith."

"Yes, Donna?" He really hated her, or was really close to hating her.

"I just wanted to touch him. Is that possible?" She reached for Sean again, and this time her hand was allowed to caress his hair. "I will put him to bed. I am sure that you have plans."

"It is quite alright. Patrick, come with me." Patrick followed behind trying to avoid what he could not understand with his youthful mind. While they attended to Sean, Donna sat and waited on their return to the room.

Her thoughts took her back to her weekend, and the time she shared with people she did not know. What would Keith have to say about her weekend? She would love to tell him, but she did not want to feel his coldness. So the question of telling him left her quickly. Halley mentioned that they would return in a month or so if Donna was up to it.

"Mommy, Sean is in the bed now." Patrick joined her on the sofa.

"I am going to leave now." Keith walked toward the door. "Listen Donna, Carolyn and I will be traveling quite a bit in the next couple of months, and I would like for the boys to join us on a couple of trips."

"Where will you be going?" Donna tucked her heart away so that it would not be injured by his words.

"We may travel to Disney World in Orlando, and then on to New York."

"What about school?"

"I don't think that 3 or 4 days out of school is going to make that much of a difference."

"Keith, Patrick has already missed 2 weeks. Can this not wait until the summer break?" Donna could see from the look in Keith's eyes that he would not accept her answer.

"Donna, we will wait until the summer break. I will see you on the weekend." Keith closed the door without saying anymore. Donna stood still hoping for reality to be not what it had just shown to her, but nothing happened.

"Mommy, did daddy leave?"

Patrick spoke softly, and the sound of his voice served as the catapult to bring Donna back to life. "Yes, baby, he did."

"I miss daddy, mommy." Patrick hugged Donna. "And Sean misses him, too. We want him to come back home."

Donna wasn't sure of what to say. Patrick's words struck her heart with extreme pain. She took his hand and walked with him to the sofa. "I don't want to hurt you and Sean anymore than I already have, but your daddy will not be coming home with us. Our lives are now separated." Patrick began to cry. "Baby, I am so sorry. Please, listen to me. Neither your dad nor I want this to hurt you or brother this much. I have done a horrible job of protecting you and Sean from all of this." Patrick could only look up at her. His eyes carried a look that she had not seen before, except during times when she took a toy from him or stopped him from doing something he wanted to do. Maybe he did blame her for the hurt that surrounded and captured his heart. It was right to blame her. She did this, whatever it is to him and Sean. She was to blame.

"Mommy."

Patrick could not be controlled, and neither could the pain in Donna's heart. No one deserved what she was putting her boys through. Even after much talking, his tears still cover his sweet face.

When the sun's light shone through the room Donna remembered her night, and quickly got out of bed and ran to the boy's room. They remained asleep, which was an answered prayer. Much of her night was spent trying to reach Keith, who never answered her calls. Thereafter she resolved to do some work for her new client.

After breakfast, they readied the boys for the school and left the apartment. She thought that Patrick would again bring up the conversation about when their father would return home, but he was busy playing take away with Sean.

After dropping the boys off at their school, she tried calling Keith, but still there was no answer. Donna did not notice the car until it was too late. The sound of the cars crashing is what pulled her attention from the thoughts of last night's past injury. But the pain in her neck is what she remembered before she saw darkness.

"Ms.? Ms., are you ok? Ms., can you hear me?"

Donna struggle to see the person who was talking, but the struggle was without result. Her last thoughts, before completely going out were about the boys, her boys. Who would take care of her boys?

Nineteen

"Donna, can you hear me?" Darren's voice was familiar, but not whose she wanted to hear. "Donna, can you hear me?"

"Darren, where are my boys?"

"They're in school. You were alone in the car. The doctor said that you will be ok." Darren still held gently to her hand. "Just rest. I called Keith's office, and he will be here, shortly."

Donna tried to move, but the pain of it stricken her attempt. "What happened?"

"You were in a car accident. Some kids were playing around in their parent's car and lost control of the car. They hit you head on. Your car was totaled." His eyes were soft and meaningful. "I talked with the doctor, and one of your ankles is broken. You have a few fractured ribs, and a substantial concussion."

"I can't breathe."

"Donna, listen, the impact to your chest is causing some complications. The doctors are concerned that you may be bleeding internally. They are running some test now."

"I am so cold." Donna could only hear him slightly. "I...."

"Donna!"

This place where she rested seemed more important to her than any place she had ever been. There were others there but she did not know them. Everyone seemed happy, joyful. Donna sat on a stone enjoying the view of the sea, and watching the people go by. No one was unhappy. As a matter of fact, no one seemed to even notice her there. Where was this place? The sky was so clear and yet the sun was not shining. It was a beautiful place. The feeling of peace filled her body. There was no pain, or any semblance of pain. In her mind's ear she could hear Darren speaking loudly, yet softly to her. She could hear him saying come back, don't leave and saying her name over and over again. What was going on? Why was Darren telling her to come back? She was just fine?

Donna decided to stop one of the persons passing by her as she sat on the stone. She started to stand, but was startled by the sound of darkness that swept across the sky. It was like a bang, a huge bang. The people ran screaming. At least it sounded like screaming.

"Ms. Pennington, can you hear me?" Donna could hear, but could not respond. She did not want to leave this place.

"Ms. Pennington, can you hear me? Squeeze my hand if you can hear me?" Nothing. "Ms. Pennington, squeeze my hand if you can hear me?"

"Donna, please squeeze his hand." Darren was frantic, but also control. How was he able to do that? "Donna, please you have to squeeze his hand."

"Mr. Duncan, she is in a coma." The doctor turned to face Darren after releasing his hand from that of Donna's. "We can only wait now."

"What do you mean wait? She could be dying."

"Her vitals are stable. The tests do not show any signs of internal bleeding, so she is out of danger."

"She is out of danger! What do you mean? She isn't talking! She isn't responding!"

"Mr. Duncan, she did suffer a severe concussion, but no trauma to the brain. Her brain activity is within standards." The doctor was calm. "We can only wait now."

"Donna." Keith walked into the room, and directly to her bed. Darren did not see him when he entered. "Donna, please you can't leave me now. Please."

"I take it you are Mr. Pennington?" The doctor asked.

"Donna, I know that you can hear me. Please don't leave me again. Not like this."

"Mr. Pennington." The doctor tried again.

"Donna, I'm here. Please come back."

"Keith." Darren decided he would try. "Keith, the doctor needs to talk with you."

Keith turned to the direction of Darren's voice. "What happened to my wife?"

"A couple of kids, rear ended her car. She was only a couple of blocks from the office."

"Where are the kids?"

"The police have them in custody. Their parents have been called." Both men spoke in calm, yet cautious tones. "Keith you will need to speak with the doctor."

"Mr. Pennington."

"Keith, please."

"Keith, your wife is in a coma. She is stable right now." The doctor slowed his words. "Your wife has suffered a broken ankle, and will need rehabilitation upon her recovery."

"Why is she in a coma?"

"We believe the coma is due to the concussion she suffered. However, there is also the trauma to her chest, which caused the fracture of her rib cage."

"How long?"

"How long what?"

"How long will she be in this coma?"

"We don't know."

"Keith." Darren interrupted.

"You may leave now."

"Excuse me."

"You heard me, you may leave now." Keith spoke firmly, but angrily. "I don't think that you should be here."

Darren looked at Donna. She looked vulnerable. "I will not leave her."

"Mr. Duncan, if you are asked to leave by a family member, then you will have to leave." The doctor instructed.

"Keith is not a family member. They are divorced."

"Is that true, Keith?"

Keith hesitated to answer. "Listen, he is her employer, and the reason she is here. If his company had not hired her she wouldn't be here."

"Keith, how ridiculous is that." Darren insisted. "Listen, I will leave, but only to give you time to come to your senses. I know that you probably need to spend some time with her, but you cannot stop me from visiting. You have no rights in this matter."

"I have every right. She is the mother of my two sons."

"And that is all that she is."

"Please, we must keep this room calm." The doctor advised. "Both of you will need to leave, now."

"I am not going anywhere." Keith seemed frozen in time.

Darren looked at him with eyes of inquisitiveness. "Keith, you stay, I will leave." Darren gave in, surrendered to the hurt he saw in Keith's heart. He saw it, felt it and then pushed it away from his. "Have you contacted your family? I am speaking in terms of the care of your children."

"Yes, my sister Jenny will pick them up from the center. Thank you."

"Not a problem." Darren walked to the door. "She is the mother of your boys. She is only my friend. I think mother trumps friend on any day." He began to walk out of the room, but stopped. "Keith may I asked that you call me should there be any changes."

"I will." Keith respected. "Darren, thank you."

The air was fresh and not a speckle of trash existed in this place. Donna could now only hear Keith's voice beckoning her to come back. Still she could not move toward it. She decided to stop trying. She sought only to sit in the peace of her present existence. The people still were unknown to her. There were some who walked alongside the seashore, and then there were some who did as she did which was to take a seat on a stone. Every one, however, was by themselves. They weren't alone, just by themselves. There were smiles and eyes of peace, love and joy. Even the grass was of pure dark green. No smog, no smoke, no sadness, no pain, no anything that would cause discomfort.

No one spoke to the other, but no one seemed lonely. "Donna, please don't do this. Come back." Keith's words went without response. There was this knowing that settled itself deep within her heart, a knowing of her imminent return to the place of where she left. But for now she would remain lost to the world she left.

"Keith, what are you going to do about the boys?" Mrs. Pennington asked.

"What do you mean?"

"I think that you know."

"No, you tell me."

"Keith, don't make me say this to you."

"Mother, since you seem to have all of the answers, I think that it is best that you do. Educate me."

Donna had not come out of the coma for over a month now, and Keith had run out of words explaining to them what had happened to their mother. He thought that maybe their visiting her in the hospital would miraculously make her come to, but nothing happened. He began to think that maybe she was purposely staying away from them just as she had purposely left him. When he spoke with the doctors about the possibility of her refusing to answer, they explained to him of the impossibility of it. When faced with the implication of asking such a thing, Keith hid from himself his doubt. At this point He was just so angry with her for taking away his family that he was willing to believe anything. She was selfish and self-absorbed. So what if they were of different racial backgrounds. So what if their skin colors were different. So what! So what! So what! Damn it, Donna!

"Keith, I love Donna like she was my daughter, but even I know at some point a decision has to be made. You have to tell the boys that the possibility of their mother coming back home is short to none."

"Mother, I will not do that." Keith had only made it into the house for a few minutes before Mrs. Pennington laid into him. He had been spending every day since the accident with Donna. He would talk to her, tell her of the memories that they shared together. Anything he thought would bring her back to him, he would do it, but nothing worked. He had made it to his living room sofa. The last thing that he needed was his mother's demands. He needed peace and quiet. He needed to think.

"Keith, I don't know what you are waiting on, but you have to do something other than what you are doing now. Decisions have to be made."

265

Mrs. Pennington followed Keith into the living room. She had been watching the boys for him, as the rest of the family had been since the accident. "Son, I am not trying to sound mean, I just know that at some point you are going to have to do something. Your sons don't deserve being left out like this."

"Mother, they wouldn't understand even if I tried to tell them." Keith fell onto the sofa. He began to rub through his hair searching for a way to escape his mother's tirade.

"Son, what have the doctors told you to do?"

"They haven't told me to do anything yet. They have been watching her vitals and that is it."

"I can't believe that that is true. It has been over a month."

"Well believe it, mother." Keith's frustration had turned to anger. "Her brain activity is still normal. There is no indication that she has suffered any brain damage. She will wake up."

"But when, son?"

"I don't know!" Keith stood and began walking out of the room. "All I do know is that she will wake up. And when she does, I will be there, and so will our sons. Please leave now, mother. I need to get some rest."

"Keith. Keith." Mrs. Pennington yelled for him to stay. "Keith, I don't want this to...."

"Mother, you know your way out." Keith walked out of the room and then up the stairs. When Mrs. Pennington heard the door slam, she left the home. Keith fell onto the bed and waited for sleep to clear his mind. Jenny had called earlier to let him know that she had the boys, and would keep them through the night. Keith thought of his heated discord with his mother, and how it left him feeling empty. She did not understand what he was feeling. Hell, he didn't understand himself. All he knew was that he did not want Donna to die, and when he heard of her accident his whole world stopped. It just stopped. Since that day nothing else mattered but Donna coming back. But to who, and to what?

Twenty

"Donna, hey this is Halley. Can you hear me?" Halley visited each week, and each day of the week. She spent more than a couple of hours on each visit. She would pray, hold Donna's hand, and pray even more. "I just want you to know that you are driving my brother crazy. He can't stand that you are not in your office any longer. You have to come back. Do you hear me?"

"The doctor said that she can hear us." Keith came into the room without Halley noticing his arrival. "Are you a friend of my wife?"

"Your wife? I thought Donna was divorced?" Halley held tightly to Donna's hand. "Excuse me, my name is Halley Duncan." Halley reached out her hand to shake his. Keith accepted her gesture as he walked to Donna's side.

"Duncan? Are you related to Darren Duncan?"

"I am. He is my older brother. And you are Keith, I presume?"

"Yes, I am."

"May I ask if the doctors have given you any further information on her condition?"

"Actually, no, they haven't." Keith kissed Donna on her forehead. "They haven't shared any further information, but I am still hopeful." He turned to face Halley. "I've not seen you here before."

"Neither I, you." Halley still held on to Donna's hand. "I have visited her every day since she came in. Maybe we have just missed each other."

"How odd is that?" Keith smiled as much as he could.

"I would say quite, but then I am not surprised."

"Meaning?"

"Meaning, if we were to have met any other time, we would have. All things are cool though. It is nice finally meeting you."

"I wish that I could say the same. I did not know that you existed."

"Old news. Is there anything that you need?"

Darren was thrown aback by her bluntness. "Are all Black women like this?"

"Are you sure that is the question that you want to ask?"

"Yes, I am positively sure."

"I don't believe that it is, so I will excuse your ignorance."

"What am I supposed to know that I don't know about Black people? I can't take this anymore." Keith demanded. "My wife left me because of this mess. And now, look at her lying here! Does it matter now that she is Black? No, it doesn't. Damn it, where did all this come from? I had nothing to do with slavery. My family had nothing to do with slavery. Yet, here we are today suffering for the evil actions of people we do not know, and because of the color of our skin!"

"Mr. Pennington....

"Now, you refer to me as Mr."

"Yes, I think that it is best that I do." Halley thought it better to move away from Donna. "It is apparent to me that we are as professional as we can be right now."

"Why is that?"

"Because you don't know me, and I don't know you. Yet, you have managed to spurt out racially motivated inflictions against me without realizing the propensity of your venom." Halley spoke with a calculating tone. "Our acting in a professional manner will allow what is said by either of us to be taken less painfully personal. And I would say Mr. Pennington, you at this point should be relieved to know that is how I am taking it."

"You know Ms. Duncan, or is it Mrs.? Whatever it is, I really don't feel it necessary to be relieved at however you are taking what I have to say. I am finished with the issue of race. I am finished with it because it has no impact on my life."

"If that is the case, why is it that Donna has fallen so deeply away from your marriage that she left you to find out exactly what it means to her to be a Black woman?"

"Because of people like you." Keith spoke with exactness. "You people who run around promoting the color of your skin, and not the actions of a person's heart. You people, who only think what matters in this world is, the color of a person's skin."

"The irony of this moment right here is that I came to visit my friend, and to pray for her waking up and full recovery. Yet, I have been met with a reality check of my own personality. Kind of makes a person wonder if indeed they should be praying for anyone." Halley took her purse from the end of the bed. "What I think I will do right now is leave before my reality check leads me to do or say something that I will later regret."

"Darren." Donna's weak soft voice spoke from what seem like a distance. "Darren, where am I?"

"Donna." Keith turned around, and rushed to the bed. "Donna, baby can you hear me?"

"Keith. Keith. Where am I?" Donna tried moving, but was too weak to make any relevant move.

"You're in the hospital. There was a car accident."

"I will get the nurse." Halley ran out of the room.

"Are the boys okay?" Donna asked. "Where are they?"

"The boys are fine. Please rest. Don't try to do too much. Halley went for the nurse."

"Halley?"

"Yes, Halley. Now please rest." Keith tried tenderly to care for her until the nurse came into the room. "You still have a cast on your leg. Your ankle was broken in the accident."

Just then the doctor and nurses came into the room, with Halley closely behind. They checked her vitals and listened to her questions without answering.

"How does she look?" Keith asked nervously.

"Her vitals look good. How do you feel, Ms. Pennington?"

"I don't know. How am I supposed to feel?" Donna spoke very softly. She could feel some irritation on her leg but wasn't sure if she should say anything about it. She was afraid to hear what the doctor would say.

"You have been away for a little over a month now. Your brain activity is functioning as it should, and there doesn't appear to be any adverse observations. I would say you are doing wonderfully." The doctor smiled.

"When can I leave?"

"Now you just came out of a coma, so we will need to keep you here to watch your vitals for at least a week or so."

"When can I see my boys?" Donna looked at Keith.

"Donna, I don't know if that is a good idea." Keith wanted the assurance from the doctor before bringing the boys to see her. But the doctor remained on mute. "I will pick them up today and bring them to see you later this evening."

"Donna, it is more than wonderful to have you back. How was your trip?" Halley smiled, cheerfully. "I have missed you."

"Halley." Donna returned the smile.

"Donna, I think that it is best that you rest now. Don't you think so doctor?" Keith interrupted. Donna looked at Keith without the face of the smile that she had only moments earlier expressed to Halley. "I am only thinking of your recovery."

"Halley, how are you?" Donna removed her hand from Keith and extended it to Halley, who took it cautiously. "It is good to see you."

"It is better to hear your voice again." A moment of acute possible sadness passed as quickly as it appeared in her heart, but not without tears. "We are going to get you a chauffeur."

"I don't think that she needs a chauffeur." Keith's emotional pain tore through the sadness that was leaving the room.

"I was only joking Keith." Halley's voice remained sweet. "My friend is awake from her long sleep, and I am just at a lost for the right thing to say."

"That could never be possible, you, at a lost for the right thing to say." Donna spoke weakly.

"Yes, most would think that. But then of course I was afraid that I would not be able to hear your voice again, and the thought of that...."

"Spend only a few more minutes with her and then I will insist that Ms. Pennington gets her rest."

"Doctor, about my ankle?"

"We will look at removing the cast. However you are going to require extensive therapy. You had quite a bit of damage."

"Therapy?" Donna asked. "Will I be able to do this from home?"

"Yes, it can be outpatient. But I am afraid that you will need home nursing care. Or you will need someone to take care of you."

"I will have some of your things moved back to the house."

"Keith." Donna resisted.

"Okay, I am going to insist that my patient gets her rest now."

"I will talk with you tomorrow. I promise." Halley held tightly to Donna's hand, and then walked out of the room to give some alone time for Keith.

The house looked different, felt different and even had the markings of something that she did not want to enter. Two more weeks went by before the doctor would release Donna, and they were the longest two weeks, she felt had ever existed in her life. Keith went home the night of her waking up and brought the boys to see her. They cried, she cried and then they all laughed throughout the night. Or rather until the nurse came and told Keith that they had to leave because Donna needed her rest. The rest of her days in the hospital were met with rehab and pain.

She still was not able to put too much weight on her ankle, but was getting stronger each day. Now here she was in the driveway of the home she shared with Keith and the boys. The home that was their home away from the world, and yet she did not want to go in. "Keith, I don't want to be here." She said sadly.

"What's wrong?" Keith put the gear in park.

"I just don't want to be here." Tears began to fall from her eyes. "Please, Keith, take me home."

"Donna, this is your home. This is our home."

"Not anymore." Keith melted away from the pain in his heart.

"Donna, how are you going to get around?"

"I will hire a therapist."

"And the boys? What will I tell them?"

"Until I can get around on my own, I think that the boys should stay here with you." She heard the words come out of her mouth, but she refused to feel what saying them made her feel. "I can't take care of them now."

"Donna, please don't do this. We don't have to share the same bed."

"Keith, I can't stay here." She insisted.

"Do you hate me that much? I mean does the color of my skin bother you to disgust that you don't want to stay in our house?"

"Keith, I don't hate you. I don't know what is going on inside of me. I just know that this doesn't feel right."

"How can you be so selfish?"

"Keith, please, just take me home."

"Let me go in and get the boys. I am sure they want to see you." Keith opened the door. "Donna, I don't know what to say or do anymore. When I received that call that you were in an accident, my life drained from me. And when I got to the hospital and they told me you were in a coma, I thought maybe you would wake up and all of this would be over. Each day I visited and nursed you with my heart and my love, but still your eyes remained close. Each day I cried, cried for my life without you and the boy's life without their mother. I never thought that you would awaken and still not want to be with us, yet that is exactly what is happening. Even when you woke, and the name you called out was that of another man, I still wanted to be with you. I still thought there was hope for us. What have I done to you to cause you so much hurt?" He stared off into the brightness of the sun. "I have loved you and I still love you, immensely. I will give you anything that you want to make whatever this is stop, but I don't know what to give. I look at you and everything I ever wanted I see in your eyes, even now I see those things. I don't understand how I could love you so much, and you not feel the same. How could love be so cruel to me?"

Twenty-one

"How do you feel today Ms. Pennington?" The therapist was young and energetic.

"I feel much better than I did three months ago." Donna had therapy, at least an hour's worth three times weekly, and sometimes more depending on her tolerance of the pain. "I can stand longer without the assistance of these crutches."

"That is great! We are going to look at more strength training. Thereafter, you will be required to walk without the crutches. Do you think you can you handle that?"

"I am going to have too. Besides, my boys need someone who can keep up with them."

"Busy bodies?"

"That's saying the least." Donna had begun to work again from her home. But only as a researcher. Darren had not called or come by since she came home. She was not surprised at his behavior, but she did miss his presence.

"What say we start with stretching, and then onto the weights?" Mark, her therapist from hell she thought, was always ready to punish her. At least that is how she looked at it. He of course considered their sessions to be needful to a greater end. "I know you don't want too, but it is a must. You do want your boys back right?"

"Actually, I was hoping that there was some way to get them for the weekend. What do you think?"

"Let's see how you do today."

"Been some time sister." Halley walked through the door like the wind, but with a glorious band behind her. She was all that Donna would dream to be, but more than she could ever conceive in her own mind. They had talked on the telephone daily, but Halley would never come by, even when Donna insisted.

After an emotional hug, Donna looked deeply into Halley's eyes, "Why has that been the reality?"

"Actually, I am not exactly sure. But I do know that it will not continue to be." Halley promised. "Now may I come and sit for a bit? Halley knew that she had been distant because of Keith, and his seemingly cold attitude toward her. "Besides we can't live for yesterday. Yesterday is gone. We only have today." Donna smiled happily. "So, I see you are not using your crutches."

"No, I am not." Donna directed Halley to the sofa. "I have actively tried to refrain from using them."

"You aren't moving faster than you should, are you? I mean the office can wait. Besides, my brother is taking care of everything."

"It's not for the office. I want my boys back." Donna took her place on the sofa next to Halley. She was happy to see her.

"What are you talking about? I thought your boys were with you."

"They are with their father until I am able to care for them."

"Well then, you still have them."

"I don't have them with me."

Halley studied Donna's face. "Dear, what exactly are you trying to prove to yourself?"

"I have nothing to prove to anyone."

"Are you sure of that?"

"Yes, I am positive." The discomfort that comes with hiding your thoughts quickly entered into the room, and into Donna's heart. Honesty was to be the only remedy. "I don't know if it is proof, or definition."

"Defining what or who?"

"Halley, I told you that I have had a struggle going on within me for the past year or two now, and that has been the case, and I guess that's what you are seeing."

"I know that you think that is what's going on inside of you, but....

"Hey wait, aren't you the person who told me not to let anyone tell that it doesn't matter?"

"And I meant that, as I mean it now. What I'm trying to say is maybe it is not going on inside alone."

"What?"

"No, who? Keith." Donna shrugged doubtfully. "This is a horrible place to put him. He is agonizing over this. I don't know him, but he seems to love you more than life itself."

"And I love him."

"Can you tell me something?" Donna answered with a nod. "How did you do this? I mean leave someone who loves you more than his own life?" Halley took her hand. "Donna, Keith loves you. He loves you immensely. Hell, even I began to question my decisions in life."

"Halley, I too love him, but something broke inside of me. Something that his love or our love for each other could not cure."

"How is that even possible? Love conquers all things."

"I haven't stopped loving him. I don't know if that is even possible. Keith saved me from a dark world, a world that I did not know. Albeit I was just beginning to learn it. He came in and showed me a different world, and he loved me into it." She smiled, and could begin to feel the tears building in her eyes. Convincingly she let go of Halley's hand. "Halley, something broke inside, and when it did, I immediately went to him, because he has always saved me. We have always saved each other. But he could not repair the damage. No matter how hard he tried. In fact, it would seem that everything that he tried only made the damage worse."

"Because of his skin color?"

"Partly. But mainly because I did not know the answers myself." Donna stood and slowly walked away. Her strength was better, as well as her tolerance for pain. "I understand now that sometimes there are situations in life that will strike your very being, and take from you

283

all that you thought and believed were there. And when you go looking for answers to alleviate this disruption, no one can provide it for you. You actually have to go through the darkness alone."

"Donna."

"Halley, you don't have to judge me. I judge me every day. This seems to be an extremely selfish thing that I have done. Maybe it is, but it is where I am. No matter what I try to do to leave it behind me, I can't let it go. Therefore now, I won't let it go."

"Do you remember the file that Darren offered to you? The one that had your parent's information in it?" Donna had forgotten about that day. "Donna, you need to review that information. And you need to do it soon."

"What is going on? What are you not telling me?" Donna came back to the sofa. "Have you reviewed the information? Do you know who my parents are?"

"Of course not. I would never do such a thing without your permission. But...."

"But what? Did Darren?"

"No, neither did my big brother. However, he did tell me about the file, and the private detective. Whatever the information is, it was obtained out of Atlanta."

"How do you know this?"

"When Darren told me about the file, he told me that the detective told him that she is in Atlanta."

"She?"

"Your mother."

"My mother?" The news hit an immediate target, her mind. "My mother." Her dreams. "What do you want me to do?"

"Donna, if you are looking to save what is left of your life with Keith, you need to look into that file."

"Have you talked with Keith?"

"No. Keith doesn't talk with any Duncans. He hates us for your working with us." She smiled. "Donna, I am a civil rights attorney. I chose this career because of my need to be of assistance to those who do not have anyone to fight for them, or cannot afford one. I have fought for many people, but none like your Keith."

"Did he hire you as his attorney?"

Halley stood this time, and begin to walk away, but turned back to face Donna. "While you were away, I visited you every day, every week, and not once did Keith and I meet each other. But one day we did, and it was the day that you woke." Her smile was there again. "We had an interesting tit for tat. And the one thing that resonates beyond all is the desperation in his voice. He is totally oblivious to what is going on with you, and it is destroying him. He has no one to help him through this, not even you." She sat. "He is like many clients I have fought for."

"What is the basis of your fight?"

"Your marriage." Nothing. "I don't want you to give it away. And the only way that I can think of to fight for it is to get you on the right path to saving yourself, before you lose everything that truly matters to you. You are my friend, my sister. If I can't fight to save you, why fight for the others."

"How long will you be gone?" Donna knew that the visit with Keith would not be an easy one, but it was needed. "What am I to tell the boys?"

"I am not sure. A week or so. I don't know."

"Is Dr. Bavelich agreeing with this? What about your therapy?"

"Keith, my therapy is going great. I will only be gone for a week or so." Donna sat in the sitting room that she had shared with him for eleven years. Many memories of laughter and love conquered her mind. "Keith, I have to do this."

"Keith." Carolyn's voice awakened darkness to the room. "Oh, I apologize. I didn't know that you were still here."

"Yes, well that is fine. Neither did I know you were still here." Donna retorted.

"Carolyn, could you please give Donna and me a moment."

"Of course. I will be in the kitchen." Carolyn turned to walk out of the hallway. Her words sought and found her target. "I was just letting you know that dinner is ready. The boys are washing up now."

Target destroyed. "Carolyn, I will be there in a moment. Also please have the boys come in to see their mother." Target resurrected.

"Thank you." Target spoke.

"I don't need your thanks. Not without you being attached to it anyway. You are their mother, and no one can, or will I allow them to take that away." This is why she loved him. "Carolyn is a friend. She has walked with me

287

through this, whatever this is. She is angry with you. That is my fault. I have shown and shared with her the pain that you have caused. But that pain has yet to take my love or my body from you." He thought to himself before continuing. "That is the problem with sharing, sometimes the friends don't always come to terms with what you share. Even though you do."

"Keith."

"Donna, it is not okay that you have done this to us. It is not okay at all. But it is our reality. If you want or need to go to Atlanta to seek out your mother, do so, and do so with my blessings."

"Keith." She wanted to hold him, but her feet would not move. She wanted to tell him that she loved him, but it did not seem fair to say I love you, knowing that she was causing him so much pain. "I don't know what to say."

"Neither do I." Keith walked away toward the hall to wait for the boys. "All I know is that you have broken me down to crumbs. I have only begun to bring myself back together since the boys have lived here with me. I could not be crumbs when they need for me to be whole."

"Daddy. Daddy." Patrick made it first. "Where is mommy?"

"Here I am, Patrick." Donna stood, and Patrick ran to her like she was forgotten and now remembered. Sean on the other hand, stood behind. He held onto Keith's hand. "Sean, may I have a hug?"

"Sean, go to your mother, and give her a big hug."

"I will come to you instead." As Donna began walking toward Sean and Keith, Patrick took hold of her hand, and walked with her. "Mommy, Sean is mad with you. He said that you are being mean, and do not want us anymore."

"Sean, I am so sorry. Mommy is making some very difficult decisions, but never do those decisions mean that I don't love you, or want you in my life." Donna spoke softly, as she took Sean's hand from his father leg and wrapped her arms around his small frame. "Do you hear me?"

"Yes, but...."

"There are no buts. I love you." Sean began to cry. "Baby, I am so sorry."

Sean still was silent. Only his tears spoke for him. Darren stood still and quiet as well. Patrick continued to hold on to his mother, but neither did he speak. Donna could not find any more to say, but that she was sorry. What else could be said that a child of seven would understand? Only, 'I'm sorry' is palatable to the heart when a child is in pain.

Twenty-two

The flight to Atlanta was covered with tears. She left immediately after leaving her home which used to be her home. She figured immediacy would prove better for situation than waiting another day. Because she failed to make it to the office before leaving, Donna had yet to open the file. Darren was asked to overnight it to her in Atlanta. Halley offered their jet and family home, and Donna accepted without hesitation. Halley had promised to join her in a day or so, giving her a day or so to clear her mind, or at least ready her mind for what was coming.

Sean never resolved to accept Donna's apology. As pissed poor as it was, he did understand that it was not enough for him. Patrick, on the other hand only wanted his mother. He reminded Donna of her promise to never leave them. Donna in turn assured him that her going to Atlanta was not permanent, and that she would be back. Patrick was willing to accept what she said, and melted into her arms.

As she considered the possibility of loss of her family, she was even more strengthened to seek her mother and solve the questions inside of her. She wanted to believe that finding her mother would, indeed, solve all of her problems, and she would be back with her Keith, and her boys. He did tell her that his body was still hers, and she was not going to let that revelation slip by. It freed her fear of him sharing himself with Carolyn. She knew now that that was not the case. But why put her through all of the doubt. It is possible to know that she deserved it, or maybe even he had considered his life with Carolyn. Whatever the reason she was more than happy to know that he was waiting on her return.

"Ms. Pennington. I hope that the flight was to your liking." Dave greeted her with a smile of welcome. August in Atlanta is nice. Not too warm, and yet cool when need be.

"It was Dave. Thank you." Donna stepped from the Mercedes actually wanting to see a smiling face, and Dave provided her wants. "Thank you for allowing me to visit with you."

"With me? I do believe that your visit will actually be with Ms. Duncan."

"Yes, it will, but you will be here, won't you?" Dave warmly suggested that he would be, but to serve not to partake in the activities of the house guest.

As the day progressed, Donna waited anxiously for the mail to arrive in her thoughts. She had showered and changed into more comfortable clothing for the evening. She knew that it would not be until Monday to expect the file, but she could not rest. Monday was two days away. How was this woman who was her mother? Why did she leave her to be raised by the State? How did she look? Who was her father? More and more questions ruled her thoughts, but none to be answered for at least a day.

When she considered her life as a child, much loneliness was found. Even though sought by many different families, she was never adopted by any. Although she made friends, none did she keep in touch with. She found that she really wasn't as interested in finding out who her parents were, as much as she was in finding out who she was. What made her so, to her parents anyway, so unworthy of their love that they would leave her behind to a world that did not want her in it?

As much as it mattered now, it would never have the weight it had on her life as it did when she was ten, and living with a foster family, who had decided that they no longer could keep her. Actually, it wasn't her they could not keep, rather each other. The couple whom she had known for three years of her life had decided that they did not love each other more than they loved the people that they were seeing outside of their marriage.

Donna remembered the pain she felt. She also remembered being very confused. Confused at what they were saying about not loving each other anymore. Did that mean that they didn't love her anymore, too? Did she cause them to not love her? She remembered feeling rejected, rejected when the foster care worker came to the home and returned her to the agency. The mother did not fight to keep her home, and the father had already left to be with his new family. She remembered being angry, then sad, then angry, then sad, until finally she just stopped talking for three years, and refused to let her heart believe again in hope.

Had she caused this hell to enter into the mind of Sean? She knew that what she saw in his eyes she had seen before, but it was looked in the mirror as a child. The clock read 3:00 a.m., but she wanted to let Sean know that she would return to him, and that she had not rejected him. She wanted to let him know that his mother had made the biggest decision to destroy his life, but that it was never meant to be. She wanted to hold him, keep him protected from her selfishness, and mental dysfunctions. When she picked up her cell phone, she knew that it would be wrong, or at least not enough to satisfy the heart of seven year old. As she closed her eyes, she watched the words of prayer surrender themselves to God in hopes that He would answer. She had not spent much time with Him. So whether or not He knew her was of no consequence to her, but she had heard of Him from her childhood, as the one you call on when things were out of your control. So it was God who she talked with throughout the rest of the early morning.

"Are we going to sleep the day away, or do we have things to do, and people to see?" Halley's voice was the alarm clock that thwarted calm to a day that had purposed a painful revelation. Before finally allowing sleep to capture her, Donna vaguely remembered the softness of the

1000 thread count Egyptian cotton sheets. She remembered how great they felt when she last slept in that bed. It was a welcome comfort from the thoughts that haunted her mind and heart.

"Halley. How are you?" Donna tried to wake from her sleep. She had only been asleep three hours before she heard the voice. "When did you get here?"

"I just walked in." Halley was smiling cautiously. "Tell me something, are you free tonight?"

"Why do you ask?"

"Well, if you are, I have somewhere that I would like for you to accompany me."

"Now, this isn't one of those surprise places like before, is it?" Donna sat up the in huge king size bed. "I mean I would not want to deal with that with what I have ahead of me."

"Actually, it is something else." Halley smiled cautiously. "It is a speaking engagement."

"Whose is the speaker?'

"I am."

"Where, and for what occasion?" She relaxed herself on the huge pillows. Halley stood and began walking toward one of the two windows.

"Actually, I was asked to speak at this particular group's annual celebration once before, but I was always too busy."

"And now?"

"Now, I am not too busy." Halley spoke matter of fact.

"Halley, is there another reason why you are here?" Donna could see something in Halley's eyes, some particular spot of evasiveness that she has not seen before with her. Normally, Halley is quite open, but her voice was silenced. "Truly there is something more to this. What is it?"

"Donna, your accident conjured many thoughts for me. Some I have either repressed or maybe even ignored. Whatever the reason is, your accident forced me to face them. It has not been an easy revelation."

"Halley, what's going on?"

Halley returned to the bedside, and smiled softly. "Life is an interesting book of tales. I have found that if we wait for the story to unfold we will find much there. At least that has been my reality. Thomas and I are getting married."

"Really!"

"Are you sure that is your question?"

"What happened?"

"Your accident happened?" Halley hesitated for strength. "It is strange, but then death or the close possibility of it tries confidence. I thought of leaving this place with no one who had my heart in their possession, and it caused quite a pause. Thomas and I have set a date?"

"Halley, are you serious?"

"I realized that I did not want to be alone anymore. I remember hearing you awaken, and hearing you call out to Darren. I wandered who would I have to call out too? Who would be there for me?" Her eyes were lonely. "Of course my parents and my brother would be there. But who would be fighting sleep each night because of the lack of feeling my body next to his? Who would be praying to the Almighty God to take him, instead of me? Who would be smiling when the world sees, but crying when the doors were closed? Who would want me to awaken so that we could go on living together? There was no one. And then I thought about Thomas."

"Did you tell him all of this?" Donna held back her excitement.

"Immediately! I mean, I called him up and asked if it was okay for me to visit him? It was a week day, and he was still at work." Her eyes filled with hoped and wonderment. "It wasn't easy once I saw him. I realized that much of what I thought was strength, was actually weakness. I thought that being alone, and free of attachment was truly what I wanted in this life, but the reality of it was that I was afraid, afraid of having to be responsible for someone other than myself, afraid of that someone leaving me with a broken heart, or even worse, a broken soul. I just did not want to take the chance on it. So I made myself believe that I was this lone warrior, who did not need to consummate my womanhood, or my humanity. But what good is womanhood, without the smoldering touch of a man to mold my heart, or humanity without the striking blow of love. I needed to be attached. I needed to feel responsible for someone other than me. I needed to feel needed, wanted, loved. I needed Thomas." She lost herself in the thoughts of her mind. "Donna, when I look back on all the times I have shared with this wonderful man, I just know that our future together will be even greater. He loves me without love."

"What?"

"What I mean is that, if love had not been the word to use for what is in his heart for me I would still be there, in his heart, living and breathing. He wants to grow with me. He welcomes and caresses my individuality. My strengths, he makes stronger. My weaknesses, he forgives and erases. My passions, he embraces as his own, and so much more. He desires me, and I no longer want to hold back from the waterfall of dreams that is offered in his heart for me. I want to wake up with him every day. I want to fall asleep with him every night. I want to feel him inside of me, dancing the dance of lovemaking. I want to have more children with him. I want to grow old with him. I want him."

"Wow!" Donna got out of the bed. "Halley, you really surprise me. I just don't understand you sometimes."

"Are you the only woman who is allowed to search for a better meaning of life? I needed this growth spurt." Halley limited her thoughts to the events of her life past travels. "Besides, I am excited about this new place."

"And Thomas?"

"Thomas. This is what he is always hoped for." Halley answered. "He is a funny man though. I mean, he only smiled at me the entire time I spoke. It was as if he knew that I would concede."

"Halley, it is as you said, he loves you. And when you love someone, you wait on them to come to their senses when they lose them."

"Maybe, maybe not. Either way I am happy to oblige him." Enough said. "Now, about my speech tonight."

"Oh yes. The speech."

"I sense some doubt. You don't think that I actually have a speech to make, do you?"

"You could say that."

"Well, I do. And I would love it if you came along."

"Halley, I don't know. I was hoping to receive the information regarding my parents on tomorrow, and I need some time to get my head wrapped around that."

"Sitting around this place isn't going to bring you the serenity that you need. Come with me. You will enjoy yourself, and maybe even someone who is struggling more than you."

"Is that punt at me?"

"Actually, no, it isn't. You see Donna, I am the kind of person who believes in looking beyond my source of anguish and into the lives of others, and their problems. Sometimes that helps me to find a resolution to my own hurt."

"Halley, I really do not want to entertain the problems of others right now."

"Well, then don't, but come with me anyway. Besides, your package won't be here until tomorrow. If I know better the waiting is going to be murder. I need your company."

"Good evening everyone, my name is Halley Marie Duncan." The church was huge, and filled with many people of all races. Upon deciding to accompany Halley to her speaking engagement, Donna searched through her clothing to find something appropriate to wear. Halley did not, again, tell her what the occasion would be, just to dress nicely. When she saw that it was a church, she only looked at Halley sarcastically, and then exited the Mercedes.

Donna remembered the last time she visited a church was at her wedding. Keith's parents were members at the St. Mark Baptist Church of Birmingham. It had one of the largest congregation in the city, and many wealthy members. When asked where their wedding would be held, it was to be the only place, even if Donna was not a believer. Keith would tell her story of his childhood and having to be in attendance each Sunday. However, when he became an adult, he forsook his attendance for golf. His parents were God fearing people and were not happy with Keith's departure from the family's Sunday ritual. His sisters, including their husbands continued their attendance, except when Jenny had to work. But all in all, they seemed to have enjoy themselves.

After their wedding, Keith's failed attendance continued, and Donna was fine with its failure. It wasn't until Patrick's birth and dedication, that Keith wanted them to begin attending services. Donna went, but not because she wanted to. She was not familiar with this God person that their preacher spoke of passionately, except through her talks with a chaplain at the home. She could not recall any family who had taken her in to be believers, either. As for her personal connection with Him, she hadn't decided to make it real. Did she believe in Him, yes? Did she believe that He sent His Son to die for her,

303

and others, yes? She believed this because the chaplain showed it to her in the Bible, not because she had taken Him into her heart.

"Please accept my indulgence, as I would very much like to introduce to everyone my beloved sister friend, Donna Pennington. Donna please stand." As the congregation salute Donna with clapping and smiles, she slowly stood to greet them with a gracious thank you, at least that is what it felt like to her. The fear was that she really was not hearing what Halley was saying, and was standing in front of everyone looking like the fool. "Thank you so much. As it is, my acceptance of your speaking request came in time when my friend was here in Atlanta, and without too much convincing on my part, she accepted my requested accompaniment invitation. Therefore, I must show my appreciation by introducing her to you." Halley's words told her that indeed she really was hearing what she hoped she had not. She looked up, and saw Halley's smile and then took her seat quickly. "I must admit this is quite an honor to be here today with you. Please join me as we walk through the paradise found in God's Holy Word. Now, you know that I am not a pastor, a preacher, nor a teacher. I am simply, but most prophetically, a speaker. My mother told me when I was a child that I would speak in front of millions, and counting you all today, I am really close to that first million." She paused for the congregation's applause, and then she continued. "I would like to speak to you today about the word, freedom. You know when Pastor Shea asked me to speak during this occasion of celebration, I really did not know what to say. Each year, for the past ten years, he would contact me and offer the same considerations. I speak, and he listens." Laughter sounded throughout the entire church. There had to be over 30,000 people in attendance. It was the celebration of their mortgage payoff. Each year since they paid the loan in full, they have celebrated their freedom from debt. "So, I see you have the same opinion that I have. A pastor, who actually lets someone else do the talking. Is that actually possible?" From the audience it could be heard a loud 'no'. Donna was enjoying herself, and enjoying the people around her. They were polite. She could feel joy inside of her heart. It had replaced the loneliness. "It happened one day as I was reading from the

Word of God, in the book of Jeremiah. It was in the first chapter, verse 5. If I may read it to your hearing, *Before I formed you in the belly I knew thee; and before thou camest forth out of the womb I sanctified thee, and I ordained thee a prophet unto the nations.* This understanding shaken my soul, for it was then that I came into the knowing that I was once God's imaginary friend." She paused for their examination of her words. After seeing their eyes brighten, she continued. "You understand, as a child, we, well some of us always contrive within our minds that special friend that no one can see. We fashion this friend in the way that we would have them to be. We give them a name. We give them a face. We give them life inside of our minds, and hearts. So it was an overwhelming revelation for me to see that God, our Creator, created this phenomenon, with the difference being, He gave to His friend actual, physical life. Shaken to my core, I, was, once God's imaginary friend, whom He created to be your sister in Christ." She paused again for their organization of thoughts, and reception. And again after she could see the brightening of their eyes, she continued. "Accepting and believing in this creation, I knew that I must be obedient to do what He has commanded me to do in verses 9-10, *Then the Lord put forth His hand, and touched my mouth. And the Lord said unto me, Behold, I have put words in thy mouth. See, I have this day set thee over the nations and over the kingdoms to root out, and to pull down, and to destroy, and to throw down, to build, and to plant.* This is why I am here, to tell you what the Lord said."

The congregation exploded with praise to God and adulation for Halley. She waited patiently for their completion of praise, and continued. "Freedom does not come without the existence of obligation, which we sometimes forsake due to our aspirations. Don't leave me now. Freedom was, and has always being fought for because of aspiration, but it cannot be celebrated, or appreciated without securing what is our obligation. Take the aspired decision of discipleship, in this wedding relationship with Christ, each of us who accept Him must reconcile ourselves with the responsibilities of keeping the relationship fresh and filled with potential for others to know Him, this is our obligation." Fascinating words of wisdom, Donna thought to herself. Her remembrance of choosing Christ had not left her heart, but it did her aspirations. Being a member of Keith's family quite frankly left newcomers no choice in the matter, for they all were believers. "I am sure that this is a truth that Pastor Shea has spoken of more than frequently. So what now do we have here, in this congregation? We have people who have already been taught what freedom is, and with this wisdom you will make your choices in life. What about those who do not know? Today you celebrate the anniversary of your freedom from a burdened past." Donna remembered why she was in Atlanta.

"If I were to say to you that the past you left behind was not at all what held you captive by some isolated enemy, but you? Would you agree? If I was to say to you that it is never release from bondage that we seek from freedom, but release from fear. Would you agree? If I was to say to you that in our purest of hearts it is never the corporate sins of others that hurt us, but the individual sins of one that leads to corporate pain. Would you agree?" Much of what was shown on the faces of the people that Halley could see was uncertainty. It was the faces of those who shared in her answers that encourage her continuance. "The problem is that in most given times when freedom is offered, received and lived, we individually begin to long for those things that forsook the freedom in the first place. We begin to reach back in time for those things that albeit brought us pain, felt better than the place that has given us freedom. We do this because we fail in securing and doing what is our obligation to hold on to freedom in the first place. Freedom is costly. Don't let anyone tell you that it isn't. It is very costly. Lives are lost or destroyed. Hearts are frozen to stone or to selfish pride. Dreams are turned to nightmares. And hope is sacrificed for despair." Donna listening ears began to reach even deeper for clarity of voice. She had decided not to let her memory of why she was in Atlanta take from Halley an opportunity for positive reception of a true friend. "But here comes the wisdom of our understanding what freedom is. It is that wisdom that should lead us in making the right choices in life. It is that wisdom that should govern us even in our deepest moments of pains. When we have been taught something, we must, or we should live by its application. I am not telling us that we should not look back on our past. History is a teaching organism. But progression means moving forward, and freedom requires that we do just that, move forward." Donna marveled at Halley's speech. The people around her seem to have had the same admiration. Including Pastor Shea, there were seven more people who sat on the pulpit's stage. As Donna surveyed them, each one who caught her eye would provide a smile of approval for her friend's gift of words.

"What I have seen in the eyes of our community is the darkness of the light that we have given away to yesterday. Freedom is our possibility from our ignorance. Freedom is our grand privilege of reaching out to the world around us. Freedom is the love we show to each other when life's trials overcome us. When we are faced with a situation that we are not able to surpass in our own strength, freedom is the tool that we use to give way to pain, lost and confusion. It may not, at the time feel good, but when we look back to the decision we made to give freedom a try, we will find that like the life of Christ, rarely do we find feeling good to the be epitome of the right decision. Pain most often accompanies freedom. It must, for if it is freedom we are seeking, oppression is what we are suffering. And the captor never wants to give away its prey, so there is a battle." Donna found that she was even asserting to words spoken in her hears. For years she felt like a prisoner in her mind, but the oppressor she did not know. Until she was met with the examination of who she was did she give freedom a try, and it has been painful. "As you look into your hearts and into the history of this church, seek to find ways to fight against the possibility of imprisonment for the generations to come. Let not your fight end with your comfort of today, for today is already gone, and those who live in tomorrow should be able to look back at what you have done to make their plight less painful. This is the life of Christians, is it not? I thank you."

Halley stepped away from the podium, and like that, after much praise and applause from the congregation and those who sat with her, it was over. The magnificence of her words shattered any thoughts of forgetting exactly what she spoke. Donna could see from the faces of those around her that Halley had garnered much respect and humble admiration for the people. When Pastor Shea stood to speak in continuity of the program, the congregation graciously refused to silence their praise of Halley. There was something great in her spirit, in her voice, in her vessel of humanity, and Donna knew that it was that something which made admiring her seemed unequaled for what she possessed. When the praise finally came to a slow halt, Pastor Shea gave the benediction, but not before expressing his appreciation and offering Halley another opportunity for her to speak. No response of acceptance showed on Halley's face, but she did gesture to her acceptance of his praise.

Donna met her at the bottom step of the pulpit, only to be greeted by a lady who graciously stepped in front of Halley to take Donna's hand.

"Hello Donna. I have waited for this day since you were taken from my arms. I am the woman who gave birth to you 33 years ago. I am who you would refer to as your mother. My name is Patricia Taylor."

Twenty-three

No one really knew what to say, at least not Donna, anyway. As far as Halley was concerned, words left her mind, but did not follow the track to her lips. Patricia Taylor on the other hand stood very still with a smile on her face, and tears streaming down her cheeks.

Donna looked deeply into her eyes, deeper than she has ever looked at anyone. She searched for the sign in them to confirm Patricia's proclamation. Out of the over 30,000 people in the church, no sound could be heard. Even though Donna was sure that there was much talking going on, she could not hear it.

"Patricia, Ms. Taylor, why don't we walk over here?" Halley spoke, awakening Donna's hearing of the crowd. She pointed toward the outer doors of the church.

"Donna, I must tell you that I am…"

"Ms. Taylor, I don't believe that here is where this conversation should take place."

"No, it may not be, but we are here." Patricia kept watch on Donna's eyes, not given any attention to Halley.

"Halley, it is fine." Donna found her voice. "Ms. Taylor, I am in agreement with Halley, this is not the right place for this conversation."

"It is why you are here isn't it?" Patricia questioned. "But then it has been 33 years. I don't see why another day will hurt?" Patricia quenched her anxiousness. "If I may ask, how long will you be here in Atlanta?"

"Actually, I am here for the week."

"Good, then we have much time to talk. May we meet somewhere? Or would it be improper to invite you to my home? I am sure that your father would love to meet you as well."

Donna was again, or had barely come out of the shock of meeting her, and here she stood telling of a man who was to be her father. A man that she has never met, has never known to be alive and was her father. Was she really that callous, or was she just a fool.

"Donna, I know that this is all shocking news to you. I do hope that you accept my apology for being so blunt. I, too, am very nervous. Actually, I am more than nervous, but I don't want this night to end without you knowing of who I am and who your father is?"

"I don't know what to say."

"Neither do I." Halley agreed. "Listen, Ms. Taylor, I truly do believe that we need to seek another time for this. Donna, are you alright?"

"Halley, I am fine." Donna looked away from Patricia and into Halley's eyes. "Did you know anything about this? Did you know that she would be here? I mean, is this some kind of sick surprise of yours'?"

"Donna, of course not." Halley protested. "I don't know this woman."

"But you know Pastor Shea, and she sits in the pulpit with him. How could you not know her?"

"Donna, Pastor Shea is a friend of my family, and a client of my father's firm. I would never do something as self-serving as to set you up like this. How could you believe that I would do this?"

"Donna, I am a pastor here. However, I have never met Halley. Tonight was our first time ever haven met."

"You are a pastor." Donna spoke with harsh judgment. "I can't take this. I have to go."

"Donna, please, we must talk." Patricia grabbed her hand restricting any further movement. "Please, can we talk?"

"No, we cannot." Donna jerked her hand from Patricia's grasp. "I would appreciate if you would not touch me."

"Donna." Halley cautioned her. "Donna, be careful."

"Be careful of what?"

"Be careful of your anger." Halley took her hand. "Ms. Taylor, can you provide a number for us, and we will call you tomorrow."

"Sure I can." Patricia wrote the number on the program cover. "I do hope that we will hear from you." She handed the program to Donna, who refused to move. "Donna, please know that it was never our intentions to leave you in this world alone."

"How is that when alone is exactly how you left me?"

"Ms. Taylor, please have a nice evening."

As long as the ride was to the Duncan's home, it was not as long as the distant between reality and the nightmare that was in Donna's mind. Halley tried without success to bring Donna to a pleasant place. Donna's refusal to join her for a walk through Destiny's Lane proved to be a trivial stage of words. Even worse was Donna's exit from the vehicle upon their arrival, and then she remain held up in the room throughout the night.

Halley decided not to attempt any further contact with Donna for the rest of the evening. Her calls to Duncan were met with no answer, neither did he return any calls. She thought of calling Keith, but what would that prove? After settling for a quick walk past Donna's room door, she went on to bed.

Donna on the other hand, stared at the ceiling waiting on a sign from a God she had not introduced herself to, to give her some answers about the night's happenings. How cruel this new person met with her heart, and the darkness of it. She did not have a dream of how she was to feel, as a matter of fact, she had not had the time to consider even the moment of her meeting. She felt an assault to her senses, all of them. She sought for comfort, clarity and escape.

"Hello Keith." Keith was the person who always gave her what she needed. "I know that it is late, but I need someone to talk too. Please forgive me."

"Is everything alright?" Keith was not sleeping. He had not slept in two years.

"Keith, I met my mother, or at least someone who introduced herself as my mother."

"Isn't that what you wanted?"

"Yes, I guess." She hesitated calmly. "I don't know any longer."

"Donna what is it that you want from me? Why did you call?"

"Keith, please I need... I need you."

"Not right now. I can't be the one you need."

"Maybe not." She began to cry. "Listen, I am sorry to wake you. Please let the boys know that I love them, and that I will be home soon."

"Donna,...I will tell them. Good bye."

"Who are you? Where are you? I remember talking about you. But who are you?" Donna found her way to the floor. It was the floor's touch that gave her comfort. While on the floor she looked up at the ceiling seeking again this God. "Whomever, wherever you are, I need you now! Please help me! Please help me!" Her tears were more than she could control. The pain in her chest was more than she could breathe through. "I need you! Please help me! I don't know what to do! I have broken my family! I have lost the only man that I ever loved, and who once loved me more than himself! I have lost it all, and for what!" She crumbled under the pain of her realizations. "God, I need you! Tell me what to do!"

Twenty-four

"Donna, are you ok?" Halley questioned as she entered into the room to see Donna getting up from the floor.

"I am. The floor may not be, but I am." Donna slept on the floor. The God she tried to reach showed up with comfort, not an answer, but sleep. And she only realized that when she woke and saw that it was morning, which led to her remembrance of last night's introductions.

"Then I take it you slept well?"

"Actually, I did. No bad dreams, just sleep." Donna rested her body on the bed. Halley followed. "You know, last night was something."

"Something is putting it mildly."

"I want to call her today." When she heard the words come out her of mouth, she then realized that maybe He did give her an answer. "I need to talk with both of them."

"Are you sure about this?"

"Yes, I am. I am losing my family. And if I don't get past this, I may lose them forever. I can't risk that."

"Donna, did something last night?" Halley began to search Donna's eyes. "I stopped by a couple of times, but there was no answer."

"Halley, I called Keith last night. I told him that I met Patricia."

"What did he say?"

"Nothing, he only commented that it was what I wanted." She began to cry. "He hates me, and he has a right to. What I have done to our marriage, our family is not forgivable."

"Donna, everything is forgivable."

"Can you tell Keith that?" Donna smiled behind the tears. "I have really messed up here, Halley. I mean really messed up. I feel like this place that I have been in is coming to a head, and I am about to lose everything, and everyone in it."

"Did you plan on losing?"

"I didn't plan on anything. I just knew that I felt lost in a world that did not know me." Memories of the forgotten besieged her mind. "The more lost I felt, the more I ran away from the pain, but then I had to stop running. It became more important for me to face the animal chasing me to destruction. But as it was, the animal did not do the damage, I did."

321

"What are you proposing to do now? I mean, even after you have called Patricia, do you know what you are going to ask, or what you are going to say?"

"Not really. I need your help with that."

"Whatever you need."

"Will you please call her, I mean, them? Tell them that we would like for them to come here or we can meet them somewhere."

"Why don't we go there? I think it will be better. The drive will do your mind and heart some good."

"Yes, you may be right. Let's do it now, so that we can get there and get back."

"Donna, you do realize that you may not come back as you leave here. It may not be as easy as your coming back and leaving for Birmingham?"

"I know, but I can't think about that right now. Halley, I have to get back home. Keith is leaving my heart, or at least he is letting me leave his heart. I can't live like that. I don't want to live like that." She appeared hopeful. "I just want to know from them why they left me behind, and did they love me? I want to know if I am able to forgive their answers of leaving me behind. Can we make the family work, today? I don't have any further plans outside of that."

"Sounds good to me." Halley stood. "Let me go and make that call now."

"Halley, thank you."

"No problem." Halley smiled. "Hey, aren't you supposed to receive your file today? Maybe we can wait until after we receive that before we make the call. Maybe it has some information that will benefit you in the meeting. What do you think?"

"I had actually forgotten all about the file." Donna's tears had dried and she was ready for the world again. "What time does the mail run here?"

"UPS delivers usually around 10. It's 8:30 now."

"Okay, then we will wait."

By the time the knock happened on the door, both Donna and Halley were sitting in the library. They tried to spread conversation around the empties of the room, but it was difficult to do. Halley quickly ran from the room to take the envelope out of Dave's hands. With courage, Donna stood waiting to receive the envelope and the venom that was in it.

323

"Are you sure you're ready for this?"

"No, but I have to look at it." Donna took the envelope and slowly opened it. "Patricia Taylor, mother and Donald Taylor, father." Stop. Breathe. "Donald. I guess I was named after him."

Donna took a seat, but then stood again. "This is my birth certificate. I've never seen it before." Stop. Breathe. "I was born in Birmingham General Hospital. I was 7 pounds, 5 ounces and 20 inches long." Stop. Tears. "Halley do you know what this means? I was actually born. I actually had parents."

"Donna." Halley shared in her tears. "Donna, that is so precious."

"I know that this must sound silly to you, but I...."

"No, I don't think that it is silly, not at all."

"I have parents. I was born. I have an existence."

"What else is there?"

Donna starred more at her birth certificate before going on to the next page. "They got married in 1976, right after they gave birth to me. I don't understand why did they not keep me?" More paper. "I don't know what to make of this. Was I that unworthy of their love? They never had any other children. He is a graduate of Auburn University, and she graduated from some theology university in Georgia."

"This explains why she was in the pulpit." Halley remembered. "What does he do for a living?"

"Donald, my father is a doctor. He did his residency here in Atlanta. He is a heart surgeon." Donna sat down breathlessly. "I don't understand. They just did not want me at all. He is one of best known, most sought after heart surgeons in this country. How could they do this to me?"

"Donna, before we assume anything let's just call them. Then you can ask them all of the questions you ever had to ask."

"Halley, they don't live far from here. The address is located here in your neighborhood. I can't believe this. These people are wealthy." Donna stood angrily. "I don't want to see these people!"

"Donna, please, let's just make the call, and go over. You can't let your assumption steal this opportunity from you. Remember, your family is in Birmingham. You have to get through this."

"You're right. I guess this is all taking me by surprise. I never really had a story in my dreams about them. I just decided that they did not want me, and that was all. I mean what reason is good enough to give up your baby. Besides, I had heard enough dreams stolen from the people I shared my life with. Each one of them had some sob story of a parent who did not care about them. I didn't want that for me, so I refused to even dream about them."

"May I call now?"

"Please do. I want to get this over with. I have a family that I have to get back together." Donna watched as Halley picked up her cell phone to make the call. There was a part of her that still held on to fear. Fear of knowing that she was never wanted. Fear that the people who gave her away never wanted her to be born at all. "Hello, Mrs. Taylor. This is Halley Duncan. I am calling for Donna. We need to know, if now is a good time for you?" Halley pretended to write the address that Mrs. Taylor was giving to her. She looked at Donna who was seemed to her like a little child, waiting for that crucial moment when the parent says no to a gift the child so desires to have. "Yes, I have it. Actually, we are only a few homes from you. We will see you in ten minutes if that is okay?" She smiled at Donna. "We will see you in ten. Thank you."

"Halley, can we walk there? I need to make some space in my head and my heart for this. Driving won't give me that time."

"Of course." Halley took her hand. "Listen, I'm here if you need me. I know that this cannot be easy for you, but if you need anything, just say the word."

Twenty-five

"How can I...."

"Don't worry you will be fine." Halley reassured Donna, as they looked up toward the huge home. They decided it would be better to drive since the distance from Halley's family home and the Taylors proved to be over two miles. "Just asked the questions to the answers you need. If you need me just give me the signal."

"What is the signal?"

"We will both walk out of the door." Halley laughed softly. "Really, everything will be just fine."

"Okay, let's do this." Before the door could open fully, Donna could see the man who looked like her.

"Donna!" He screamed her name as he walked quickly toward her. Patricia came to the door soon after. "Donna! I am Donald Taylor. I am your father." He reached to hug her. But she pulled away quickly. "My apologies. I know that it has been some time, and I probably should not act as if we are your actual parents, but I am just so excited. Please come in. Who did you bring with you? I believe my Patricia said your name is Halley. You spoke last night."

"Hello, Mr. Taylor. Please to meet you." Halley was always perfect in what to say.

"I understand that you are quite a motivator." He continued.

"I do alright. The people seem to like it." Halley tried to be humble.

"Truly, words that motivate can only come from someone who seeks to bring clarity and hope. So, it is much more than the words Ms. Duncan. It is the heart."

"Well hello you two." Finally Patricia makes her way to the car. "Isn't it only God who provided such a fortuitous time. But then again, nothing happens by chance when God's timing is at hand. May I give you a comfort of a hug?"

"Of course." Halley stepped up to the plate and hugged Patricia tightly.

"Why don't we all go into the house? We have quite a bit to talk about." Donald suggested.

The walk up the driveway was long and quiet. But it did not match the beauty that was found in their home. Donna felt overwhelmed with class and prestige. "Believe it or not, Donald decorated the entire house himself. It is his hobby. Interior decorating is like heart surgery for him."

"Your home is beautiful." Halley again spoke. Donna had yet to find the words. "Totally beautiful."

"Thank you so much, Halley." Patricia looked at Donna. "What do you think, Donna? I mean this will all be yours one day, along with many other properties and such."

"I don't believe that I will need any of it." Donna forced the words out of her mouth. Donald directed their steps into a room filled with the scent of blossoms. It was the sitting room. Many books were aligned to the shelves on the wall. Candles were about the room as well. Each candle had been lit and a small flame gave way to the sweet, blossom fragrance.

"Of course you don't, but still it will be." Donald stated. He politely gestured for them to sit. "Now that we know that you are our daughter, there is much that we want to share with you."

"Baby, this may be too much for Donna to deal with right now. Let's take it slowly, and do only what she requests." Patricia spoke nicely as she took her seat next to Donald. They loved each other. It was evident in their manner of speaking to each other. It was evident in the way they looked at each other.

"Yes, you're right. Tell us Donna what would you like to know?"

Donna waivered a little, but then found the strength to go on. "Why did you leave me?"

"Right to it, I like that." Donald smiled. "Well, how can we put it without sounding like two selfish young adults? I guess there really isn't any way to do that." He took hold of Patricia's hand, and began to speak. "Your mother and I made the most difficult decision in our lives the day that we decided that we would leave you behind, but it was a decision we thought best at the time." He looked sweetly at Patricia. "The day that you came into the world was twofold for us. We loved you instantly, but knew that we could not keep you with us. I delivered you myself, and then took you to the hospital and gave you to the emergency room nurse. Your mother recovered in the hotel room. When I return to her, she was not well so I had to take her back to the hospital that I had just departed from. You were the only baby

I have ever delivered, and the only one that I ever will."

"I don't understand."

"Let me bring you clarity. When we decided that we were to give you up it was because we wanted to focus on our careers. At the time we both were medical students. Your mother was quite a surgeon of the heart for some years, but then she decided that she could no longer wrestle with the torment of her own heart. She left our practice and began her study in theology, and welcomed into our lives the warmth of God."

"You make it sound like some romantic story between the two of you. You left me behind to focus on yourselves. You did not care what happened to me."

"Actually, that is not true at all. We did care. We cared enough to know that should you remain with us, you would be forsaken more times that we could count. We knew that our careers meant more to us to fulfill than the requirements of parenthood. Of course, it was a selfish act. We did not guard ourselves from the pain and guilt of the decision."

"What?"

"Donna, I speak of it easily now because we have already suffered the pain and guilt of leaving you behind over 30 years ago. We made a very selfish decision in leaving you behind. It was very selfish in deed." He was calm. Patricia sat quietly listening and attentively staring at Donna. "But at the time, we thought it was necessary."

"Necessary?"

"Maybe necessary is too harsh, but it is the truth. Our careers were too important to us. We wanted to cure the world of its ills. We had dreams and aspirations that did not include caring for a baby." There was a sullen pause. "That decision did not come over well with our hearts, but we fought our emotional battle until we could no longer feel its sting." No one said anything. "For your mother, it was worse and I believe to this day that it was the pain of leaving you that began her interested and thereafter, walk with Christ." Patricia still remained without words of her own. "In fact, I know it to be true."

"What about your parents?" Donna didn't know if they were still living, but she had to ask.

"It was not expected, but her parents, never argued with her about it. Neither did mine." Donald answered quickly.

"Where are they now? Her parents I mean?" Donna asked, still wandering why Patricia had remained so quiet.

"Both of our parents live only a few miles from here." Donald answered. "They never knew about you until years after you were born. We thought it would break their hearts if we told them that your mother was pregnant. They wanted so much for us to be doctors. But much to our dismay, they were excited. For some time we search for you, but none of the investigators could offer us promise. The hospital refused to provide the name of the agency that took you in. They would only tell us that you were adopted by a nice family, and was well cared for. Was there any truth to that?"

"Not actually." Donna remembered the loneliness of the home. "Most couples weren't interested in baby girls. I spent my entire life in the orphanage." She could feel the anger building inside of her. "There were foster homes, but no adoptions."

"Donna, please forgive us." Patricia comes out her silence.

"Forgive you?"

"Yes, forgive us." Patricia repeated. "I have spent a lifetime of regretting what we did. Your father is right about my chosen profession. I could find no peace, no comfort in leaving you behind. Each night my heart would break. Each day my mind would crumple into pieces. I did not know what to do but to call on God. It wasn't until then that I could feel unbroken." She began to cry. "There is nothing we can do to give to you what we have taken, but we can offer you a future in getting to know you. I mean if that is what you want. If not, then we can end right now and go on with our respective lives."

"Just like that, everything is forgotten, forgiven?"

"Of course not. Tell me something. Are you here in Atlanta just to accompany your friend, or is there some other reason?"

Donna considered her answer. "Actually, I am here because I was looking for you."

"How did you know that we were here?"

"Halley's brother hired a detective who found you here in Atlanta."

"So you have been looking for us?"

"I have been looking for me." Donna looked at Halley. She could tell that she was happy with her response. "I am married to a man who is Caucasian and loves me beyond all measure of love. We have two beautiful boys. For over eleven years we have been married. But then I lost myself, and then I lost him, and now, them."

"Donna?"

"I just did not know who I was, and I began to realize that I never knew who I was supposed to be. All I knew was how to live in his world and how to survive in his world. For some time that was okay, but when it stopped being okay, it broke. Rather, I broke. And the man that I had loved and who had loved me could not put me back together."

"Donna, I am not sure what this had to with looking for us." Donald had yet to put it together.

"It had everything with finding you." Donna found she could no longer sit. She stood and walked toward the large windows. The day was wonderfully bright. The house was indeed in a perfect place for the sun to shine through.

The furnishing for the sitting room was quite contemporary for the Taylors' age, but they fit. Donald has great taste in furnishing. Black fine leather for the sofa sectional and the walls were painted with a touch of brownish colors. None were too dark, but were soft and gentle for the moment. "I had, for years in and out of the orphanage only one or two friends, Black girls who went on to be adopted, or moved to a different state. I was a very lonely child, never really comfortable with the world or people outside of me. My entire life up to eighteen years of age was lonely. Then, two years later I was greeted with a smile from a man who would later change my life from the lonely victim, to the sprouting butterfly. The only difference was that I did not know that my death would come years later, rather than moments later." She wanted to stop talking but she had to stop the words from mind making their way to her heart. She wanted to release, to heal. "I didn't know that I had so much lost of me inside of my head, but I did. It has brought me to this very moment. And I must say that I actually feel a sprout of confidence building inside of me."

"Donna, what exactly are you saying?" Patricia asked.

"What I am saying is that I have given up my family in search of my parents, and now that I have found them, I want to go home. I want my family back."

"But?"

"But what?" Donna interrupted. "What is to come of you, of us?"

"Yes." Patricia answered. "Donna we never wanted to leave you behind, and we don't want to do that now. But we are no longer in the position of choosing here, but you are. I am asking you to please don't leave us as we did you."

Donna remained still. "I am in the position to make the choice this time." She took her seat next to Halley, again. "My friend here has taught me a great lesson in this life. If I were to do what the pain in me dictates, I will have suffered this walk in vain." A small pause filled the room. "I am here for the rest of the week and for that time I want to spend much time learning all that I can about you, and my grandparents."

"Are you serious?"

"Patricia, I have spent more time than I want to imagine away from my husband. I have lost him to another woman."

"Are you sure of this?" Donald inquired.

"Yes. I have met her."

"Donna, if you say this man has loved you, and has also taught you to love, I find it difficult to believe that he would stop loving you."

"Well, you didn't leave him."

"No, we did not. But we did leave you. And here you stand giving us a second chance."

"Yes, here I am, but what I have done to my family is more than he can withstand."

"I don't believe it to be true."

"I would rather not believe it myself, but it is my reality." Donna tried to smile but her lips refused the muscular stroke required to pull it off. "Would you like to see pictures?"

"Of course we would. But first may we pray for you." Patricia requested.

"I don't think God much listens to the cares of my heart. I haven't spent any time with Him for Him to care what happens to me."

"Donna, look where you are right now. Do you really think that you planned this to happen? That everything just fell into place because it was supposed to? Sweetheart, nothing happens just because." Patricia sat up on the sofa, releasing Donald's hand. "Everything that occurs in this world is governed by God's sovereign authority over all things. You must understand that."

"What I understand and what I know are distinctively two different things. But that is what my future holds."

"Donna, you are not going to give up." Halley came out of her silence. "I have told you that you are not to give up. Everything in its time will happen."

"You are right, Halley." Donald agreed. "We will deal with today and let tomorrow take care of itself." Her smile came boldly. "Where do you want to start? We have much to do, and a small amount hours to do them." Donald stood. "Halley will you be joining us?"

"Please, Halley. I want you to stay with me."

Halley hesitated. "I am not sure if I can do that. Maybe for a day or so."

"Thank you so much. I really don't want to do this alone. In fact, I don't think that I can."

"Donna, you are not alone any longer. We are here to stay." Donald assured her.

"I do hope and pray that you are right." She was saddened by the thought of Donald's words being lost in the pain that she inflicted on Keith. "What I have done to our family has hurt him to the core. And I don't know if I will ever be forgiven for what I have done. So, I am going to need someone to stand by me when the reality of his nonexistence in my life truly becomes my reality."

Twenty-six

As Donna looked into the mirror, she could see more than who she once saw. There was a figure of happiness looking back at her. She reached toward the mirror and began to trace the structure of the face she saw. She looked deeply into the eyes of the face. Happiness, confidence, gentleness, and love abided. How could this be? Such a happy face, and yet there was loneliness. What she had shared with Donald and Patricia in the past couple of days was more than she could understand. Photo albums, stories of old, meeting grandparents she did not know, but who gravitated to her as she had been with them since her birth. They even welcomed Halley into their hearts as their own. Her life was regenerated. Her ethnicity had become her possession.

Halley remained as she said, and took part in the family beginnings. Her presence made it easier for the reception of this new family into Donna's heart. And seeing that her new family had also accepted her as their own, and as Donna's sister, made the journey sweeter.

"Who are you looking at?" Halley asked. She was standing at the door of the room.

Donna turned to face Halley. "My new friend."

"New friend."

"Well, not exactly new. Halley I am so happy. I can't remember feeling so vulnerable to life, and yet I am happy beyond belief."

"That is living, isn't it now?"

"Is it really? I have never known it to be." She welcomed Halley into the room. "I never considered that vulnerability was an instrument to happiness. But that is exactly how I am feeling, vulnerable."

"I can't really say that I have experienced vulnerability. Your revelation is mine as well."

"Truly."

"Truly." Halley situated her seating on the bed. "Halley, I have lived a life of power, celebrity recognition, uncommon wealth and selfish provocation. I have never had the need for vulnerability. Everything around me. Everyone around me were those of strength in some position in life. Remember, I have only recently allowed myself to accept Thomas' proposal. I didn't know that it was vulnerability that I was running from. I thought it was the grandiose fight to hold onto me." She smiled to her spoken words. "I have grown to understand that we don't like feeling vulnerable, even at the expense of losing our love ones. It makes us weak, and that makes us fearfully, angry. But since my acceptance, Thomas and I have talked every day with my heart deeply longing to be near him, to feel him next to me, holding me with his love." Did she really just say that? She inhaled with romance. "I love talking to him now. Not that I didn't before, but now, now it does something to my heart and body when I hear his voice. Now if that is vulnerability, I will take loads of it."

"Well, now." Donna enjoyed Halley's revelations. She left the mirror of herself. "That is living, isn't it?"

"Funny." Halley stood. "So what do we have planned for today?"

"My parents…

"You like that, don't you?"

"Yes, I do, mind you." Donna turned again to the mirror. "My parents have asked that we meet them at home, and the day is ours."

"Okay then that is what we will do." Halley agreed joyfully. They behaved like teenagers.

"Donna, listen, I am going to leave tomorrow night."

"Missing Thomas, are we?"

"Exactly. And I do have a job." Halley answered. "Are you going to be okay?"

"Yes, I will be fine." She walked to the door where Halley was standing to leave. "Halley, thank you for staying. You are truly a friend. Actually you have become my sister. Thank you."

"That is living, isn't it?"

Twenty-seven

Halley's departure left much room for contemplation. Donna assured her that she would be alright, and that if not she would call her. Even though there was only two days left before she herself headed back home, she wanted to do as much with her parents as she could. But she knew that no matter how much they did, it would not be enough to stop the thoughts that were already taking their turns at bat against her heart.

Donna had managed to put aside the hurt that waited her in Birmingham. She had managed to hold the thoughts in her heart with joy. Talking about Keith and the boys with Donald and Patricia, and her grandparents also provide much hope. They reminded her of their own passages through the windows of love. They reiterated that if it is real love, true and pure, then all would be well.

Donna chose to believe them because it was necessary to, and it made her feel hopeful. She knew the damage she had caused. She also knew that she would not stand for Keith to have done to her what she had done. But she wanted to believe that Keith was better than she was.

She had also learned a lot about marriage and commitment from watching her parents relate to each other. They shared a dedication to each other and their marriage that made Donna dream of her tomorrows with Keith.

They told her to put her trust in a God that she had only come to accept as God. That, too, she had been met with quite a bit in times with them. They talked about Him always. At first, Donna rejected their constant words of His salvation, His glory, His Son, and His love. She even went so far as to change the conversation when they brought Him up. It wasn't that He was all they talked about, it was more that she did not want to hear what they had to say about Him. His existence made her examine her life and all she could see were her failures. She did not like that because she had to look at her failures every day, and she did not need some God reminding her of them.

But there was hope. Hope that came from her meeting the parents that she never knew, and seeing them so happy and loving together. It made her wonder even more so how could two people, who appeared to be filled with so much love for each other, and those around them, could leave their child behind. And as she looked at them now they did not carry what is usually thought to be the outcome, the guilt of yesterday's decisions. Maybe Patricia was truthful when she said that they had already fought their way back from the pain of leaving her behind. Maybe there was hope for her after all, even having made such a decisively horrible choice to leave her husband. Maybe it was possible to come back from regrets. But then again they never said that they regretted leaving her, only that they had been selfish.

"So did Halley get home safely?" Donald asked when placing the plate of breakfast in front of Donna. He was an exceptional cook. But then so was Patricia. Cooking was something else they shared as if it was some sort of romantic voyage.

"Yes, I heard from her when she touched ground." Donna answered taking in the aroma of the plate of grits, eggs and turkey bacon. Wonderfully toasted bread laid perfectly in the small plate next to her breakfast plate. "Thomas was there to meet her."

"This Thomas, I take it he is some kind of a special man?" Patricia requested.

"I believe that is a requirement of Halley's if you wish to seek a place in her life. One must be special."

"What about you? Do you also require a special person?" Patricia smiled curiously. "I mean, we are both hoping to meet Keith, one day. Do you think that the opportunity would be possible?"

No words could match the ones that saluted in her heart. "Yes!" They screamed inside of her chest. "Yes! You will meet him. And you will meet your grandchildren! And we will all be one happy family." But reality's markings stepped in and stopped her tongue from saying anything but what was truth. "I doubt it. But you will meet your grandsons."

Patricia went to speak, but Donald took her and Donna's hand. "Let us bless the food." Heads bowed, eyes closed. "Father God, we thank you for the abundance of life, health, family and sustenance. We thank you for those who have prepared the foods, and we ask that the food which has been prepared be good nourishment to our bodies. In Jesus Holy name we pray, amen." Grace had to be said before each meal, whether in privacy of their home, or public restaurants.

349

"So, is there anything special that you would like to do today? We only have today and a short time tomorrow to share with you." Donald spoke sadly.

"You make it sound as if when I leave tomorrow, there will be no more tomorrows for us. I do hope that you will come and visit. I really want the boys to know their grandparents. And I want to know you better." Donna heard the words spoken, she just did not think that they were coming from her mouth. "I mean if you want too."

Both Donald and Patricia sat with their eyes totally centered on Donna. It was Patricia who spoke first. "Donna, if we had a choice, we would not let you live there alone. We would love for you to move here with us. You and the boys."

"Move here? But what about my job? I can't just leave without notice."

"We don't mean to leave without notice. We mean after you return home, and get your things together. If you find that it is truly over for you and Keith, we want you to come and live with us." Donald offered.

Donna thought seriously then of her return to the place where the love of her heart lives to reject it. "We will see. I mean, I still have my job to consider."

"Consider, yes, but you can always find a law firm here to work. Or maybe even work for the Duncan's firm here. I am sure that they would have no problems transferring someone with as much drive as you have to a city like Atlanta." Patricia took a deep breath. "Donna, we really want to get to know you as our daughter. We have missed so much of your life."

"And you will. But I doubt that my moving here is going to be a possibility. At least not right now."

"Well, we have today. So, let us enjoy it." Donald said joyfully.

Twenty-eight

"So are we going to see you back in Birmingham anytime soon?" There he stood, showered in masculinity, sprinkled with the salt of passion and adorned with beauty of Solomon, who she read of from the Bible. Darren was too much for her body to receive. He made her feel things that she was unsure of, but enjoyed. He was a danger to the chemistry of her. He was too much. She could not say anything to him. "So are you?"

"Am I what?" She watched him move closer to her. She had been sitting in the large reading room of his family home. Her day with her parents ended sooner than she wanted, but it was needed so that she could rest for her flight on tomorrow.

"Are you coming back to Birmingham?" He moved closer. His statured made his steps appear to be choreograph by his next move. "I mean if you are not, then we need to do something about your office."

"Do you want me to come back?"

"I want you."

"What?" Donna placed the book onto the shelf. She wasn't reading it anyway. She was only waiting for sleep to claim her. The silk gown that she wore posed a problem for her as it did not conceal those places on her body that were necessary to hide from another man. She reached for the protection of the matching robe, but could see that Darren was aware of her unmentionables. The only place left to run and hide was in her mind, so there she ran. "You want me?"

"Yes, I do." Darren took further steps in her direction. "That is what you want to hear, isn't it?" He was dressed in a pair black slacks and a light short sleeve grey sweater that touched his body gently. He was gorgeous.

"Let's supposed that it is. How much more could I bargain with you?"

"Oh, you are talking about money?" He was there, standing right in front of her.

"Is there anything more?" She reached for his hand. He took possession of her waist. There was that feeling again running through her like a sharp measure of electric shock and spasmodic sensation. Where does it come from? And why is it that it only happens when Darren is around?

He hugged her closer and tighter. "It is good to see you."

"It is good to see you, too." Her head pressed against his right side of his chest. She could feel his well sculptured pectoral muscle. It was firm, thick, but not too big. He was wonderfully made. "What brings you here?" Donna gently pulled away from his grip.

"Well, I was wondering how you were doing?" He released his hands gently, and watched her move away from him.

"Halley, didn't tell you that I was doing great?" She tried to not pay attention to the stirring inside of her, but she had nowhere to control its simmering.

"Actually, Halley did not speak of you at all. She was too busy with Thomas."

Donna sat. "Please have a seat. It is, therefore, your home." She could feel his presence more than she wanted. It was his weapon of conquering would be prey and judges. He sat on the sofa in front of her. "I am not surprised. She really was ready to get back to him." Donna still was at a lost as to how he made her feel. "It was good to see. I mean, Halley, happy and so in love."

"Why is that?"

"Why not? Everyone should experience it at least once in their lives." She felt as if she was walking into a trap, but could not pull herself away from its snare.

"If you say so."

"Darren, why are you here?" He had no bags with him. At least none that she could see. "I mean your presence was not expected, and yet you are here."

"I did not realize that I had to make an appointment to visit my family's home."

"That isn't what I am asking, and you know it. What is it that you are looking for?" She stood slowly. "I am leaving tomorrow night, so if you had plans to meet with someone before then, I can get a hotel. Or I could stay with my parents."

"So, I take it that all is going well with your parents?"

"Yes, it is. So, really if you need your home to yourself, it is okay with me."

"Donna, I came here because I wanted to see you." He spoke without a break in sentence. "I have missed you, and I wanted to see you. I believe that I have waited long enough."

"What does that mean?"

"It means that I find myself caught between a rock and a hard place." He slowly stood and began to walk in her direction. "I...."

"Darren, I think that maybe I should go now." She tried to slip by him, but he stopped her.

"Are you running from me?"

"No, I am not running from you. I am running from what I believe is a dangerous road for us to travel."

"Meaning?"

"Meaning, I think that it is better that I go. Please let me by."

"If you feel that I must." He moved aside. She quickly walked out of the room.

Why was he here? Why didn't he call her to let her know that he was coming? Why does he make her feel this way? Why? Why? Why? She could still hear the questions in her head when the door to the bedroom opened. He stood there looking at her. Drawing her into his snare again. Leave me alone! She screamed inside, but her lips did not move. "Donna, may I speak with you?"

"Darren, I don't see that we have anything to talk about." She was busying herself with packing.

Upon entering the bedroom, she immediately went to the closet and took out her luggage. She reached back in and took out the clothes on the rack. Then she went to the drawers to remove the garments. It was then that she heard the door, and the voice.

"Donna, I...."shrank

"Darren, please." She had to interrupt him. She knew now what her body and mind were confused about earlier. She knew now what the feeling was that kept exploring the inner most private parts of her, it was, no it could not be. It was desire. Desire to feel him holding her, touching her, kissing her in places that only Keith had been allowed to hold, touch and kiss. It was hot, intense and seducing her movements against and toward him.

"Why are you packing?"

"I think that it's best."

He walked into the room, leaving the door opened. "Donna, please let me explain." His voice was soft, not seductive, yet she wanted to be seduced by him.

"Explain what?" She did not look at him.

"Look at me, please." He touched her arm gently. "Please let me explain."

357

"Darren, there is nothing to explain. This is your house, and I will leave." She looked only for a moment, and quickly turned away.

"Donna, please you must let me explain. I need to see your face." He took a firmer hold to her arm. Gently, he physically persuaded her to turn to him. "I did not come here to tell you to leave. I wanted to see you. I needed to see you." She only stared at him. "Donna, I can't seem to stop thinking about you. You have taken over my thoughts, and I don't mind." Still she said not one word. "I need you to tell me how to deal with this. I have never wanted anyone like I want you."

"Darren." She pulled away. "Please let go of my arm."

"My apologies." He released her arm, and turned away from her. "Donna, I never wanted to feel the way that I do about you, but I have felt this way ever since the day you walked into my building."

"What do you want me to say?

"I don't know. I don't know what I'm saying. All I know is that I can't get you off of my mind. I think of you every day. Every morning I wake wanting to be near you. Every night I search for your fragrance in my bed. I can't stop this seduction of my heart, and I need you to do it."

"How can I do that?"

"How do you handle it?"

She was thrown off. "Darren...."

"Are you telling me that you don't feel what I am feeling?"

"I am not telling you anything."

"If I am wrong tell me that I am wrong."

"Darren, these are your feelings I can't tell you what you want to hear."

"So, how do you know what I want to hear?" He moved toward her again. "So, you do have some feelings for me."

"Darren, the feelings that I have for you are of friendship, and no more."

"You're lying, Donna."

"Lying."

"Yes, lying." He walked toward the window. He felt lost, foolish. "Donna, if you are not having the same feelings, there is obviously something wrong with me. And I have never been considered a fool at anything. I am willing to believe that you are hiding behind the truth." He quickly walked to her and took her into his arms and began to kiss her. She pushed away, but her body felt a surge so powerful that she weakened in his arms, and began to kiss him back.

She could feel his hand caressing her gently on the small of her back. Before he could move any further, he withdrew from her. He stared deeply into her eyes. She tried not to stare back into his, but she wanted to be there, and even closer. He chanced not for her to refuse him anymore and took her chin and lifted her lips to his. His hand trembled to her neck, gently, cautiously, tenderly. He trembled a little more, and then continued. His kiss was as powerfully sultry as the sight of him. Donna had yet to touch him. And she dared to reach for his shoulders, before realizing that her robe had fallen to the floor. He stopped, and looked at her again. The silk gown provided much possibility for visual delight of her body, and consummating fantasies of making love to her. He raised his hand slowly to trace her waist and then to her shoulders. He could see her trembling. She refused to look up at him. He took the bikini strap of the gown into his hands and released them from her shoulders. The gown slowly drifted off of her body to the floor.

He stared with strong desire to capture her. She finally looked up to find his eyes requesting to touch her, to taste her, to explore her. She could feel the fingers of his hands teasing her nipples, marveling at their hard state. He lowered his head and his mouth imprisoned her breasts methodically, as if he had known them before. His tongue danced around her nipples. She moaned. He continued. She moaned more.

When she felt her shoulder strap touching her skin again, she realized that he had stopped. "I am...I apologize." Her eyes opened to see him dressing her.

What was she to say? Her body still desired him enormously. She could not move. He placed her robe back on her, and then walked out of the room. Her body still felt unmovable, immobile. When it appeared that he was not going to return, she sat drained on the bed.

"Donna. Donna." She awakened to the voice of the same person who had only moments ago walked out her room, leaving her on the brink of sexual explosion. "Donna."

"Darren, no. Don't touch me." She screamed and tried to move away from him. Her vision was still blurry, not yet coherent of her surroundings.

She turned in the bed away from him. She did not have on a gown, just a pair of sweats, and a tank top.

"Donna, what is wrong with you?"

It was then that she realized the state of her being. It was all a dream. He had not touched her. He had not tasted her. He had not brought her to the brink of ecstasy and then walked out on her. "Darren, what are you doing here?"

"I wanted to make sure that you were okay." He moved away from the bed. "I have been calling you for over three hours now."

"Why?" She was embarrassed. She did not know how long he had been in the room, and was fearful that he may have heard her moaning.

"Well, I hadn't heard from you, and my sister has been caught up in a love fest, so I could get nothing from her, either. I wanted to know how your meeting with your parents was going."

She found her way out of the king size bed and sat on the edge of the other side, away from him. "Everything is going great." She was still somewhat in a daze. "Darren, could you please give me a moment or so?"

"That must have been some dream."

362

"Why do you say that?" Her heart began to beat faster.

"Well, look at you. You act as if you don't know where you are. Besides that, when I came in you were moaning."

"No, I was not." He was there.

"Okay, maybe you weren't moaning. May be you were just yawning, sensuously." He smiled teasingly. "So, who was this man who could persuade you to moan?"

"Darren, I was not moaning." She stood and walked into the bathroom, splashed water on her face, dried it with a towel, and then returned to the room. Darren stood waiting on her, and the answer to his question. "Really, what are you doing here?"

"I told you, I wanted to make sure that you were okay. I have missed you."

She considered his words, and his tone, and was not afraid. "You missed me?"

"Yes, I did." He walked over to her. "Donna, I believe that I have fallen in love with you."

"What did you say?"

"I said that I have fallen in love with you."

"Darren, why are you really here?" She put the towel on her shoulder, and stepped away from him.

"Donna, a lot has happened since you came into my life. A lot more than I am willing to admit." He followed her steps to where she was standing. "I thought when you told me that you were married, these feelings would go away, but they did not. But I knew that you loved your husband, even after the divorce, so I sought to repress what I felt. But I can't do this anymore. I feel like I am going to go crazy if I don't get this out. I love you, Donna. And I want to be in your life."

Twenty-nine

What happened tonight was not to happen. After Darren opened himself to her, Donna rushed out of the house without saying a word. Why would he do this to her now? She had no time to determine what it was that she was feeling for him, but hearing the words come out of his mouth told her more than she wanted to admit too.

When she saw her parent's home a smile came across her face in accepting the reality of having them to go to, in such a desperate time. It was still rather early in the evening, only around 8:30 p.m., or so. She saw the lights still sparkling in the sitting room. She knew that they would be there reading the bible or some sort of book that offered hope, salvation or something like that.

The key that they gave to her was a new adventure for her. She, instead, pressed the button for the doorbell. "Well, hello again." Donald opened the door before she could use her key. "We didn't think that we would be seeing you until tomorrow morning."

"I hope that I am not disturbing you, but I just didn't have anywhere else to go." Donna walked into the foyer as Donald took her hand.

"Is there something wrong?" They walked into the sitting room. Patricia was there to greet her.

"Not exactly. I just needed to step out to gather my thoughts."

"Donna dear, is it something that we can help you with?" Patricia spoke softly. She gestured for Donna to join them on the sofa. "Did you hear from Keith?"

"No. I wished that I had, but no I haven't heard from him." Donna then realized that she came to her parent's home for comfort, support, and wisdom. She had parents that she could consult with about her problems. "Actually, it is Darren."

"Darren?" Patricia asked.

"Darren is Halley's older brother." Donna understood that she needed to explain to them what the situation was between her and Darren, but she didn't even know herself. She had not been confronted with a dream of him before, neither did she have to contemplate any feelings for him. "He is here."

"Is that a problem?" Donald asked cautiously. Donna did not respond.

"Donna?" Patricia looked at her deeply. "Are you involved with Darren?"

"No." Donna answered quickly. "I, we are not involved, but…

"But what?" Patricia asked pointedly.

"He is something of a conundrum for me. I don't know exactly what I feel for him. At least I didn't know. But after tonight, I don't know what it is that I feel for him." Donna had not taken her seat next to her parents. She had remained very focused on the moon. She sought its wisdom of time and experience with others who had searched its foundation for answers that wrestled in their lives. She turned to face Donald and Patricia. "I am afraid that I may love him."

"What about Keith?" Donald asked.

"What do you mean?"

"I thought, well, we thought that you were hoping that two of you could make things work out."

"Keith and I are over. I don't see that happening. What I have done to our family is unforgiveable, and I can't see that he would even want me back."

"So, how does Darren feel about you? I mean have you talked with him?" Patricia asked. "Why is he here, anyway?"

"I am not sure. He said that he had been calling me, and there had been no answer, so he came."

"Are we to believe that he drove or flew this far just to make sure that you were okay?"

"That is what he said. But he followed up with other things."

"What things Donna?" Patricia asked anxiously.

"He said that he felt as if he was falling in love with me, and wanted me to do something about it." The weight of the words made her feel weak. In fact, it weakened her to sit. "And I just don't know what to do."

"Donna, do you love this man?" Patricia asked.

"I don't know.

Patricia stood and walked to stand near Donna, who refused to remove her eyes from the moon which shone brightly through the large window. "You may continue to look up there, but it is only in here where you will find your heart." Patricia pointed into the direction of the heart that Donna tried desperately to hide. "You know your father and I went through such a time as this."

Donna first dealt with the blow of knowing that she had a father. The word has a gentle feel to it. It gave her comfort, not rejection as it had in the past. Then she did what was necessary for her to do, she asked the question. "When was this time?"

"It was a year or so after you were born." Patricia turned to look at Donald who had decided to join her place in the room. "It was a difficult time for me. I ran away from Donald and the home that we shared. I just did not know what to do with the pain that was raging a war inside of me. No matter what I did, nothing and no one could remove it, until I met him."

"God?" Donna question with certainty.

"Yes, and no." Patricia began to dream of yesterday. "He was actually a student of theology, and because of our growing relationship he introduced me to God." Patricia smiled cunningly, knowing that her answer was not exactly what Donna expected to hear. Donald smiled with her, knowing the same. "I was devastated beyond all understanding when we chose to give you away. I carried you for nine months and in those nine months, I loved you more than time could realize. I knew that I wasn't supposed to, but I could not stop my heart from loving you. It was a desperate time for me that day we gave you away. It cut me through and through, and I could not be relieved. Each day brought on a new pain, a new regret. A part of me was taken, given away to another and I could not reconcile this reality."

Donna saw the pain in Patricia's eyes. The remnants of it was still quite visible when she spoke of its memory. She even appreciated its moving. She tried not to make Patricia feel any more of it by turning her gaze away from her.

"I had not known such love and pain could simultaneously take over one's heart, but it happened, and I fell apart. There wasn't anything that Donald could do for me, even though he tried all that he could, and some. I walked around like a lost soul for over a year or so, and then I met this man."

Donna interrupted. "Do you mind if I asked, what was his name?"

"Gary Shea." She smiled sweetly. Donald, who still stood near her, gently rubbed her shoulders. "He saved me. He saved my marriage with Donald." She softly touched Donald's hands. "He reminded me of love, and how sometimes it is not all roses, but still worth the life it lives in." Patricia released Donald's hand and walked over to Donna, and took her hand. "Love is love, no matter the heart it exist in. Meaning, even though things seem impossible for me, love did not stop. I only thought, and even felt like it did."

"Your mother was in a place that I could not reach her. She stopped talking to me, and begin talking at me. We no longer laughed together. Everything we did became a tour of agony for her. It left me feeling lost and defenseless. I could not help her. I could not find any help for myself." Donald had turned to face both of them. Patricia did not, at all seem surprised at what he spoke of, and Donna understood even more of how special their marriage was. "You see, I was just as lost in pain having chosen to give you away, but your mother's pain was more important to deal with. She was dying inside, and inside of her was our love. I didn't want to lose that, and for some time I thought that I had."

"Gary told me that God wanted to talk with me about my pain, my marriage and my life. And I laughed at him, because it all sounded idiotic. He sounded idiotic. But he was relentless, quietly so. He said it was placed on his heart. I, for a while thought that I was falling in love with him. He made me feel the things that your father had, but I no longer felt. I had refused to. But Gary was focused on what the call was in his life, and did not let my weaknesses become his. After a year or so, and my letting him tell of this God he loved so much, my life was changed, I opened my heart again for your father, and I changed my study to Theology. Since then, I have not heard from Gary. At least not the Gary I thought he was. I no longer feel that romantic love for him. He is my pastor, my brother in Christ, and my friend."

"Pastor Shea, is Gary?" Donna asked shockingly.

"Yes, he is." Patricia smiled pleasingly. "Gary, and I attended Theology school together. After graduation he went to pastor at his parent's church, and I continued to complete my doctorate thesis. Upon completion, Gary asked me to join his staff as an Associate Pastor. Actually, I was there as a member serving in different ministries. I had yet to walk in the calling that was placed on my life."

"Does he know about me?" Donna voice was shaken a little with the question. She gestured her head nervously, yes. She did not want to be a secret disgrace of Patricia's past.

"I told him about you the day that I trusted him, which was a year after we met."

"What did he have to say about it, about me?"

"He told me then that I had not given you away, but that I had been disobedient to God. That the life that grew inside of me was not mine to give away, but to care for and present to Jesus." She grieved at her memory. "I remember the pain I felt in my heart, I had disobeyed this God I did not know. But still there was this overwhelming pain that surfaced. I wanted to run and hide, but where was there to hide? Then he told me that God forgives a sincere, broken heart if I go to Him in faith, knowing that He would." As the tears streamed down Patricia's cheeks, her lips parted with a smile. "I went to this God, and I prayed to this God to forgive me. My heart was sincere. My heart was broken. I remembered that to pray simply meant to talk to Him, and that is what I did, I just talked." Donna saw a place of peace for her parent's decision that she had not seen before.

She could feel the memory of her separation from them taking on a different existence. She no longer saw it as a great, selfish mistake on their part, instead it was a purpose for her life. "It was in talking to Him that I began this journey of forgiveness for Donald and myself, and my walk with Him."

"What does all of this have to do with what I am dealing with tonight?"

Donald spoke softly. "Dear, your mother and I too had a time of desperate separation from each other. For months I did not know what to do for her. I loved your mother more than life, and even today that love grows. I refused to let her take that love from us."

"And?"

"And, dear daughter, if you still truly love Keith, I would suggest that you forgive yourself, tell this Darren fellow no, and return home to Keith. He is waiting for you." He smiled tenderly as he held Patricia in his arms. Her tears still controlled her heart, refusing her arms to let him go. "We will be here. Or better yet we will be there to meet him in a week."

Donna hugged them both tightly.

Thirty

Darren was still there when she return to the house. He had, however fallen asleep in the sitting room. Just as Donna reached the sofa where he laid, he awakened. There were no immediate words, only stares.

"Did you go to your parents?" Darren broke the uncomfortable silence as he sat up. "Halley told me that they lived not too far from here, in the same community."

"Darren, we need to talk."

"It is why I came all this way." Darren stood. Donna walked away from him. "I don't like this anymore than you Donna. And I don't want to feel this way, I just do."

"You just do what?"

"It is as I said before you ran out of here, I love you. Or at least, I think that I do. I want to be in your life."

"Darren, I have no life for you to be in."

"Well then, you must tell me what to do with it. Why did you cause it to be there?"

"I did not cause anything to be anywhere. I never expressed any words of love or admiration to you, Darren." Donna tried to remain calm. She spoke in a cautious, yet stern voice.

"Donna, I know that you didn't." Darren rubbed his head and sat back down. "I feel as though I am struggling through one of the worse cases in my life, and I am my only witness." He studied his thoughts and tried to begin again. "Donna, from the moment I saw you, I was moved to be with you, to hold you, and probably to love you. But I ignored those feelings, until you walked into my law firm." He stood again. "You were so beautiful. The most beautiful woman I have ever seen. And each day you grew even more beautiful to me. Even tonight when I walked into that bedroom and saw you lying there, your beauty became even more glowing to me. I saw you and wanted to take you away from here."

"Darren, please don't say these things." Donna tried not to look at him. He had made his way next to her. "Please, I can't do anything for you with this. I can't help you with this."

"Donna, I did not ask for your help with what I am feeling because I felt alone in this. I asked because I felt that you felt the same way. Am I wrong?"

"Yes, you are. This love that you express, what do you want me to do with it? I have no place to house your love."

"Well, that is all that I needed to know."

"That's it? Nothing more?"

"What do you expect me to do? I am not one who is accustomed to chasing after anyone who does not want me." He turned and walked toward the door.

"Darren."

"Yes." Darren stopped at the door, and turned to look back at her.

"Are you really going to just walk out?"

"What else is there for me to do Donna? I have opened my heart to you in such a way that it has left me feeling empty and vulnerable. And quite frankly, I don't like this feeling. I need to regroup." He turned again, and walked out of the room.

"Darren." Donna ran out of the room. "Please don't leave. Please, I must…"

"You must what?" He caught her shoulders as she almost ran into him. "I apologize for everything that I have said. I never should have put you in this position."

"Darren, I, I have to." She resisted the words as they walked through her mind. They seemed almost to choke her humanity. They threatened her with their restriction to be released from her mouth.

"Donna, it's okay, really." He tried to console her, even though he felt weakened by his revealed heart's words.

She stepped away from him, but only a little. "Darren, I don't know if it is love that I feel for you, but I do know that it is more than what I understand to be friendship." She watched his eyes. There was clarity from the storm.

"What are you saying?" His question was without intrusion.

"I am not sure." She still struggled within, but could feel the hostage of her heart being released. "Darren, I have only loved one man in my life, and he has been the only man that I have wanted to love. But you, you make me feel things that I have shared with him. Things that I only wanted to feel for him." She released the breath that stricken her heart muscles. "I have ignored these feelings since the day that I met you. I have chosen to believe that it was an illusion of sorts. I just did not want to feel such feelings for any other man."

"Donna."

"Please let me finish before my strength fails me." She looked at him directly. "You make me aware of my femininity, my heart, my vulnerability, my dreams, and my passions. All that I am as a human female, you give life too, and I hate it." She turned from him, and walked back into the room. He followed her slowly. "When I awakened tonight to find you there, my body surged with such excitement and passion that it almost cause me to collapse. I did not ask for this, but it is here, and I have to deal with it."

"Donna, do you love me?" He stood still observing her silhouette through the moon light that shown through the window. He did not want to look at her directly. He was afraid of what she would answer.

She turned to face him. "Yes, I love you."

"And Keith?"

"He is my, was my husband. Our marriage ended, but not my love for him."

"How would you like to handle this?" Still without looking at her directly, Darren was trying to be strong, but his heart fought with him. "I mean, if I am to have you, it will not be like this."

"Darren." She spoke with a gentle softness.

"Donna, I will not share your heart with another man. It isn't fair to you, and it damn sure isn't fair to me." He turned his focus to her totally. "I cannot do that."

"I don't know what to say."

"Donna, it is just like this. I will not provoke you to fight between your feelings for Keith, no more than I would want him to do that to me." He walked toward her, and took her hand into his immediately as he shortened the distance between them. "You deserved to be loved. I deserved to be loved. But that love cannot be with the wars of someone living within you. I want to have you to myself." He gently pulled her to him. "I can't have you any other way."

"Darren, it isn't that simple for me." She remained locked in his hold. "How could you expect it to be?"

"I don't. I am just letting you know what is here for me."

She looked up into his eyes. "I was dreaming of you and me together when you came tonight. It was the first time that I had. The dream felt so real, I was lost in it."

"Would you like to tell me about it?"

"What good would it do?" She moved away from his touch. "Darren, I have no place to house your love for me, any more than I have room to keep my love for you inside. It is overwhelming." She took her seat on the sofa. She was tired emotionally and mentally. Her physical strength had but gone, but she knew that she had to hold onto it or else she would be easy prey for Darren's words of eternity. "This has been a day." She relented. "Please will you join me." She pointed to the spot next to her on the sofa. Darren walked over slowly and sat with caution. "Darren, if I could say to you right now, at this very moment, that I don't love Keith, I would and joyfully walk into the moonlight with you. But I can't."

"What are you going to do?" He sat forward. Not once looking at her. Nor was she looking at him when she spoke. "Do you think that you have a chance of getting your marriage back together?"

"No, I don't, but what am I to you with the love for someone else in my heart. I want my marriage back. I want my family back. But I know now that this is not to be." She turned to him, and touched his leg to gather his focus on her. "I have a lot to work out, and I don't want to bring anyone into my life with what I have to do. It would not be right."

"Donna, what can I do?"

"Don't give up on me."

"What does that mean?"

"Simply that I don't know where my life is going right now, or in the next whatever. I feel so confused and all I can see is darkness."

"Donna, I apologize for tonight."

"Please Darren, don't apologize." The tears that had hid behind her eyes finally gave way. No longer could the levy's walls keep them restricted. "Please don't. Believe it or not, I needed this. I needed to tell you what I have been feeling for some time. You came into my life when there was no other man for me to hold. You have always been a gentleman and a friend. What you did in finding my parents for me is priceless. Your friendship has given me a new life, and new dreams. I love you dearly for that...."

"You're breaking up with me before we can date." He tried humor to temper the pain in his heart.

"Darren, if only we could have met...well, that is not to be. Yes, I am breaking up with you before we can date." She danced with his humor, because she too felt the pain of 'no' spreading throughout her system of love.

Darren smiled and held her hand for the time in space that he could without taking her at such a weakened moment for her. "Tell me then, what can I help you with." He stood, but did not move away from her.

"Are we going to be alright?" She remained seated, but held tightly to his hand. "I mean, I need you in my life, but I don't know if we can survive together without being together, per say."

"Donna, we will be just fine." He took a tone of seriousness, such as the great lawyer he was. "I love you enough to want what is better for you. In fact loving you has helped me to look outside of myself. I haven't done that in a long time. When it came to matters of the heart I have always wanted what was never too much work to have. And love is one of those realities that requires a lot of work." He still held tightly to her hand. "But you made me see that it is worth the while. I wanted to be with you for whatever work it was to require. I will admit I knew that you loved Keith, and I never expected for you to give up that love. I saw the fire in your eyes when you spoke of him, and I wanted you to have that love for me. I wanted others to see that fire in your eyes when you spoke of me." He smiled gallantly. "I had hope, and that was wrong of me. But you kept looking so inviting." He loosened his grip of her hand. "Well, we are not to be, but that doesn't mean that we can't work together, does it?"

"No, I enjoyed working with you. But are you going to be alright working with me, and not...."

"Not wanting to be with you?" He interrupted. "Donna, I will be more of a friend to you than necessary at times, but that is only because of my love. However, I don't want to lose you as a partner in the office."

"I don't know if we can make that happen without it causing problems."

"Problems? With whom?" His question was not immediately answered. "Are you looking to renew your marriage with Keith?"

"I am."

"Well, I am...happy for you."

"Really?"

"Really. I mean it. Maybe Donna, we will find that we truly share this love, I mean that it is not an intrusion in our lives. Maybe it will lead to greater possibilities for both of us."

"When did you become such a philosopher?"

"When I realized that I was in love with you." He gestured for her stand. "Donna, I am not a man who chases after women, even if she is the woman that I love. I will not do anything to cause Keith any caution of doubt. I respect marriage, and therefore will live with the love I have for you, not as if it does not exist, but that it exist for another to come." He paused. "Woman, choosing to love you has given me a new place to travel with my mind. I won't turn back from here. But, if Keith does not want you back, promise me that you will come to me. Not because you were rejected, but for the love that you have for me."

Thirty-one

"Keith, why are you here?" Donna entered into her apartment, seeking to remove the stress of where she had come from. With all that had expired in the week past, and the night before, she needed a mental and emotional sabbatical. She saw that her question placed caution in his heart. "I mean, is everything ok?"

"Yes, I wasn't sure when you were going to return, but the boys needed some more items. I hope that it is ok."

"Of course. I just was not expecting anyone to be here." Donna put her luggage on the floor. Keith was walking from the boy's room in the apartment. He began to assist her with luggage carrier, and shoulder bag. He looked prepared to leave.

"Well, I was just on my way out." He said putting the luggage against the wall of her bedroom.

"May we talk?" Keith looked as if he was about to say no, so she rushed to add to her request. "I would really love for us to reach a place in our relationship that will allow for peace."

"Peace?"

"Yes. Peace." Donna sat on the sofa. "Keith I know that you have gone on with your life. It is a fact that I am not happy about, but it is a reality just the same. With that I have to find some way to live without you."

"That is your peace?" Keith asked without sitting.

"No, it is not. But it will have to be."

"Donna."

"Keith, please let me speak. I got myself into this and must suffer the consequences." She interrupted. "When I think of my life without you in it, it is peace that I will have to find. I don't want to be without you. I don't want to be without your touch. I miss you so much. I miss us." She exhaled. "I love you more than the windows of my heart can house. There is no room for anyone else, at least not romantically. You are it."

"Donna."

"Keith, please." She felt tears, but decided not to let them fall. "If I could go back and change what I did, I doubt very seriously that I would. It is what has taught me many lessons of maturity. This life that we have been given does not exist for failure, it exist because of God's grace and mercy. I don't understand why He has allowed such a wonderful travesty of love, but He has, and nothing can be done to go back and change our steps to the present day."

"Donna."

"I know that hearing the name of God from me is in itself doubtful, but I must do it." Again the tears, but she refused their visit to her cheeks. "My mother is an associate pastor. Can you believe it? My father is a doctor, a heart surgeon, no less. One of the most renowned heart surgeons in the world, can you believe it. My mother's church is in Atlanta. It has a congregation of over 30,000 persons. For the week I was in Atlanta I visited her every day. I visited his practice every day. They told me why they gave me away to this world. They told me because of that reason they refused to bring any other children in this world. They are wealthy, happy and the best of friends. They have shared over thirty-five years together, and they are still passionately in love with each other. I was angry with them because of their happiness. I wanted to meet people who were lonely, sad, and regretful of leaving me behind, yet they were not."

"Donna." Keith still stood at the door with bags in hand.

"Keith, they were still in love with each other. They told me that they did not regret it because they did it together with the understanding that I was hindering their possibilities of personal growth. They worked harder than most, and forsaken themselves from another child. It was selfish, but it was what they wanted." She had not looked over at him since she began to talk, and still her eyes refused to give sight to his physical presence. "They are happy, and at peace with life, with the choices they made in the past." She considered her words. "I realized after understanding them, I, too, must do the same with my life's choices." She now looked at him and gave welcome to the tears that beckon to the resting place of her cheeks. "Keith, I love you. I will not ask for you to come back to me. It will be wrong of me because the decision to separate was mine, not yours. I forced you into a dark place of my confusion, emptiness, my loneliness. I did not ask for your help. I caused you pain, and weakness. I ask that you forgive me."

"Donna." He dropped the bag to the floor. "Baby, I love you."

"Keith."

"He walked over to her and fell to his knees. "Donna, please let me speak."

"Keith, I am afraid too." Her tears began to flow stronger.

"But you must."

"Keith, I am not strong enough."

"But I am." He took and held her hands tightly. "I am strong enough to forgive you. I am strong enough to tell you that I love you and did not stop loving you. I crave you every moment of the day. And at night I make love to our memories. You are my wife, my friend, my sister, my lover, my woman."

"Keith."

"Donna, my life stopped when you stopped being in it. I have not been able to go on without you, I have only existed. This peace that you speak of, I don't want it without you. I need you in my life."

"Keith." She fell to the floor to be near his lips. "Don't play with my heart now. Please don't open your world to me again, and then leave. I won't survive that pain again."

"Donna, I didn't leave you then, I ran away from what I knew to be the wrong time for us." They sat. "Listen, to me. I know how your body feels inside and out, and when we made love I knew that as much as we were together, we would not be forever. When I walked out of that door it was because I had to, not because I wanted too."

"Now?"

"Now, I knew to be here when you returned. I have been here every morning since you left, sitting, and waiting hour after hour for you to return. I wanted to be with you." He paused for only a moment of thought, and then continued. "Donna, I am responsible for how I love you, not how you love me. My father told me this shortly after you left. When he first said it I refused to accept it, but the longer we were apart, the more sense it made. So I started to wait for you in my heart. I began to pray for us, for our family. Until the day you left, I had not known what to do, but then my prayers were answered. So every day I have waited for your return."

"Every day?"

"Every day. Each day waiting for you to walk through that door, waiting to hold you in my arms again. I love you Donna."

"What has Carolyn had to say of this? I thought that you were dating."

"Carolyn is, and has been a great friend through all of this. We did talk about dating, but she knew that my heart belonged to you. After that was reaffirmed she continued to be my friend. There were moments of anger for her because of your treatment of us, but still a friend she remained."

"Do you love her?"

"Yes, I do. As a friend, and only as a friend. My heart never could come full circle to loving her beyond that place."

He questioned her next thoughts, but interrupted them. "What about Darren? I know that he loves you. I saw it in his eyes when you were in the hospital."

Donna cautioned her words. "Darren came to Atlanta."

"He went with you?" Keith's heart screamed the question before his mouth could refuse its escape. He did not want to risk losing her, especially not with outburst of anger. Even if it was rightful anger.

"No." She spoke immediately. "He arrived last night."

"Why was he there?" He whispered to his heart to be calm. His question was less extreme.

"Keith, I love you."

"And." Still calm.

"There is no, and. I love you." She realized that she was truly happy. No hesitation prompted by her confession of Darren's visit to Atlanta. She just wanted to relish in the moment of their unbreakable love, their unbreakable bond. "Keith, I love you, and I love us. I love you."

"Donna, do you love him?"

"I do. Darren reached a place in my heart where you are. Not because he tried too, but because I opened my heart to him." She remembered realizing the existence of love for Darren in her heart. "I did not know this until he came last night."

"And he? Does he love you?"

"He expressed that he did." The memory of last night still rested in her heart. It was a strangely beautiful place. A place that she knew was not to be home. "Keith, I have and will continue to love you forever. Darren knows this to be the truth, and did not try to change my mind from it. He has been a friend to me. His family has been a family to me. And Halley has become my sister. I don't want to give them up, but if you ask me too, I will. I refuse to let anyone come between us again."

"What about your job? Are you still practicing law with their firm?"

"Yes, I am." She could not tell if her answer failed his test of trust. "Keith, I...."

"Donna, please, you don't have to say anything more." He stood, and walked away from her.

"Keith, I don't have to work there. I don't want to lose you again." She quickly stood and walked to him. "Please don't let me go again, please."

Keith turned to look at her deeply. "Baby, I wasn't thinking of letting you go. I was only thinking of how I was going to deal with you working with this tall, dark and handsome Black man." He smiled tenderly. "Donna, if you want to stay there, do that. I won't ask you to quit. But Darren and I will have to talk. Maybe I can introduce him to Carolyn." His smile was interesting, but Donna dared not to speak. "I don't know if you could have handled any of this differently, and right now I don't mind to care about it. But there is one thing that I need for you to know." He took her hands in his. "Donna, I never meant to seem as if I was overlooking the color of your skin, your heritage. Actually, I don't remember exploring your skin color for too long before being captivated by what was living inside of your eyes. You had room enough for me, and more. I knew then that you loved me, even if you didn't."

"And I still love you." Donna confirmed. "What I experience had nothing to do with our love, it had to do with my existence. I did not know who I was anymore, or maybe I never did." The apartment filled itself with her childhood memories. "Being asked who I was as a woman of color struck something lose in me that already been stretched beyond its elasticity before we met. The problem is I never knew it." She stood. "In so many ways after we were married, and even before while we were dating, I gave away my heritage for entry into yours."

"I never asked that of you."

"No, but neither did you ask me not to." She walked over to stand next to him. "Keith, did it ever occur to you that I had no friends of color. Probably not because I never considered it. I was living in a world that was slowly but surely becoming my safe, yet dangerous haven. I separated myself from people of color, and I did not care how it affected my life. It reminded me that I was a child given away by two persons of color who did not want me. They were my parents, and they were Black, or should I say African American. Either way I did not want to be reminded of what they did to me."

"So, am I some kind of…

"Are you some kind of what?"

"I don't know, your White knight in shining armor."

"Keith." She smiled at his question. "Keith when you walked into the restaurant that day, my thoughts were not of my parents. Neither was it of love. I was working to stay alive, and looking forward to moving forward. What love you saw in my eyes I did not know was there. I had no plans on loving anyone. How could I, I did not know what love was, or how to obtain it." Many years passed before she could gather that understanding. "No, you came into that restaurant and arrested the heart of an innocent child, living as an adult. I was excited about what was to come of my life, I just didn't know it would come so quickly. But I accepted your offer for a date, and then your proposal of marriage. It was what I needed to erase any memory of my life before you. Besides, what or who was I leaving behind. I had no friends, not close friends anyway. All I had were reminders of being known as the Black girl whose parents gave her away. My parents did not want me, and I, when old enough did not want them."

"Donna, I want you to have friends from every culture of people. I should have notice this myself, but I guess when you live in the world you live in you don't see what is actually there. I don't want to do that anymore."

"Keith, please you don't have to take the blame for my selfishness. My choice to separate my life from the people who wear the same skin color as mine was my decision, and my decision alone." She walked back to the sofa. "Befriending Halley, and even Darren has been a needed direction for my life. Between both of them, I have been reintroduced to a world that I once thought was cold and calculating. I love the skin I am in, it is the color that God chose for me."

"I am not sure what to say."

"Keith, if you are serious about taking me back, I would like to make sure that our sons are involved in both realties of their heritages. I want us to make sure of that."

"That isn't a problem."

"Are you really being truthful in saying you will take me back?" She felt it better to be near him in posing the question. "I mean what I have done to our marriage, to our family can't be undone, and has left much damage."

"You forget, I am a corporate attorney. Dealing with damage property is my way of life. Besides I love you more than life itself, and one more day without you in it is going to be much more than I could bear. I don't like being without you." He pulled her close to him. His hands gently formed around her waist. "You are what my life needs in it to breathe. If it is the color of your skin that causes that life to breathe in air from a different setting, let it be so, I will take it in." His eyes became heavy with tears. "Donna, when I declared my love for you, it was for all of you, and that would include your skin color."

"I too, am learning to love me, skin color and all. I never knew that I was suppose too. But now that I understand that I have to love me as me, then I can run the rest of this race with vigor and confidence." She reached up and kissed his lips. "With my White knight in shining armor." Their lips parted for an insatiable kiss.

"May I tell you now?" Keith asked releasing his lips from hers.

"Tell me what?" Donna was still fascinated with the feeling that was now moving inside of her. "What is that you want me to know?"

"I never filed the divorce papers." Keith spoke softly as he nibbled on her ear. "We were never divorced."

"I already knew that." She continued to kiss him.

"What do you mean you knew?" He kissed her back.

"Keith, don't you think that I followed up on the filing? She began to work with the buttons on his shirt. "I am an attorney."

"Why didn't you say something?" He pulled her blouse over her head.

"What was I to say? It wasn't the divorce papers that separated us, it was I." She felt his fingers teasing her sweetly. "When I signed those papers, it was like signing my life away. But it wasn't until I could no longer feel your touch that I knew that we were no more."

"Donna, I love you." She caressed his chest gently.

"And I you Keith." Donna could hear Phyllis Hyman singing their song again. She was renewed. They were reborn. It was their wedding night. This man that walked into her life some eleven years ago. This White man, who walked into her heart over eleven years ago. This human man who told her of his eternal love for her only a minute ago, had no idea of how his professed love caused a serenade of that song in Donna's heart. She looked deeply into his eyes. They were blue, filled with passion, love, loyalty, friendship and so, so much more. More than Donna could ever describe or share with anyone. He loved her, and she loved him. And as they met each other on the moon, again consummating that love, she surrendered to the hope of their love. She surrendered to the desperation of the season. She surrendered.